GHOST DUST

Susan Slater

Books by Susan Slater

THE BEN PECOS MYSTERY SERIES

The Pumpkin Seed Massacre
Yellow Lies
Thunderbird
Firedancer
Under A Mulberry Moon
The Thaw
Ghost Dust
A Way to the Manger (a Christmas novella)

THE DAN MAHONEY MYSTERY SERIES

Flash Flood
Rollover
Hair of the Dog
Epiphany

STANDALONE NOVELS

0-60
Five O'Clock Shadow

GHOST DUST

Ben Pecos Mysteries, Book 7

Susan Slater

Secret Staircase Books

Ghost Dust
Published by Secret Staircase Books, an imprint of
Columbine Publishing Group LLC
PO Box 416, Angel Fire, NM 87710

This book is a work of fiction. Names, characters, places and
incidents are either the product of the author's imagination or are
used fictitiously. Any resemblance to actual events or locales or
persons, living or dead, is entirely coincidental.

Book layout and design by Secret Staircase Books

First trade paperback edition: December, 2020
First e-book editions: December, 2020

Publisher's Cataloging-in-Publication Data

Slater, Susan
Ghost Dust / by Susan Slater
p. cm.
ISBN 978-1649140432 (paperback)
ISBN 978-1649140449 (e-book)

1. Pecos, Ben (Fictitious character)—Fiction. 2. Native
American—Fiction. 3. Navajo people—Fiction. I. Title

Ben Pecos Mystery Series : Book 7
Slater, Susan, Ben Pecos mysteries.

BISAC : FICTION / Mystery & Detective.
813/.54

If there had not been a Tony Hillerman, there would never have been a Susan Slater!
No one could have been more supportive, more generous in his praise, and more patient with a newcomer's naive questions all those years ago.

Thank you, Tony. I hope I continue to do the genre justice.

Chapter 1

A hundred and ninety-two miles west of Albuquerque, the wind kicked up. Fairly gentle at first, just a buffeting of pumice-like grit, better known as desert top soil. The white F-150, on loan from the Indian Health Service, was starting to turn pinkish tan, and fine sand was beginning to collect and crater beneath the windshield wipers. A *Haboob*—the scourge of every desert—a storm at once dangerous in intensity, but usually fleeting, was seldom forgotten.

It wasn't Ben's first sandstorm. He respected their strength—had *felt* their strength. He knew it was a force that could lower visibility to zero, unpredictably killing by luring disoriented drivers to leave the highway. Yet, dry as the wind was, he knew they resulted from thunderstorm formation when winds moved in a direction opposite to a storm's trajectory. After precipitation begins to fall, the wind reverses and moves outward from the center of the storm but remains strongest following the direction the storm travels along a gravitational pull. Often precipitation doesn't even reach the ground but dissipates, actually evaporating, becoming *virga*. Another of those Southwest phenomena that seeing is believing—at the center of its strength, there could be a wall of blowing sand several stories high.

The wind was picking up sharply. Ben slowed the truck. These sandstorms could carry winds of over sixty miles per hour. Sometimes up to the force of an F-1 tornado. Not the type of circumstance where you took safety for granted.

"Zac, we should reach a roadside rest area about a mile ahead just before we enter the Navajo reservation. I'm going to pull off there. I think we'd be safer if we rode out the storm away from the highway."

"Probably, but it's just ghost dust sent by *Silla*." The eleven-year-old was looking out the back window of the cab as the billowing clouds of silt swept across the bed of the truck. "Aunty Uki said *Silla* sends a storm so we can get its power and stay strong. Everybody's power comes from the wind."

Ben nodded. There was so much he didn't know about Alaskan Native beliefs—many that probably predated his own Pueblo ancestors' teachings. Didn't the Alaskan Natives proudly proclaim that they had been there since the world was formed? That they welcomed others who walked across the Bering Strait to join them? He owed it to the boy to find out about these beliefs. This trip had been all about introducing Zac to his Pueblo heritage in New Mexico. A late eleventh birthday present that would include fishing, maybe a hot-air balloon ride, and lots of New Mexican cuisine. All favorite things that Ben missed, but he was finding that he was learning a lot, too. Starting with getting used to the fact that the young man sitting beside him was his son.

August. It had been a crazy year so far—a shocking time. In February Indian Health Service had contracted him to the medical services in Moose Flats, Alaska, to start a clinic dealing with the opioid crisis raging across that state. A challenge in the best of times out on the tundra in a village sinking into the ocean, but couple that with finding out he had a son, a then ten-year-old by an old girlfriend, and his life had been turned upside down.

Now with his wife, Julie, in Hollywood, Florida, setting up their permanent home, and Ben in New Mexico treating Zac to this pre-back-to-school trip—suddenly, the world as he had known it, no longer existed. All because of a pandemic that no one was prepared for, but made new rules for living mandatory. Everyone was separated not just by distance but by a lock-down in place due to this world-wide spread of a virulent virus. No internal or external travel—not even across county lines—let alone state borders by car or any place by air. Only a special permit would get you beyond five miles of your home. Interstate truckers were exempt if they were hauling necessities, as were people who had to travel twenty miles or more within state boundaries for work or supplies. This part of the state was out in no-man's land. You wouldn't be stopped from going to a grocery store, or if you needed emergency medical or dental care, but socializing outside one's immediate family—and they had to live under the same roof—was forbidden.

In the years that it had taken Ben to go from completing an internship in the Tewa Pueblo to a PhD in psychology, there had been two pandemics. The first claimed his last close relative, his grandmother. The Hantavirus—originating in a lab, perpetuated in the wild by a host, deer mice, crossed to human beings thanks to some contaminated pumpkin seeds. Deadly and threatening but relatively short-lived compared to the virus that the world was struggling with now. Once again, a host from the wild. This time bats were blamed with transferring the deadly disease to humans.

If there was anything good to come out of that time in Tewa a few years ago, it was meeting Julie Conlin, local TV reporter. Wild, curly, red hair, tight skirts above the knee, smarts and talent. And now Ms. Conlin was Mrs. Pecos. This current separation was a killer. He couldn't stop worrying about her being in south Florida, the hotbed of the illness with no visitation in the foreseeable future. He couldn't go there; she couldn't come here. Stuck, that's the way he felt.

He and Zac had landed in New Mexico one week ago. Time for a little fishing on the Jemez River, several days in the Tewa Pueblo and what was going to be a quick visit to the IHS hospital in Albuquerque. But once back in the city, Dr. Black, his old IHS boss, jumped at the chance to send Ben to the war zone, as he called it, and enlist his help that was so desperately needed.

The sprawling Navajo reservation was struggling. The huge expanse of land covered some twenty-seven thousand miles, touched three states, and included the Hopi reservation. Not all homes were clustered together. Most were spread out across this wide expanse of land—many hogans and modern mobile homes were without running water or sanitation. Almost all were far from the few, understaffed hospitals and clinics and dependent upon food and supply sources that had literally dried up. To say that help was needed was a grave understatement.

Ben would not have refused even if he could. All able hands—doctors, nurses, support staff—everyone who could be spared in IHS was being sent to the Navajo reservation. The major concern for Ben? He would have to take Zac. On the one hand, what a learning opportunity. On the other, the threat of the virus, the close proximity to life-threatening danger scared him. Becoming a parent had some real drawbacks and came with tremendous responsibility. Would an eleven-year-old be wary of danger that he couldn't see? Always remember to wear a mask and gloves? Socially distance or simply stay sequestered if required?

But maybe he wasn't giving Zac enough credit. And it wasn't like the situation was permanent. At least he hoped not. Zac's school started in two weeks in Bellingham, Washington. There were supplies to purchase, clothing, soccer practice—supposedly to be held on that city's professional field. He knew Zac was really looking forward to that. Ben was probably worrying for nothing. Hopefully, he'd be able to send Zac back within the two-week timeframe. But who knew how long the lock-down would stay in effect? A virus wasn't necessarily predictable. Should he at least plan ahead, a just-in-case scenario? Was home schooling a possibility? A necessity? Ben had a fleeting image of how his life had changed forever. He was tired of hearing people talk about the 'new normal' when he couldn't really accurately remember the 'old normal'. He knew he had Julie's support; he just didn't have Julie with him.

"Dad, quick, look." Zac had pivoted to point out the passenger's side window which he was quickly lowering before leaning out. "What is it? A deer?"

"Antelope, a Pronghorn." The roughly hundred and forty pound animal was running parallel to the truck—and keeping up. Ben glanced at the speedometer, sixty-two MPH. Not exactly a cheetah, but not shabby either. Ben eased off the gas and watched the animal match its stride to the truck's motion. The Pronghorn was literally three feet from Zac and staring at him—running forward but with his head turned to lock eyes with the boy. The animal was known for its overly large, almost bulbous eyes with a three-hundred and twenty-degree field of vision.

"It's like he knows me. Hey, Dude, I'm Zac."

Ben further backed off the gas, but the antelope also slowed. The last thing Ben wanted was for it to try to cross the road in front of the truck. At least they had turned off I-40. There was little or no traffic on this artery that connected with the reservation. But what a bizarre encounter—a wild animal literally interacting with humans. It must be the storm. Under duress animals sometimes reacted differently than what would be considered normal. He knew Pronghorns weren't jumpers; they were built for speed—lightweight bones, hollow hair shafts, and two-toed flexible hooves. To save the antelope from getting caught in fences, area ranchers would often remove the bottom foot or so of their fencing so that the animals could slip underneath without injury and not risk possible death by becoming entangled going over the top.

Zac was enthralled and couldn't keep his eyes off of his new friend. Finally, Ben coasted to a stop alongside the antelope. Only then did the Pronghorn snort and paw at the ground before walking gingerly across the road in front of the truck, looking back once before immediately being swallowed up in the grit-filled haze.

"That was pretty neat. Do you think he's somebody's pet?"

"I wouldn't think so but he did seem tame, didn't he?"

"I wish he'd come back." Zac stared out the windshield trying to catch a glimpse of the antelope. "It's too dark; I can't see anything."

Zac was right. For three o'clock in the afternoon, it might as well be dusk. The sun was almost completely blocked by the storm, offering only a hazy, yellowish light like a flashlight whose batteries were going dead. Ben flipped on his lights, but the truck's headlights were useless—high beams only bounced against the wall of dust, not penetrating it, and low beams had a radius of six feet. Ben put the truck in gear and started forward. They were close to the turn-off, the road that would put them on reservation land; he just didn't know exactly how close.

He had barely accelerated when the rest area sign appeared and Ben braked to make the turn off of the highway. He pulled onto the side road with other signage that proclaimed they'd find restrooms and showers just ahead. Finally, he could relax a little. Pulling off the highway had been the best thing to do. He slowly followed two cars in front of him to a large, but almost full, parking area.

When the dust briefly lifted, he could see that it

appeared the highway had been blocked. It was barricaded and guarded by Native police, armed and in uniform. About twenty pickups and cars were parked in a cluster just to the right of the restrooms, more cars and one eighteen-wheeler were closer to the road. What was odd was that no one seemed to be waiting in their cars. Then it dawned on Ben that this was some kind of protest. The storm must have interrupted a stand-off. But if he understood the new rules, this was a group of obviously more than ten people and wasn't that against the recent mandate? And there wasn't one mask in sight.

He hadn't paid attention to the signs being carried by several people walking along the highway near the turnoff—four-by-four-foot square poster-board attached to wooden slats. In the rest area itself, several signs were propped up against cars, while some were held aloft. The one that gave a shout-out to Woody Guthrie, with a slight adjustment, by announcing "This Land Ain't Your Land," caught his attention. Whose side was the sign carrier on, Indian or Anglo? He kicked himself for not paying attention to the news. He'd been too busy to even turn a TV on. Speaking of which there were two news vans—one local and one sporting NBC signage. Whatever was happening must be big; big enough to vie for national attention.

At least the wind had died down. They would probably be ready to head out again in thirty-minutes or so. He'd use this time to sweep out the bed of the truck and make sure the tarp over their luggage and the supplies from the hospital was secure.

"Hey, Dad, I'm going to go to the restroom."

"Okay, Zac. I hope we can get out of here in a half hour. Be careful. Come straight back to the truck when you're through—I don't like the look of that crowd. Promise me you won't get any closer to them than you are now, and keep your mask on."

"Yeah, Dad."

Was that an eye-roll? How could an eleven-year-old master the withering look so early in life? But maybe Ben was being a little overly cautious and overly protective to Zac's way of thinking. He needed to back off, not do so much overseeing when it probably wasn't needed.

"Sorry, Zac, I don't mean to preach; I just want to keep you safe."

"It's okay. What are they doing?"

"I don't know. Protesting over something. I think I'll try to find out though."

Zac nodded, opened the truck's door and slipped to the ground.

Chapter 2

Weird. That was the only word that Zac could think of as he walked to the squat, tan building with the ends of trees sticking out of the walls in what he had learned was something called "adobe style" and those tree trunks were *vigas*. He'd bet that inside there were small pieces of wood between the *vigas* and those were called *latillas*. To be fair, if his ancestors had figured out how to make homes from snow and ice, he guessed these people had a right to build houses out of mud and tree stumps. But they were strange—floors made of bricks and walls two-feet thick. It was a lot to get used to. He pulled open the heavy, natural wood door to the men's restroom. Sand crunched under his sneakers as he walked in. At least the room had light. Two naked bulbs hung from cords that stretched to the ceiling. If the bulbs had ever had any kind of glass covering, the shades were gone now. Sheets of metal acted as mirrors and lined the wall above and behind the urinals and the trough-like sink to the right. The metal wasn't a good replacement for glass and offered only a fuzzy outline of the room's contents at best.

He had walked to the nearest urinal before realizing he was being watched; someone was in the stall directly behind him. His eye caught the movement of the stall's door in the distorted reflection of the pretend-mirror. He turned to look and saw an eye quickly disappear as the door shut and a pair of dusty biker boots step back. Could be some pervert. They had had a video in health class last year about men doing things to boys in places like this. Or maybe the guy was just curious. Zac wasn't going to let it bother him. He wasn't afraid. He'd just finish up and walk back out to the truck. He didn't even turn around again.

Zac zipped up his jeans and stepped to the sink. The long trough had four faucets. Not one of them turned on—no water; he tried all four. This time the door to the first stall opened and a really big guy stepped out. He was as tall as Dad but lots fatter and he had a beard instead of hair on his head. His beard reached to his chest and had beads braided in it. That looked weird. The guy shaved his head but decorated his beard and the beads were all red, white, or blue.

Zac knew this guy was called a skinhead and not just because his head was shaved; his T-shirt had a confederate flag on it. He bet he rode a Harley or drove a truck. Bad-ass. The term just popped into his head, but Zac bet it was the truth. This guy looked like he got off on being mean.

"Hey, kid, you an Indian?"

"Yeah, are you?" The remark brought a loud guffaw.

"Oh, sure kid, maybe your red-ass needs a whupping for having a smart mouth."

Zac shrugged, pushed his mask up over his nose, and took a couple steps toward the door.

"Not so fast. I'm getting me an idea." The man stepped in front of the door and blocked it. "I think you just might be able to help me out."

"How?"

"I think I'll call it running interference."

"What does that mean?"

"It means that you sorry-ass red suckers are going to let me drive my rig onto your land so I can get to Shiprock before night."

"Why can't you just go?" This wasn't making sense.

"'Cause they gotta take your temperature and a history of what you've been doing, that's why—in case you're bringing the illness with you. And if you're white, you're shit out of luck. You gotta turn around and drive another hundred miles out of your way just to get where you're going—temperature, or no temperature."

"It's called sovereignty. A tribe has sovereign rights. If they don't want you on their land, they can keep you off."

"Oh yeah? You think you and all your red relatives have the right to screw up my day? Cost me a day's wages? Well, you got another think coming."

The guy was beginning to bug Zac. He took a step forward only to be grabbed and spun around with his left arm doubled behind his back.

"Ow. You're hurting me."

"You'll hurt a lot more if you try to get away. Don't mess with me. Only good Indian is a dead one to my way of thinking. Now we're going to walk out of here with you in front of me—close, real close. Don't try anything cute, 'cause I got this 9mm pointed at your head. You understand, kid?" He waited until Zac nodded, then added, "Okay, then, open the door. We're going out." The barrel of the gun was cold and Zac believed his threat. He pushed the door outward.

In the fifteen minutes he'd been inside, the wind had fallen away to just an intermittent soft gust here and there, and the sun was seventy-five percent back to full strength—blindingly bright and beating down on the parking area.

"You see that truck over there? Got Rocky Mountain Transport on the sides in red letters. We're gonna walk over there and the two of us climb up in the cab. Then I'm gonna fire her up and we're gonna bust through that barricade and just keep on going. You do anything stupid, you're out of here. Like in a box. You know what I'm saying?"

Zac nodded. He knew he was shaking but he couldn't stop. And his arm really hurt. The guy had it jerked up high against his back. He only pressed harder if Zac tried to lean away from the pressure.

"Okay then, let's go."

* * *

Ben watched Zac walk toward the restrooms. What had he been like at eleven? Much the same if he remembered correctly. A little arrogance that comes from being a cute, smart kid with a doting grandmother or, in Zac's case a grandmother, an aunt *and* a mother. Neither Zac nor Ben had a father growing up. That was going to change for Zac,

Ben promised himself—it wasn't too late to fill a void.

The six people nearest the roadblock were Navajo men—three were in the uniform of tribal police and judging from the stack of crates and boxes behind them, they were safeguarding a cache of supplies waiting to be taken onto the reservation. He didn't see a pickup or two behind them or any other method of transportation though. The eighteen-wheeler idling to the side appeared to be an interstate transport judging from the tags. They must be waiting for someone from off the Rez to pick them up.

The four-foot-high stacks of worn tires made an effective barricade stretching across both lanes. Two Ford Broncos with Navajo police insignia were parked to the side with two more uniformed men leaning against the hood of the nearest SUV. It was a decent show of power Ben thought, enough to discourage any acting out by motorists surprised at being stopped, or protestors who got out of line. The sandstorm had called a halt to all activity and the protestors were just now picking up their signs and gathering at the road's edge. They seemed to be protesting the situation—a major artery being blocked—not the fact that their travel had been interrupted. And it looked like a few people were getting their fifteen minutes of fame. Two men from NBC had their cameras rolling as they moved among the crowd. One stopped to focus on an interview taking place.

The Navajo man in uniform closest to Ben walked over. "Billie Benally, local Chief of Police." He stretched out his hand and shook Ben's. "Sorry about the handshake; I just used sanitizer. Wasn't sure you were up for an elbow bump." The chief laughed, "I was notified that a Dr.

Pecos was heading this way with supplies for the FEMA settlement? Am I right in thinking that's you?"

"I'm Dr. Pecos and if that's where I need to deliver supplies from IHS, then, yes, I'm your man."

"Good meeting you. We already have supplies just sitting and waiting on transport. The guys picking these up had car trouble—truck just quit on them. We've got another truck going over to the Rez from here, but they can't take everything. Would six of those crates fit in the bed of your truck? We'd appreciate the help."

"Sure. I'll make room. Let me get the truck."

In ten minutes everything was snugged in tight and covered with a large, tie-down blue canvas tarp. "I'll have two of my guys hitch a ride in that sedan with the school teacher." He pointed in the direction of an elderly blue Toyota Corolla much in need of a new paint job. "That way somebody will be at the settlement to help unload. Can't guarantee any help being at the camp. But that's right, you have no idea where you're going or what you're getting into. Well, welcome to FEMA's best mucked up attempt to help the Natives."

"Sorry, I'm not following. FEMA? A camp?"

"You'll get your choice from about fifteen trailers, maybe more by now. Cast-offs, most of them used. Remember Katrina? Well, that's what we've got going out here. Rows of trailers out in the middle of nowhere. Three hospital tents not even completely erected yet and they need more—an additional three are supposed to be delivered today. Spotty electricity, even though they've got some guys working on it, running water every other day until they can clean out the only functioning well—there's talk of a new well, but that depends on whether they can get a rig out here. I'll bet you that could be thirty days. And who's going to pay for it? The bright spot is that you'll have broadband access. Got that set up, tower and all, last year. Yeah, that's a nice modern touch but overall, it's not going to be what you're used to. Well, you get the picture--you'll be roughing it."

"Didn't you mention the woman over there is a school teacher?"

"Yeah, Miss Otter, Miss Carolyn Otter. Single woman. These kids, K through twelve, are her life. Won't find anyone more dedicated to their work."

"Otter? Is she Native?"

Billie laughed. "No, but I'll tell you how she got her name—from the kids. Carolyn was flattered to death—her real name was McKowski, hard for the kids to pronounce or even remember; so, they gave her the name of Otter. But come to find out the name had special meaning. Tell me, Dr. Pecos, you ever smell an otter?"

Ben shook his head. A vision of cute furry animals floating around a pond on their backs holding each other's paws came to mind.

"Well, let me tell you, they smell. No, STINK is more like it. Don't know if it's all the fish they eat and they're just pooping out rancid cod liver oil or it's something in their fur but you don't want to put your nose on one."

"So, the schoolteacher had no idea that giving her that name might be a comment on her personal hygiene?"

"None. She loved it. Even had her name changed legally to Otter. That's been years ago. If she ever found out she'd been the brunt of Indian humor, she never said. It's been so long no one even thinks about it anymore. She's just Miss Carolyn Otter, teacher. We're lucky to have her."

"Her school is nearby?"

"Yeah, the camp is about five miles from a cluster of family dwellings that includes the school—as the crow flies. You'll find that's a favorite Anglo saying out here. Tough to find a direct path to most things. Most times the straight line takes miles off the journey, but meandering is the only thing that will get you where you're going. The school attracts quite a roster; some students come in from up to fifteen miles away. The building that houses the school is old, but functional. The camp is going to tap off of its electricity—they're running some temporary poles between the two areas. Water's being trucked over from their community well now. It will all get fixed—it's just not fixed now."

"Miss Otter lives out here?"

"Drives back and forth from Shiprock. She's out here today getting her classroom ready for school to start. My kids are pissed. Their friends over in Gallup won't be starting school on time this year. But the Rez has its own rules. And everybody's got to be front and center come Monday next week." Billie laughed. "Nobody said being Indian was easy."

Ben laughed with him. He liked this easy-going man who wore his dark hair pulled back in a ponytail and had a turquoise and silver bracelet that covered his entire left wrist.

"Gallup is a ways from here."

"Yeah, but it's about the closest big city." Again that laugh. Gallup being a 'big city' was a stretch, Ben knew. "I have to go over once or twice a month. In addition to wearing this uniform and taking care of everything that comes with it, I'm a silversmith and need to keep my sellers happy. I got three stores that sell my stuff. Need to top up their inventory pretty regularly. Those tourists want their trinkets."

"Not sure this year there'll be a lot of tourists."

"That's a fact. The virus hasn't done us any favors. Maybe you heard that Gallup was completely closed off to all visitors earlier this spring. If you were on I-40, there was no stopping."

"What's the protesting about?" A woman walked by carrying a sign that read 'The Highway is MY way' and pushed past a group of protestors to get closer to the barricade.

"Navajo elders, and backed by the Navajo Nations' President, aren't allowing anyone to cross or enter Indian land who's not a resident or doesn't have a good reason to be here. Granted this highway's the fastest way to Shiprock but there are ways around. It's just one step in trying to keep the virus from spreading. Once on Indian land, we all wear masks and adhere to a strict curfew. You'll get fined if you're out running around after nine—unless you're on hospital business, of course. We're ill-equipped to fight the virus once it takes up residence on the Rez. We're lucky. We've got a President who's taken the illness seriously and moved quickly to contain it." Billie turned to survey the parking lot. "Most of these people are outsiders. Some are just seeking excitement. Some think they need to travel north and pissed that they can't. Like that skinhead. Oh, shit, that looks like trouble." Billie pulled his two-way radio off of his belt and barked into it, "Heads up, coming your way. You got my six?" Then took off, still giving orders that Ben couldn't hear.

Ben turned in the direction Billie was headed. A

mountain of a man, three hundred pounds if he was an ounce, bald head now shining in a ray of sunlight, his T-shirt proclaiming his affiliation, was striding purposefully toward the lone eighteen-wheeler in the lot. He was holding a gun on a kid, pushing that kid in front of him. *Oh my God, the man had Zac.*

"My son! The guy's got my son." Ben caught up with Billie.

"Stay back. I'll handle this." Billie jogged across the highway slowing to a walk keeping his hands out in front of him, but Ben was staying parallel to him and moving at the same rate of speed. There was no way he was going to hang back. He fought to keep the panic down. It would be okay, he would reason with the guy, the cops would let the truck go through—thoughts were coming fast one piled on top of another. *Please, God, don't let anything happen to Zac.*

Chapter 3

"Let him go. Take me." Ben was now about twelve feet from Zac and his abductor.

"I'll let him go when I'm ready." They were nearing the transport. "Back off. I ain't warning you again."

"Dad, no, go back. He'll shoot."

"Okay everyone, let's just calm down. I can guarantee you safe passage. I'll even give you an escort, but you've got to let the young man go." Billie still held out his hands in front of him, palms up. "I'm not armed. I'll give the order and my men will drop their guns, too."

"You think I'm crazy? I'm going to ditch my insurance policy 'cause you promise something? I wouldn't get a mile down the road before you'd sic your posse on me."

Stay calm. Watch. Keep your mouth shut. Ben's internal

dialogue wasn't doing much to soothe his frayed nerves. The guy was tall enough so that Zac's head barely came up to mid-chest. Room for a sharp-shooter to get a round off. But he'd run the risk of a reflex reaction and the gunman would pull the trigger. There was an area—a triangle running from the edge of an eye to the middle of the cartilage between the nasal passages that meant a quick death. A bull's eye hit in this area produced an immediate kill and negated the flinch reflex. Or so he'd heard. It would take some target-perfect marksmanship.

Suddenly he thought he had lost his hearing. The shot was deafening. But the visual of the explosion and burst of bone and blood spraying outward as the body of the trucker was thrown backwards would never leave him. The police lieutenant prone on top of the SUV was literally dead-on from forty feet; it was a sniper's shot with probably an F-Class rifle. Billie must have given orders when he first saw what was happening.

Billie picked up the trucker's gun as Zac hurled himself into Ben's arms.

"I was scared, Dad, I was really scared."

"I was, too, son. You're safe now." And no more words were needed. Ben just hugged his son to him. Even Billie didn't interrupt. When Ben looked up, he realized that the NBC reporter was motioning for him to join the TV crew, but Ben declined. It was obvious that the cameraman had captured all the action. He felt certain that they had made the six o'clock news as it was. His comment or even Zac's wasn't needed. Zac's mother, Raven, would be on the phone the minute she saw what had happened anyway. And Julie? She'd be scared to death. He'd call her the minute they were free to go.

But that wasn't for another two hours. A lot of questions, a lot of paper work. A tow truck finally showed up to take the eighteen-wheeler to an impound. The body was released to be taken to the county coroner's office back in Gallup. There was a little confusion about jurisdiction, and the FBI would inevitably get involved, eventually. Rules and regs for Indian land could be confusing. Finally, they were released to go. It was after five in the afternoon and they still had an hour of driving, then unloading and setting up a place to live.

Ben had been given a list of items they'd need—all household goods, pots and pans, bed linen, towels—duplicates of everything he and Julie had in storage. They'd set up delivery to occur when they had a place in south Florida. Who knew Ben would need household goods now? And it made him think that IHS wasn't treating this as a short-term assignment—not just a long weekend anyway. He'd worry about the timeframe later; right now he needed to make certain that Zac was strong enough to put this incident behind him and not suffer any further trauma. PTSD was real and a possibility. Talking now would be helpful in keeping it in check.

* * *

The ride to camp passed quickly. Ben gave Zac a chance to talk, ask questions or whatever, but he rode quietly, only once commenting on how pissed his mother was going to be and followed up the comment with a grin before he asked if Ben really thought they'd be on TV.

"Yeah, but I nixed the *Today* show for tomorrow morning."

"Really?"

"No, I'm just kidding. Even if they called, we're going to be busy setting up camp for the next week, maybe longer."

And that turned out to be an understatement.

The tiny dots in the distance grew larger until the thirty FEMA trailers fanned out in front of them. Wasn't that a dozen more than the chief had said there would be? There was a distinct 'circle the wagons' effect to the placement of the temporary living quarters—they all faced six huge white tents in their center; again, Chief Billie said six would be in place, that is, if all of them were hospital tents. The tents had to be able to hold twenty to thirty beds. That would be up to a hundred and eighty very sick people at capacity. At least the tents offered more room than the trailers. Important when bulky hospital beds and equipment were required. The magnitude of it all was beginning to sink in. This was preparation for a worst-case scenario. And that could very well be where they were headed.

According to insignia and the half dozen military-type vehicles to the side of the road, both New Mexico's and Arizona's National Guard were the builders of the tent city. Several men were carrying basic items of hospital furniture into the two tents closest to Ben's truck. All were masked and maintaining six feet of distance between them.

In addition, there were several outbuildings—one marked showers, several others obviously toilets. Had he been warned that the plumbing was really just outhouses? No. Would it have made a difference? No, he was here to help. And it looked like he was getting in on the ground-floor, judging by the flurry of activity everywhere he looked. It appeared that digging was in progress for what appeared to be container septic tanks. Heavy plastic and metal receptacles were stacked to the side of the first row of trailers. The set-up had a feeling of being new, and had a certain lack of permanence. The health care units, tents, in front of him marked a temporary settlement, much needed and well-planned but not set up to last indefinitely. How long would the temporary hospital tents be needed? Ben was certain he wasn't the only one who wished he knew.

A cluster of hogans, plus wooden sheds—some possibly homes—were about a quarter-mile farther to the west. But that was the beginning and the end of established civilization. A corral and a makeshift building with eight stalls was to the right of the first FEMA trailer marked 'Office'. He supposed out here horsepower was just that—a way to get around provided by a horse. Someone had graded a makeshift road and thrown some gravel on it. The road crisscrossed in and out between the trailers, the office, and the existing hogans, before meeting the asphalt that they'd driven in on.

"Looks like that's where we need to go first." Ben pointed to the office. Four men sat on the steps, one getting up when he saw Ben pull in and motioning for him to park closer to the building and back in.

"This is our temporary storage until we finish the hospital area. We crammed a couple desks in the front here and left the rest of this building vacant for keeping the necessities close at hand."

"Do you know which of the trailers is yours?" Another man walked forward. "I'd be glad to help you unload."

"I don't have a clue." No one had given Ben the particulars—he'd packed a suitcase, borrowed a truck loaded with hospital supplies, and taken off. Maybe he should have been better prepared. Now he wasn't sure why he hadn't purchased some basic household goods—storage or not. It probably wouldn't have hurt to have doubled up on basics. They might be sleeping on bare mattresses until he could get Julie to unpack what they needed out of storage and send it. Looked like his first job would be to take inventory and make a list. One thing he hadn't even given a thought to was what they would eat. He'd bet money on the trailer not being stocked. And he'd stake his life on the fact that there wasn't a restaurant within fifty miles, let alone a grocery store.

"Well, let's go in and find out where we've been assigned." Ben parked to the side of the office trailer.

"Coming?" Ben turned back to ask Zac.

"I'll wait here." Ben nodded. There was a certain security to waiting in the pickup. He heard Zac lock the doors behind him as he followed the man up the steps.

Chapter 4

Let me get you some hospital sheets and a couple pillows. You can return them when you get your own stuff. I don't fault Dr. Black for not saying anything; I'm sure he has no idea how strapped for supplies we are out here. The trailers are pretty bare—only the basics—but the fridge, stove and microwave are new. We just don't have the electricity to run them—not fulltime and only after a generator is fired up. So, right now, they're just nice to look at. Each trailer does have a propane tank for the stove. At least that's something." The woman who seemed to belong to the desk in trailer one laughed. She had introduced herself as Trini Lovato, Administrative Assistant to the FEMA appointed logistics marshal. Probably forty-something with a messy bun on top of her head of shiny black hair, Trini was holding a phone to her ear with one hand while the other was rummaging through the top drawer of a file cabinet.

"I know I put the keys to the supply trailer in here somewhere. We'll get you all set up. I really should be apologizing but we've been promised water and electricity late tomorrow. Fingers crossed that's not a fib. We're so indebted to Dr. Black for sending people to help. I don't want you to think the only thing I can do is bitch. I really mean it when I say thank you for coming."

"I want to help. We'll be fine; I have my eleven-year-old son with me and it will be a great experience for him."

"Camping like he's never seen it before." She chuckled. "He'll survive. Kids are so much better at adapting than we are."

"I tend to believe you, but I'd feel better if I knew how I was going to get groceries."

"Oh, I'm glad you reminded me, the supply truck will be going into Gallup tomorrow. Make a grocery list and the driver will pick up what you need. If you can have the list to me by nine in the morning, he'll pick it up before he leaves and should have your order to you by mid-afternoon. Now, let me see which trailer I've put you in. Trailer three. Come with me; I'll walk you over."

Zac had jumped out of the truck to join them by the time they'd walked across the open area and passed trailer two.

"Here we are—home sweet home and in the front row. You're lucky getting in here a day early. By tomorrow, all thirty trailers will have occupants. We're having to squash families of four or five into two-bedroom trailers—the relatives of those being hospitalized—their own communities so riddled with disease that they need a place of safety. And I've been told we can expect our second wave of virus patients—another twenty-five this afternoon. That first hospital tent is already full and the second will be a hive of activity soon. And, I'm sorry to say, it will instantly fill to capacity. We just can't stay ahead of the illness."

Ben liked being in the front row and not stuck a few trailers deep. He could only imagine this place once it became populated. "I can see why getting the electricity connected is a high priority."

"Absolutely. Right now generators are saving our bacon, but they're only meant to be short term and for back-up when needed. Here, I'll get the door." She pulled a ring of keys out of her pocket, slipping two off and unlocking the front door before turning to Ben. "Here you go, keys to the front door and back door. No rules about locking up— probably no reason to out here. We're all working together for a common cause. I think we can be trusted."

"Does anyone have a bike I could borrow?" Zac stepped up beside Ben.

"Bikes for transportation aren't nearly as plentiful as horses. And horses make more sense. Say you fall off somewhere a ways from camp; that horse will always come home to eat, letting everyone know something happened. Are you a rider?"

"I've been on a horse once." Ben could tell Zac wasn't too excited about relying on a horse to get around.

"Well, I'm sure we can find you one to learn on. I'll put the word out."

"That would be great, wouldn't you agree, Zac?" Ben got a very tepid nod in return.

"Let's make sure everything's in order." Trini pushed the door open and stepped inside.

The single-wide was more of a modular than a trailer—sturdier, for one thing. And it was clean. Ben was surprised. He had pretty much counted on borrowing cleaning equipment and spending an exciting first evening just getting the place ready to move in, but outside of a little dust that had seeped in under the door, the place sparkled.

As if she could read his mind, Trini added, "It looks pretty good. It's been disinfected and you'll find a generous stash of Clorox wipes and hand disinfectant under the sink. Make yourselves at home. I'll be back with the linen." She left the door open, and Ben watched as she headed toward the office. Trini was thin, sinewy, with the long and lean body of a runner. From the back, a couple of tendrils of her black hair had escaped the bun to dangle past her shoulders. But it was her jewelry that caught his eye. It was spectacular—rows of pin shell *heishe* that belied a Pueblo heritage, interspersed with hand-carved Zuni fetishes of bone, amber, and semi-precious stones. In the center was a string of round, etched, hand-made, sterling silver beads graduating in size from a penny to a quarter. His grandmother used to call necklaces like that, 'Navajo Pearls'.

Ben turned to Zac. "What do you think?"

"Makes me think I'm in Alaska—you know, tiny houses?"

Ben smiled. "I hadn't thought of that. You're right, these would fit right in. So which bedroom do you want—your choice."

"Can I have the bedroom in front with the window and the bunk beds?"

"It's yours. Want to help me bring our stuff in?" The second bedroom had a queen-sized bed—much more appropriate if Julie ever visited. Ben smiled. Bunk beds wouldn't really have worked out.

In addition to their two suitcases and a box of patient files that Dr. Black would be picking up, was the last of their lunch fixings—half a loaf of bread, a jar of peanut butter, one of strawberry jam, chips, and another bag of stale Ritz crackers. Looked like this would have to do for dinner also.

Trini delivered the sheets and towels and had a young maintenance man bring over a cooler with ice, soft drinks and a half gallon of milk. "I begged a box of Cheerios off of Oscar here. He just got back from town so the ice should keep overnight and the milk will still be fresh. Don't forget to get me your grocery list. Here's a flashlight, and I'll have Oscar fire up the generator so you'll have lights tonight." With that she was gone.

"Is there a TV?"

"No, we may not have reception out here." Ben was glad he'd charged up their phones in the truck before they got to the camp. No electricity was beginning to become a problem. Oscar reported that the generator that would get them by didn't seem to have gas. He'd check into it in the morning. And he wasn't sure that the promise that there would be broadband support had been entirely truthful either. When he checked a map for T-Mobile on his phone, it showed only eighty-five percent of the reservation had service. If they didn't have service, he wouldn't have to listen to Raven and hear what a bad parent he was for endangering their son.

But there was enough power for Raven's call to get

through and between her yelling and tears, Ben was finally able to assure her that the situation on the highway was a fluke. They were now safe in camp and would continue to be safe. Zac talked to his mother and then handed the phone back so Ben could promise a call a day--if the electricity was turned on and they could charge their phones, and if they had more than half a bar of available service; otherwise, he said he'd make a trip into civilization and make sure they connected and she got an update. Appeased, or giving up—Ben couldn't tell which—Raven hung up.

Ben walked out to the truck to call Julie. Amazing how clear the air was—not even a hint of the sandstorm just a couple hours before. Without clouds, the sky simply sparkled. He was tempted to stop and try to name some constellations, but it was getting late and tomorrow promised to be busy. He'd make a note to look up some material on star formations. Star-gazing might be a fun thing to do with Zac.

Chapter 5

Ben woke with that disturbing feeling of being disoriented. The sheets smelled slightly of disinfectant and the room was stuffy—hot, without moving air. It crossed his mind to jump in the shower before he remembered that there wasn't any running water. Oscar Begay, who seemed to be in charge of maintenance and delivery of supplies, had brought two five-gallon containers of drinking water last night before they went to bed and left them on the porch. Ben hoped they wouldn't have to rely on bottled water for too long. He checked his watch, seven straight up. They'd gone to bed at ten and slept soundly; at least, he had. The quiet of the desert had a lulling effect, soothing actually, but he had a feeling it wouldn't last once the camp filled with people. This might have been his last full night of sleep.

"Hey, Dad, you want some Cheerios?" Zac's voice carried easily through the thin, hollow-core bedroom door.

"Sure, pour me a bowl, I'll be out in a minute."

Zac was sitting at the counter working on what might have been his second bowl of the breakfast food when Ben pulled up a stool in front of his own bowl of Cheerios.

"Can we get some eggs and bacon? Maybe orange juice? And bread, can we get white? I don't like whole wheat."

"Glad you reminded me. I'll grab pencil and paper and we can make a grocery list right now."

Coffee was high on the list, as well as paper towels, toilet paper, and dish soap. Ben nixed ice cream, reminding Zac that coming from Gallup or Shiprock, it would arrive in a puddle and he wasn't sure they'd have a freezer—at least not by the end of the day. The generator would keep things cool for a short time, but ice cream would be a challenge. Finally, the list was finished. Additions of popcorn, sliced luncheon meats, and cheese, bread, mayo, mustard and a large bag of chips took care of lunches along with a few cans of soup. It would be hard to go wrong with toasted cheese sandwiches and Campbell's tomato soup. The kitchen wasn't exactly his place to shine, but Ben thought he could keep them from starving.

"I'm going to run this over to Trini. I'll be right back. If they don't need me here, let's do some exploring, get acquainted with the reservation—sound like a plan?"

"Yeah, that'd be great."

* * *

It was not quite eight but Trini's truck was parked beside trailer one. Already two ambulances were parked behind the first hospital tent next to a good-sized truck hauling a flatbed trailer. Several National Guardsmen were unloading what looked to be hospital equipment—crates that might contain compressors, or ventilators, and IV paraphernalia alongside beds. Several others in scrubs—doctors, techs or nurses—seemed to be giving directions as to which tent needed which equipment. Trini had been right, there was a lot of activity. The promising sight was the New Mexico Power and Light truck that pulled in with a trailer holding a huge spool of cable. Now that looked positive. Maybe there would be electricity by the end of the day.

He pushed open the door to the office and was surprised to see Chief Billie sitting across from Trini.

Chief Billie looked up. "Dr. Pecos, just the man I want to see. Got a minute?"

"Sure."

"Let's step outside."

Ben handed his grocery list to Trini and followed the chief back out the door.

"First, I've got some information I think you might be interested in. Secondly, I'm going to ask a favor."

"Okay."

"Let's sit in the Bronco. We won't be bothered there."

Ben had to admit he was curious. He sensed that the chief was a no-nonsense type and he had no idea what kind of favor he would ask. The Bronco had seen better days, but riding around the reservation would age any vehicle. Ben climbed in and closed the passenger-side door.

"We got the report on that skinhead who grabbed your son. Seems he wasn't just the trucker he pretended to be. His eighteen-wheeler was loaded with supplies that were meant for this camp. We found the driver—or the driver's body, I should say—in a dumpster in Gallup. Apparently, our guy had killed the man, highjacked the truck, and was headed for Colorado. He had a rap sheet a mile long. Coroner put his prints in the system and what a surprise." Chief Billie paused. "What I'm going to share with you needs to stay between us. Do I have your word on that?"

Ben nodded. "Of course."

"If the run-in with the trucker had been an isolated incident, I wouldn't be having this conversation, but it wasn't. In the three weeks that we've been putting together this camp, we've lost three shipments of supplies—the one we just confiscated would have been number four. Somehow the shipping schedule is leaked and Personal Protection Equipment bound for this area is diverted either coming out of Gallup or Albuquerque. We've lost twenty-five crates of ventilators. We were lucky to be able to have access to several donated by hospitals in Colorado. They should have arrived this morning. PPE, made up of masks, gowns, foot coverings, gloves—even sanitizer and disinfectant—are also in high demand and disappearing in bulk."

"Where does the PPE go?"

"To the highest bidder, for starters. It's repackaged and shipped across the US—maybe even to other countries as far as I know. It's big money. Millions usually. There's a center, a warehouse actually, that accepts the contraband. The FBI has it under surveillance, but those behind the crime ring have managed to elude capture."

"And the favor you were going to ask of me?"

"I need a plant—someone who can freely travel this area. IHS is a perfect cover. Your time won't be one hundred percent dedicated to the hospital here; I suspect you'll be free to move around and you'd have a reason to be involved with ordering supplies. I need an ear to the ground. Someone who knows his way around the medical world and can speak 'doctor'."

"Remember, I have my son with me."

"All the better. A child just broadens the scope of your interests and ability to join groups. We're going to need a spokesperson to act as liaison with the government over the stimulus payments. Someone who can bargain from a position of knowledge of what's needed. That same person would need to interact with the local tribal chief; actually, we call him President—a Native, someone who wouldn't be suspect. Do I need to say that you would be perfect?"

"Thanks for the vote of confidence."

"Is that a yes? You'll do it?"

Ben nodded. He might not be so willing had Zac not had his life threatened. Finding out that incident was just part of a dangerous crime ring preying on the reservation swayed his decision. The murder of the real transport driver was shocking. Theft was one thing, but killing put a sinister and ruthless spin to it. And it didn't sound like the theft would stop—not without intervention. He wasn't sure what he could do, but he'd be the chief's inside contact.

"If I need to get a message to you, I'll send Oscar Begay. I think you've met the kid who makes deliveries around here. Your code name is 'shrinkwrap'—I'm sure you see the connection? Seems perfect for a psychologist. If Oscar brings in a grocery list requesting shrinkwrap, I'll know you need to talk and I'll be making a trip out here pronto."

Ben fought an impulse to laugh; the chief was deadly

serious. Codename Shrinkwrap? Had he just auditioned and won a part in a bad *CSI* episode? "Clever," was all he thought of to say.

"Don't write anything down unless you have to—unless it's something you might forget or screw up. A license plate, a phone number, for example. I'd like you to check the deliveries—what's been ordered and what arrives. I'd like you to get me a list of staff—volunteers and IHS transplants. Who comes out here, who goes. Maybe the thefts are completely inside jobs. Maybe it's delivery people, even government or state workers getting us all wired up for the future and are in a position to know what's being ordered. Can't put a stop to what you don't know. So, if something seems odd, out-of-place maybe—and I don't care how trivial—let me know about it. People gossip. Over the years that I've been in police work, I've found much of it is worth following up on. So, as I said, keep an ear to the ground. Questions?"

"I'm sure there will be; I just can't think of any now."

"I can't tell you how pleased I am. This takes a big weight off my shoulders. I've been at a disadvantage in that I can't be here all the time—I have a pretty large territory to cover and this is just one part of it. So, I have to say this makes me believe in prayer—I've been searching for a remedy and here it is. I need to stop talking and get on out of here now. Funny how there's always an urgency to police work. It doesn't wait until you can get around to doing something. Most situations need answers yesterday. Good luck, Dr. Pecos. I'm counting on you."

No pressure, Ben thought as he opened the Bronco's passenger-side door and stepped to the ground. Just help keep the operation safe and productive and catch the bad guys. He had to admit he was flattered; he felt useful. He watched as Chief Billie turned toward the road, gunned the Bronco, and disappeared into a cloud of dust.

Chapter 6

When he got back to the trailer, it was unlocked and empty. He probably needed to see about having another set of keys made or just give Zac the back door key and have him enter and leave that way. That was easier. Ben was replaying the conversation with Chief Billie and beginning to feel the need to outline a plan of action. Not to write down but just to think through before acting. Trini would be invaluable. If anyone could help him with the comings and goings of supply deliveries, it would be Trini. He'd just taken a cool bottle of water from the ice chest and pulled up a stool to the breakfast bar when Zac burst in.

"Dad, I got somebody I want you to meet. This is my friend, Nathan. Nathan Yazzie."

Ben had been gone an hour and already Zac had made a friend. A young boy stepped out from behind Zac. Ben was immediately struck by large brown eyes and black hair shaved on one side of his head leaving a pretty impressive comb-over that brushed his shoulder on the opposite side. If it were the seventies, the cut would be a type of Mohawk—named for Mohawk Indians fighting wars with bows and arrows who would shave the side of their heads where the bow-string would be pulled back. If Nathan was a warrior today, he'd be announcing to the world that he was right-handed. He was probably Zac's age or close, but pre-teen boys grew in varying spurts. Even though Zac was tall for eleven years, Nathan was two inches taller.

"Nathan, it's nice to meet you. Do you live here in the camp?"

"I rode in the ambulance with my grandmother this morning. She's got a bad heart and it's safer for her to be in the hospital with all the sickness. I don't know where I'll stay. Is there someone I should ask?"

"Let's go check in with Trini at the office. I bet she'll have the answers."

* * *

But Trini didn't. The three of them crowded into her office and waited until she finished a phone call to see where relatives of patients would be staying.

"It's just one more thing we didn't plan on. Single family members. We need a dormitory setup. I don't know why FEMA thought all patients would be by themselves and magically get here, check themselves in and hop into bed after taking their own temperature. And if anyone came with them, it would be two or more adult family members. We have a lot to learn and a lot to do better. We just don't have accommodations for anyone under eighteen."

"Dad, why couldn't Nathan stay with us? My room has bunk beds. We've got room."

"Oh, Dr. Pecos, if you could see your way to take Nathan in, that would be wonderful. He lives over four miles from here with his grandmother, and now even if he could get back and forth, he'd be alone."

"I think Zac's suggestion would work out fine. Nathan? What do you think?" Ben asked.

As an answer Nathan simply looked up at Ben and nodded. Ben watched as Zac gave Nathan a high five and both boys just grinned at each other. Had this been planned? It didn't matter; Ben couldn't have asked for a better turn of events. He'd been worried about leaving Zac alone or, worse, dragging him everywhere he needed to go.

"I need to bring my horses here. I saw the stalls and corral. May I put them there? I only have two."

"I don't see why not. They were installed for those traveling a long distance to visit the hospital. At least someone got that right. I'll put your name on the two stalls at the end and add your name to Dr. Pecos's trailer." Trini was writing on a yellow tablet. "I'll let Oscar know that he needs to get water to the trough at the barn. Will you be in charge of food for the animals?" This was directed to Ben.

"Yeah, I think I can manage that. I should be able to get into Gallup to a feed store when I have to."

"I need to get some things for my grandmother and pick up the horses. I've got food there, too. Zac said he could help me bring them back to camp."

This was awkward. Ben assumed he meant to ride the

horses from his home to here. He didn't think Zac had a lot of experience with horses, and riding one a few miles might be a little challenging. But he wouldn't embarrass his son by either sharing his worries or refusing to let him help. There were just some things that came under the heading of *learning experiences*. And Ben had an idea that he'd be spending a lot of time crossing his fingers.

"Oh, Dr. Pecos, I meant to ask earlier—would you be able to meet with a FEMA representative at four today?"

"Sure. That will work. What is this concerning?"

"Money. Delivery of goods. Finger-pointing—excuses as to why it hasn't gone faster. It's always the same. In the thirty days that we've been assembling this camp, the powers that be have visited one time. Took a few pictures and left. Of course, they call almost daily. Dr. Pecos, we're playing catch-up. Everything that's here today should have been in place a month ago. I'm tired of the promises and no action. And I'm tired of everything being our fault. I'm glad you'll be dealing with them and not me anymore."

* * *

Ben followed Nathan's directions and headed the truck west and south. He wouldn't make good time; the road was washboard rough. In fact, he wasn't so much on a road as he was on packed clay that had been worn down by foot trade, vehicles, and more than a few horses with riders. Every rain, which luckily wasn't often, saw rivulets run across the road leaving a wavy surface when dry. Just one of those things Natives were stuck with without road-grading equipment.

Once again he felt himself caught up in the vast

expanse of land and sky and natural monuments in the distance. Pinks, oranges, and golds defined the landscape of mesas and rolling hills. There just wasn't very much that was green—some scrub brush but nothing taller than his waist. Yet the landscape was arresting—something a visitor would never forget. The boundaries of New Mexico and Arizona were blended together out here. If he were to turn more directly south, Chinle would command the skyline— that stove-pipe shaped rock outcropping several stories high, a symbol synonymous with the Southwest. This Indian land just a couple hundred miles from his birthplace was so different. The Pueblos of Ben's childhood were true villages with their squat adobe dwellings, most sharing an interior wall clustered together to form one community with a plaza in the center and a church and burial ground at the edge. Or, like Taos, the first apartment house style of adobe buildings with a second floor.

In contrast, the Navajo reservation was a collection of scattered residences, separate hogans or wooden lean-tos, housing that defined autonomy with distance from one another. More than one hundred and seventy-five thousand citizens in an area the size of West Virginia. Ben could see the worry about a virus running rampant across such a vast area. What plan had been set in place to contact these outliers? Who was checking on families like Nathan's?

"Nathan, how did you get an ambulance for your grandmother?"

"I went to my uncle's house last night and told him his sister had fainted and was complaining about pain in her chest. He promised to have someone come out this morning. He's a member of the tribal council, so he can make things happen." He suddenly pointed out the truck's windshield. "There. See the water tank and windmill? Turn to your right. You can see the hogan from here."

It was evident that this dwelling was a summer house with a bark roof and one side open. But again the entryway faced east to capture the sunrise and good blessings. Much of everyday life was enjoyed outdoors for a part of the year—even weaving. Under a thatched hut to the side of the dwelling was a loom and a half-finished rug or blanket— he couldn't tell which. A cooking pit was also outside; otherwise the structure consisted of wooden beams, large sticks actually, covered with weeds and grasses and covered over with an earth mixture of natural 'plaster'.

Behind the summer house was the foundation and debris of what had been an octagonal hogan, now destroyed. Ben knew without asking that the house had been demolished because there had been a death. When someone dies in his or her house, ghosts prevent it from ever being lived in again. But the real surprise was the forty-foot travel trailer, an expensive-looking camper with two pop-out rooms and a covered porch that commanded a good portion of the loosely fenced yard. The old and the new. Somehow this living arrangement seemed to sum up modern life on the reservation.

"My cousin won that at the Flowing Water Casino last year. My uncle wouldn't let him put it on his land so he gave it to his sister, my grandmother. I like it. The beds are really nice."

"Isn't Flowing Water by Shiprock?"

"Yeah."

Ben paused. Odd. Indians usually weren't gamblers. There were all those sayings about what the Indians gave the White Man, like tobacco, which the White Man couldn't handle and casinos where the White Man lost his money. The downside of those sayings, however, was the fact that the White Man gave the Indian alcohol and the result of that was history. Only now, Ben would add opioids to the list.

"Looks like a nice winter home." And it looked new. He wasn't up on his recreational camping equipment, but this looked like a thirty to forty-thousand-dollar model. The cousin made a nice win.

"It is, but my grandmother still cooks outside and grinds corn on a metate. See, there." Nathan pointed to a spot just outside the door to the summer house. "And she's working on a Two Grey Hills rug over there. She won't work inside the trailer, says the light isn't good."

Or more likely, changing old ways wasn't easy, Ben thought. The spirits that might dwell in an aluminum-sided camper trailer wouldn't be the kind of old spirits that the rug would need in order to be in balance with nature. The sound of a whinny interrupted his thoughts.

"That's Apache. He knows I'm home. Zac, come with me." Nathan took off for a lone stand of trees next to a corral of rough-hewn boards. A lean-to propped up by several bales of alfalfa provided shelter and two horses hung their heads over the top railing of the fence, seeming to anticipate some petting.

"C'mon, Dad." Zac hurried after Nathan.

"Apache is the buckskin." Nathan had already climbed up on the fence and was stroking Apache's neck. "This is Rain. He's a grullo." He pointed to the silver-gray horse with dark points and a dark dorsal stripe, the coloration on his legs was mottled with white stockings on his hind legs.

"I think I might have named him drizzle." Ben said

mostly to himself not meaning Zac to hear, but too late. Zac had already turned 'dad' into two syllables.

"Da-ad, Rain is a great name. He's going to be my horse."

"Okay, but Nathan, what's a grullo?"

"His mother is a dun and his father is a black and white pinto. It's a really special color. Plus, he won't get too big because his mother is a Fjord—that's a horse from Norway."

Already Ben knew he was out of his element, but he did have one last question. "I'm curious, Nathan, why does Apache have a red ribbon braided into his tail? Any special meaning? Or just decoration?"

Nathan laughed. "Uh, you don't do a lot of riding, do you?" Ben shook his head. Ponies were scarce in the Pueblo; growing up, all his friends wanted dirt-bikes. "Any time you see a horse with a red ribbon in his tail, it means he's a kicker. Don't walk around him too close and don't ride your horse up behind him or you'll both get kicked. Apache likes to cow-kick, you know, that sideways thrust that can cripple you—I mean like break a kneecap, it's so fast and strong."

Ben was developing a new admiration for the horse that was standing with its weight on three legs, fourth leg bent with a tip of the hoof barely touching the ground—relaxed to the point of dozing off. It was hard to imagine the horse was a kicker.

"Zac and I should get started back to camp."

"Want me to follow you?"

"No, I'm going to show Zac around a little. We're going to go up to the foothills. But I would like some help loading these bales of alfalfa onto your truck. And I don't want to forget the mash and some brushes and their water buckets. I'll just put the tack we're going to need today out in the corral."

Ben watched Nathan retrieve two saddles from the makeshift barn attached to the two open stalls, and in three trips, saddles, bridles and blankets were all positioned at one end of the fenced area. Ben moved the pickup around to the back of the corral, getting as close as he could to the stash of alfalfa before jumping out and lowering the tailgate.

"Nathan, I'm going to be snoopy. How old are you?" Ben watched him grab a sixty-pound bale and hoist it up onto the tailgate.

"Almost thirteen. I'm a year ahead in school. Miss Otter has promised to put me into the upper middle school group. There are three of us. Will Zac be starting school on Monday?"

"Yeah, Dad, can I?"

Ben hadn't thought about it, but it might not be such a bad idea. It would give Zac some structure, and Ben would be free to do whatever needed to be done for Chief Billie. For six to eight hours out of the day, he wouldn't have to wonder what the two boys were doing. "I don't see why not. If enough kids might be interested, ask Miss Otter if she'd like me to set up a soccer field—that is, if there's room. I wouldn't mind getting in some coaching time."

"That's great." Ben could tell Zac was thrilled. Even Nathan enthusiastically nodded.

"We need to get you some supplies. Nathan, do you know what Zac will need?"

"No problem. I always have extra. I'm sure I have enough. We're supposed to have Wi-Fi this year; so, he'll need a tablet. That's maybe the most important thing."

"Got one."

"Sounds like you're set." Ben sighed. Just in case there were other supplies that Zac might need, he'd try to touch base with Miss Otter and double-check that Zac was prepared. It could be a great learning experience. He moved the pickup closer to the barn and helped Nathan load all the food and horse gear. Then Nathan led both horses out into the corral and Ben stood back to watch.

"I'll saddle Apache first. Watch what I do and copy me. I'll help if you need it."

Both horses were wearing halters. Nathan snapped a lead rope in place then unbuckled Apache's halter, slipping it back behind his ears to work as a collar around his neck. He fastened the end of the rope in a looping knot over the fence post. He warned Zac that it was important to have his horse tethered in place before saddling especially in a community barn or around others. So, next came the bridle, he started at the mouth, a thumb in the corner to get Apache to open and take the bit, then up and over his ears, putting the crown of the bridle over one ear at a time. Lastly, he buckled both straps—the throat latch and the strap across and under the nose.

Two saddles were propped on the ground and two brightly woven wool blankets had been thrown over the fence. Nathan handed Zac a saddle blanket, before putting one on Apache. Next, he picked up the saddle, set it on the horse's back with one stirrup over the pommel along with a girth strap, the other girth strap hanging down the opposite side. He ducked under the horse and pulled the far strap to meet the strap closest to him before slipping the end through the buckle, tightening it by pulling back hard, his knee against the horse's belly for leverage. Lastly, he adjusted the stirrups.

"Now, it's your turn."

Ben had to admit that Zac was good. He remembered everything; only the girth needed to be tightened. Nathan redid the strap by once again putting a knee against the horse and pulling hard, then he wiggled the saddle to test its stability.

"Done." Nathan laced his fingers together palms up, bowed his arms and slightly leaned forward. Zac lightly stepped on the makeshift booster step and pushed off, grabbing the pommel and pulling himself into the saddle. A slight adjustment to the stirrups and they were ready to go.

"Good job. You could become a real Indian." Nathan was grinning so no harm intended, Ben thought. And Zac was just as quick on the uptake.

"Yeah? Come to my house someday and learn how to kill a walrus. That's real Indian stuff." Both boys were laughing as they rode out of the yard.

Ben could hear Nathan continuing Zac's riding lesson. "… you don't want too much slack in the reins but don't pull on his mouth either …" Finally, they were out of range, but it looked like the lesson was continuing. He watched Nathan bend forward explaining something about the bridle or, at least, that's what it looked like.

Ben knew of all the fun things that he might think up to do on this vacation, Zac would put horseback riding and meeting Nathan first. And he couldn't say that he blamed him. Good friends were to be valued. Ben started the truck and turned toward the road. He didn't even turn back to watch the two boys ride in the opposite direction. He admonished himself to stop worrying. Kids everywhere learned to ride horses. And Zac had a private teacher. And a smart one, too. Kids needed to learn things on their own; they didn't need helicopter parents. Of course, he'd decided all those things before he became a parent. Funny how reality put a new spin on things.

But he needed to get to work—get back to camp and talk with Trini before meeting with the government representative. There was a lot that he didn't know. On the job training wasn't going to work in this situation—preparedness, or simply having the upper hand, would be important.

Chapter 7

Ben walked into Trini's office just as she was opening a lunch box with Star Wars characters on the sides. He was pretty certain it was a hand-me-down from grandkids.

"Just because it's old doesn't mean it should be thrown out." Noticing his interest, she pointed at the lunchbox. "I think that's a good attitude to have until I look around my house—I'm not a hoarder, but it looks like I'm in training." She laughed. "I used to work for the Mission School out your way; Franciscans never throw anything away. I always say their habits rubbed off on me."

"I meant to ask this morning but wasn't comfortable in front of Nathan—how is his grandmother doing?"

"Not well, I'm afraid. She'd had pneumonia last winter after a heart attack and still isn't very strong. But I'm so glad she's here, and I am so glad that you were able to take Nathan in. I don't know what's going to happen if he loses his grandmother."

"His parents aren't able to care for him?"

"Both dead. He lost both of his parents when he was five. A car accident outside Gallup; they had been drinking. I doubt if he even has a clear memory of them now. His grandmother has been his only family."

"He mentioned an uncle—grandmother's brother?"

"Yes. Interestingly the grandmother's brother did the same thing she did—took in his grandchildren when their parents died. There were two boys and it was difficult even after one of the boys passed. The uncle tries, but he's getting older now, too. And the remaining child, his grandson? Don't get me started. I'll be kind and just say he's worthless. But this is a common story on the reservation. The true extended family many times born out of necessity."

Anything further was interrupted by shouting and the banging of car doors. Some kind of confrontation was taking place right outside the office. Ben couldn't make out what was being said, but the anger was hard to miss.

"I'll be right back." Ben opened the office door and stepped onto the narrow porch just as the gun went off. "Get down." This yelled over his shoulder to Trini. "Under the desk." In the meantime, Ben hit the wooden planking and lay prone. Apparently, the shot had gone wild—maybe meant to scare and not connect. The young man getting into a silver and black Camaro was still angry, slamming the car-door shut and peeling out but not before yelling, "You want red-power? We'll show you red power. Don't mess with us."

Idle threat? Some long-term grudge? Ben was at a loss

because he didn't know the history or the players. There appeared to be two other men in the muscle car but no gun in sight. The object of the attack was a man just standing up and peering around the hood of the van parked next to the building. He squinted through thick lenses in black plastic frames. In the hot Southwest sun, he looked out of place in a black suit and red-striped tie. Ben noted the van had government tags.

But what caught Ben's attention and was absolutely mesmerizing was the sparkle as the sun hit thousands of tiny glass bottles scattered around the car and reaching to the bottom of the office steps. Glass containers that appeared to be some novelty shape—maybe miniature soda bottles? None of this made sense.

"It wasn't my fault. I want you to make a note of that. I had no idea what they were sending. None. Zip. Zero." The man slipped on the loose bottles as he came toward Ben. "This is an outrage. I agree with the hothead in the Camaro—not with firing a gun but with the anger at how the needs of thousands of people out here are being handled. Guess I should say mishandled. Charley Chase here." The man started to hold his hand out, then drew it back.

Ben kicked aside a few bottles. The pandemic had put new procedures in place for meeting and greeting. He wished the man was wearing a mask. "Would I be right in saying that this would have been literally a case of killing the messenger?"

"Well, at least the delivery person. He could have done a better job of that, if he'd wanted to. Just put a crease above the door here." He pointed to a scraped indentation in the van's white exterior on the driver's side. "I have a feeling this was a deliberate near-miss only meant to scare me, and let me tell you, he did one hell of a good job of that."

"You don't know the guy? Never seen him before?"

"Nope. First time out this way. I'm an office flunky in the IHS hospital over by Shiprock and last-minute substitute driver 'cause the regular guy called in sick."

"But miniature soda bottles? I'm at a loss here."

"Just another foreign shipment that wasn't checked when received. Another example of thousands of taxpayers' dollars wasted. You ought to see what was delivered to the warehouse bearing the name of toilet paper. Rolls about one tenth the size of what we'd call normal. Over a hundred thousand dollars' worth. Criminal. Just plain robbery."

"I'm still not sure what had been ordered here? Why you got little novelty bottles."

"Vials. Five thousand test vials for sample collection. The reservation has got to get a handle on who has the virus and who doesn't. This debacle puts them back another month—thirty more days that the illness can go unchecked."

"Who did the ordering?"

"You mean who'll own up to it. Everybody passes the buck. Committee to committee. Nobody does any wrong. But the buck should stop with FEMA."

"There should be some recourse with a government agency. Maybe take it to the courts?"

"We'll pay hell trying to make it stick. But this is a criminal act—with lives endangered."

A man in a white lab coat walked toward them, then stopped, surveyed the bottles and just shook his head. "No one even cares. I'm Dr. Henry. I'm heading up the task force out here. I volunteered to help but had no idea what I was getting into. I'm assuming there were no swabs?"

"None in this shipment."

"I can get fifty or sixty vials and swabs from Albuquerque. Lovelace Medical Center has made the offer. But fifty or sixty test setups are a far cry from the thousands of tests that need to be done. "

"How can we make this right?" Ben asked.

"Well, this goes a little beyond writing your congressman. I'll be honest; I don't know." The doctor sat down on the office steps before adjusting his mask. "I used to think I had a little pull with Washington but not this administration. We triaged ten patients over the morning. Half needed to be put on ventilators immediately—I had brought up five with me just yesterday from ABQ. That was pure luck. Now we're waiting on a shipment of ventilators and hope we don't get generators, or swimming pool pumps."

"What if we contacted lawyers in Washington, made our case, even included pictures? I'd like to think no one really knows how dire our plight is out here. I'd be willing to take on the project. I think IHS sees me as a floater—do whatever I can, wherever I can—and I'd think they could be helpful with finding personnel to represent us."

"As long as you have the time; I don't. In fact, I need to get back to the tent now. My night shift is going to be made up of nurses from Gallup General, nurses putting in a double shift. I'm setting up one of the tents as a dormitory. As long as I'm borrowing nurses and overworking them, I need to allow them some rest and a little privacy. I'm also looking into setting up a cafeteria. I'll let you know about that, and you keep me in the loop. Let me see what you send out, and if I need to make time to help, I'll try to be available." Dr. Henry stood up. "I'm glad you're here."

Ben watched as he walked back around the office. The word competent came to mind. They were lucky to have someone like that in charge. But now the work started.

He turned back to the government man in the black suit. "Mr. Chase, I'm going to need you to give me a statement. I want to know where you picked up the load of supplies, names of contact people, and I'll need copies of your bill of lading."

He showed Chase into a spare room in the office trailer, one not yet filled with supplies, and told him to make himself comfortable. Ben grabbed his laptop from his own trailer and a bottle of water from the ice chest. Wow, what a surprise—Ben heard the hum of the refrigerator. And just to make certain the electricity was on, he flipped the kitchen light switch. Lights. That was a relief. At least things wouldn't spoil. He put a half dozen bottles of water in the fridge and pulled the ice-maker bar down before remembering there was no water hook-up. Oh well, electricity was the main thing.

* * *

He gave Charley Chase the cold bottle of water and a yellow tablet and closed the door, leaving him in the makeshift office while he talked with Trini.

"Who was the guy in the black Camaro?" He had seen Trini looking out the window as the Camaro was driving away.

"J.C. Yazzie, the grandson of Nathan's uncle. It might have been a bit harsh, but I did refer to him as worthless."

"What does the J.C. stand for?"

Trini laughed. "His name is actually Jacy, the male form of the Native word for 'moon'—he was born at night under a harvest moon—it seemed fitting. When he went to school, first Gallup and then Albuquerque, initials seemed more macho, Anglicized, I suppose."

"But why shoot at a van carrying supplies?"

"Because he's bad news. This is just one example. If trouble isn't following him, then he goes and finds some. The minute the chief reads his name in your report, he's going to be pissed. This will be the third run-in Chief Billie's had with him in as many weeks. He used to say he wore out more than one Bronco during J.C.'s teen years just coming out here all the time. It was worse when there was two of them."

"Two of them?"

"Yeah, when the grandfather took them in, there were two of them. J.C. had a brother one year his junior, who became as wild as he is. He's been gone five years now, died when he'd just turned seventeen."

"What happened?"

"Rock-climbing accident. You know, that invincible age, an 'I own the world' attitude. Still...." She paused and lowered her voice, "I hate to say anything, but the accident was suspect. That kid could shinny up a telephone pole in his sleep. To pass off his death as a fall from the face of an outcropping a couple stories high that he'd been climbing since the age of five, well, it was hard to believe. But there were two witnesses and no questions were asked."

"I'm assuming one witness was J.C.?"

"And a neighbor. I think it tainted J.C.; made him wilder, more reckless. He had been close to his brother."

"That would explain a lot of his behavior, but I'm still trying to figure out why he was interested in what he must have thought was a shipment of test vials."

"Probably to steal them. Word has it that there's an active black market in virus-related goods. And a local gang of twenty-something hoodlums who elude capture by getting lost on the Rez after they fence the goods."

"Chief Billie is aware of this?"

"I'm sure J.C.'s on his list of suspects."

Ben thanked Trini for the information and went into the spare office to interview Charley Chase. The man kept good records and had lists of contacts, phone numbers and dates of deliveries—both past and those upcoming—ready for Ben. A Bill of Lading itemized the crates of vials. He idly wondered if J.C. had been tricked, too? That would give everything an interesting twist. He thanked Charley once again and assured him that Chief Billie would get a copy of his report. Ben promised to follow up and make certain the IHS hospital was kept up to date.

After Charley left, Ben wrapped up the final report in less than two hours, emailed copies to Dr. Henry, and set up a file on his laptop for future documents. Mr. Chase was scheduled to deliver a PPE order in four days and would contact Ben if that date changed. Lastly, Ben wrote a short summary of the afternoon and forwarded that and a copy of his letter seeking restitution for the mislabeled glass vials to Chief Billie along with a witness-style narrative outlining the confrontation with J.C. Yazzie. He gathered up his laptop and headed for the door.

"Oh, Dr. Pecos, I meant to tell you earlier but you were busy. Zac and Nathan stopped by to let you know they got back all right. Nathan is such a good kid. I'm glad Zac has him for a friend. Absolutely night and day different from his cousin. And guess what? We have lights."

"I heard my fridge running when I got my laptop. Do we know what time Oscar's going to get here with the groceries?"

"Not for sure but should be anytime now. I'll have him bring your order to your trailer."

A half hour later Ben was helping Oscar Begay unload his truck.

"I know you didn't order these hot dogs, but they were on sale and kids love 'em. Got some buns here, too. Looked to me like you needed something more than just ham to put that mustard on."

"I appreciate your help." Ben thanked him and gave him an extra twenty.

"There's no need to tip me. I like to help. But I thank you; it sure will come in handy."

From the jars of peanut butter and strawberry jam on the counter and milk rings left in two glasses in the sink, it looked like the boys had had lunch. Ben checked his watch. In an hour they'd be hungry again, but there was time for a quick call to Julie. He'd sent her pictures of the tents and trailers, told her about Zac starting school and riding a horse to get there and bemoaned the fact that this wasn't the way he'd envisioned their move to Florida. He missed her—a forced separation hadn't been on the agenda and no one knew how long it would last.

He'd hoped to catch her right at the end of the day, but there had been a late meeting. He left a message and promised to call back.

Ben was tempted to walk over to the corral and see if Zac and Nathan were there, but that would be too much like checking up on them. At eleven and twelve trust had to be established or you'd be playing catch-up during the teen years. He'd seen it too many times before when working with parents. He was certain Nathan would help Zac take care of Rain. They needed to walk the horses and cool them down before brushing them and feeding a flake of the grass/hay mix Nathan had brought from his house. He hoped Oscar had filled the galvanized metal water trough. But, again, trust was everything.

He'd barely had time to split the hotdogs, and put them in a skillet when the boys showed up. He'd already sliced a couple apples, put chips in a bowl and poured two glasses of milk. Dinner was a little light on veggies, but Ben figured they'd all live until he had more time to spend on cooking—or the cafeteria materialized. That would be a godsend if it happened.

Finally, dinner was on the table and the hotdogs were already disappearing.

"Dad, Nathan's half Hopi—Hopi and Navajo, like I'm Pueblo and Alaskan Native."

And you need to throw a little Anglo in there, too, Ben thought—about a quarter's worth—but didn't say anything. Ben hadn't known his father, a man his mother had met in school. Memories of his mother, dead by the time he was five, were already becoming shadowy. Had his father even known about him? Ben looked at Zac. Had history just repeated itself—fathers not knowing about the birth of their children? He hadn't thought about it before but that was a possibility.

"My mother was Hopi, Rachel Honanie. When I was real little, I used to go to her village, Moenkopi. One time we were driving there and my dad got lost and it made my mom mad. She kept saying 'just follow the cloud'. We were going to watch a rain dance. Dad stopped the car and got out. He was going to prove my mom wrong—but there it was, one single gray cloud, raining in just one spot. And it was right over the village."

"Do Pueblo Indians believe that way? I mean can they make a cloud come to make rain just for them?" Ben could see that Zac was honestly curious. It was interesting, but challenging, being from two worlds.

"Yes, rituals are much the same for all of the Southwest tribes—Utes, Pueblos, Navajo, Hopi—all have ceremonies to encourage crops to grow, and to give thanks for the harvest of them. And that's only two topics of many addressed by dancing."

"My grandmother says I'm related to White Feather," Nathan said.

"Who's that?" Zac asked through a mouthful of hotdog.

"Sort of the Southwest Indians' Nostradamus," Ben said.

"Huh?" This time mustard escaped the corner of Zac's mouth and he dabbed at his chin with a square of paper towel. "Nostros ... who?"

"Throughout history all peoples have had their seers—those who can predict the future. Native people are no different. Correct me if I'm wrong, Nathan, but White Feather saw many of the changes that came true for this country. He saw the coming of foreign men who would kill for the Indian's land; he saw the snaking of pathways across the land as in railroads and highways, as well as wires in the air that would stretch from coast to coast that would carry words."

"Yeah, my grandfather was talking about how he saw the virus coming, too. How a pandemic is just the earth cleaning itself, renewing itself to start over. When man violates the earth, even its animals revert to attacking one another and then attacking man. This pandemic came from animals, bats and some weird animal that looks sort of like an armadillo. But because man didn't honor his Mother, the earth, he needed to be taught a lesson."

"Wow. White Feather knew all that?" Zac was obviously impressed.

"Yeah, and he told all these stories so that we wouldn't forget the power of our Mother Earth. My grandmother still tells these stories today."

Ben put a half dozen chocolate cupcakes on a plate, brought them to the table and refilled milk glasses. "What's on the schedule for tonight?"

"I need to go back out to my house and get school supplies and some clothes."

"Okay, we can do that." There went a quiet evening with a long conversation with Julie, but he could always call her later. He knew she'd understand. Parenthood was pretty much 24/7 and he was surprised just how much he liked it.

* * *

There were four cars parked in front of the camper-trailer—one was the black and silver Camaro. Four men were drinking beer around a fire pit, having dragged up logs as chairs. There were two women, well, probably more like teen girls, also with beers coming down the steps. Their jeans looked spray-painted on, with halter-tops that left little to the imagination. Ben couldn't believe himself—six months of fatherhood and already in favor of dress codes. He didn't see J.C., but there were others in the camper.

"Damn. I hate him. He shouldn't be here." It was said quietly, but Nathan was dead serious. Hadn't Trini referred to J.C. as 'worthless' and a trouble-maker? Had to be a reason he wasn't winning popularity contests, being where he wasn't wanted. It appeared he'd broken into Nathan's home. Shooting at a delivery van should have gotten Chief Billie's attention. Ben didn't have proof that J.C. did the shooting, only that he was there and seemed to be in charge. Ben wondered if Chief Billie had read his report on the afternoon's incident.

Ben coasted to a stop by the last car in the row, a red Mustang convertible that was parked next to a couple dark blue Dodge Chargers. Looked like a meeting of a muscle-car club. The men sitting around the fire eyed them as they got out, but made no attempt to even say 'hello'. Only the girls acknowledged Ben and the two boys with a nod. Nathan walked ahead up the steps and pulled open the camper's door.

"Get out of my house." He had to almost shout it to be heard above the music, some old grunge rock band that Ben wasn't familiar with. And that's when he saw J.C. coming out of the bedroom. Shirtless and barefoot, jeans low on his hips, holding yet another beer in one hand, the other grasping the waist of a teen girl in Daisy Dukes with black hair cascading to her waist trying unsuccessfully to button her blouse.

Ben had to give it to J.C. —he was good-looking in a bad-boy sort of way. The kid had the abs and the toned arms coupled with black hair slicked straight back to his shoulders and a brooding, heavy-lidded look that girls probably thought was sexy. Even his attitude might be impressive to someone fifteen or younger. Ben was glad that Nathan could see through all the posturing.

J.C. smirked, then took a long swallow from the beer bottle but kept his hand on the girl. "Hey, little man, show some respect. You forget who got this tin can for your gramma?"

"You don't live here."

"You better hope your gramma doesn't die, 'cause if she does, *you* won't live here."

Ben had heard enough. "That's it. This is a tough time for Nathan. Wouldn't hurt to show you care. The woman's your aunt."

A short laugh. "Would I have to mean it? Or could I just pretend?" The other two men in the camper laughed with him. The girl looked embarrassed and wiggled out of his grasp.

It'd been a long time since Ben had wanted to deck someone. He was sizing up his chances of taking J.C. out when a siren interrupted. Although the patrol car was probably a mile away, the reflection of a flashing red light was clearly illuminated in the camper's front window. Had Chief Billie read his report? He'd signed it 'shrinkwrap'.

"Shit. Ditch the beer." J.C. grabbed a six-pack off the kitchen table and pushed it under the couch. The men at the table chugged their drinks, tossed the empties in a garbage bag under the sink, then carried the bag out the back door. J.C. likewise chugged his and kicked the bottle under the couch with the six-pack.

Not all Indian tribes banned alcohol on their reservations but the Navajo did, Ben recalled. Beer and what were probably underaged females added up to trouble.

"What about my grandmother's medicines? Should I take them to her?" Nathan was standing in the doorway to the bathroom.

"That's probably a good idea. Is there anything else she might want?"

"My uncle just gave her a big bag of Werther's caramels. Those are her favorites, but she has to take her teeth out to eat them."

Ben doubted she'd be ready for candy anytime soon with or without teeth, but in a weird way it kept hope alive, indicated there might be normalcy again someday. "Good idea. You wouldn't want anybody else to get them." Ben moved his head ever so slightly to the right indicating the man behind him. The meaning wasn't lost on Nathan. He gave a sly smile and disappeared into the bedroom. The three muscle cars revved up and spun out in single file, leaving the fire in the pit glowing brightly through a cloud of dust. Everybody but J.C. had dumped and run. Even the girl who'd been in the bedroom with J.C. was gone.

Zac was pulling white garbage bags out from under the kitchen sink and heading toward Nathan in the second bedroom. Ben sighed. He was guessing the bags were for Nathan's things. Why hadn't Ben thought to bring a couple suitcases for Nathan's clothes?

Chief Billie didn't knock, just opened the door and stepped inside. "Looks like I broke up the party and, J.C., it looks like you're trespassing."

"Not me, Chief. My grandpa gave me the key to keep an eye on things. This place still belongs to his sister. It's a family thing."

"That include drinking and underage girls?"

"Look around, Chief, you see anything out of place?"

"Bet I wouldn't have to look far. And that cologne you're wearing—eau de hops?"

Ben thought the chief was pretty funny, but he was certain that the beer reference had gone right over J.C.'s head. "Let's me an' you step outside for a little talk and let these folks finish what they're doing."

J.C. shrugged but followed the chief down the front steps. Ben stepped closer to the camper's kitchen window. He couldn't hear what they were saying, but there was a lot of head shaking. Finally, J.C. opened the Camaro's trunk and took out what looked like a revolver. The chief slipped on a pair of latex gloves and took the gun from him, turned it one way, then another and with what looked to be a paper towel wiped something from the tip of the barrel before opening the cylinder and pocketing something that could have been a bullet. Finally, the chief handed the gun back and continued to talk to J.C. even after he'd gotten behind the wheel and started the Camaro. Then, with a wave, J.C. accelerated and was gone.

Ben walked out on the porch. "Nathan and Zac are collecting some school supplies. And Nathan needed to get some clothes. I was surprised to find J.C. here."

"Figures. J.C. is nothing if not an opportunist. I wouldn't have given them a warning if I hadn't run up against a flock of sheep that wouldn't move off the road. Had to light it up and turn on the siren just to nudge them along. I was planning on a nice quiet visit—catch the beer-drinking and the girls firsthand."

"J.C. told Nathan that he's out of the camper if his grandmother dies. You think there's any truth to that? Won't the grandmother's brother take over? Protect his nephew?"

"I wouldn't plan on the old man stepping in. J.C. pretty much has his grandfather wrapped around his finger. He'd probably give the camper to J.C. and expect Nathan to stay there, too. Nathan's uncle is pretty high up in tribal affairs. It's one of the reasons J.C. has had a free ride, been difficult to make a misdemeanor here and there stick. The uncle always steps in. Basically, that's why I let him go. I want him to feel comfortable, above the law—at least, not looking over his shoulder. If my hunch pays off, I'll catch him doing a lot more than a little drinking and groping of a fifteen-year-old."

"Nathan's a good kid. I wouldn't want him hanging around the drinking and groping—I don't see J.C. as a fit role model."

"Nor do I. I was pleased when I found out Nathan was staying with you. Finding a friend in your son helps buffer the concern of having his grandmother hospitalized. And if she passes, Nathan will have support. I take comfort in that. Sometimes things in life have a purpose bigger than what appears on the surface."

Ben nodded. "The kids are going to school together on Monday. I think they plan on riding the horses. Zac is having the time of his life learning to ride. I couldn't have imagined a better friend for him. And you're right; because Nathan can't visit his grandmother, their friendship fills a void. It would have been difficult for a twelve-year-old to live out here, take care of himself, and ride back and forth to the hospital every day."

"Yeah, Nathan wouldn't have been safe out here either. I'm suspecting J.C. is using the place to do more than party. I'll have a deputy swing by every other day and keep an eye on things, but I'm getting stretched thin when it comes to manpower. Go ahead and have Nathan take his belongings out tonight— anything he doesn't want stolen. Oh, and don't forget the horses; pack anything the horses might need, too."

"Good idea."

"I almost forgot—will I see you at the dances to-morrow?"

"I hadn't heard there were any being held."

"Trini's slipping. When she's not helping out during a pandemic, she's my right hand over in the Shiprock office. Not like her to forget an announcement."

"Is this a Harvest celebration?"

"No, that usually takes place in the fall—October. This is purely ceremonial, a call to our deities to stem the spread of the illness and give thanks for all that we have been given. In fact, the emphasis will be upon chanting—singing, if you will. It's our way of calling out to the deities who protect us. Remind them of our need. There might be a sand painting. I don't have all the particulars."

"Where will this be held?"

"Behind the last trailer, to the right of the last hospital tent—the one marked Triage. After today, twenty-five trailers will have families in them—all with relatives in the hospitals, and all needing to quarantine. It's filling up. But the good news is that there's a cafeteria, and the government is picking up the tab on this one. Two women who usually have a food booth at area craft fairs have moved their kitchen equipment to the camp. Doctor Henry has made a space for them. They should be fired up and ready to go tonight—I hear the special is mutton stew and fry bread. And they've promised Navajo tacos by ceremony-time tomorrow. My mouth's watering just talking about it."

Chapter 8

The old man watched the moon first pop up above the horizon and then continue noiselessly upward to hang among a sprinkling of stars. Its light formed more shadows than it illuminated in the landscape below him, yet it seemed to smooth the wrinkles from the desert floor as it spread. The pale light pushed the darkness ahead of it leaving a blanket of ivory incandescence. Were the stars merely candles in the sky? Not the Milky Way, but a phosphorescent profusion to control, if not mock, the darkness? An 'I'm better; I can show you the way. Your work would be nothing without my help. My making it possible.' He sighed and adjusted the chamois neck covering. He must offer a prayer to this helpmate.

In silhouette, standing against the outcropping of rock,

someone glancing upward to the ledge would see a majestic Pronghorn Antelope. The head fully preserved, human eyes looking outward from under a widely dark-striped forehead and nose, shaded by large bulbous, unblinking animal eyes smoldering mysteriously—all beneath the two-prong horns he was so proud of. A buck in his prime, a leader of his herd, now fittingly, his hide falling beneath the knees of his captor, taking on new life as the costume of a shape-shifter, a Skinwalker.

Was there a better-known witch in all the Southwest? He thought not. More recently reduced to scaring young children into doing good, he could still command the fear and respect of their elders. He was being blamed for this current evil that had befallen the tribe. And he must prove them wrong. A witch was always an easy scapegoat when science was beyond the grasp of most. Witches lived among the people. A witch, *Yee naaldlooshii*, translated from the Navajo means 'with it, he goes on all fours'. He was simply a part of his people's beliefs, something it would never dawn on them to question.

Some of his Skinwalker brethren were cougars, wolves, coyotes, bears, even snakes. All had the same purpose of members of the *Witchery Way*—to introduce and perpetuate evil within the tribe. Each chose an animal by capturing its spirit depending upon need—speed, strength, and stealth were popular, sought-after attributes. Often this animal impersonation was to cause death and then to use the bones of victims as tools or prepare concoctions from their bodies that would curse or harm others.

This was his seventieth year. His father, grandfather and great-grandfather had been witches. And the next generation? Had he passed on his skills? His power? A sigh. That might very well be his greatest failing. He had trusted his closest relative, his grandson, and all had not gone well.

A pledge would only be accepted by the secret society if he could perform the evilest of deeds—the killing of a close family member. Always better if it could be a sibling. The man who could do that had no boundaries, nothing to contain his evil. There could be no traces of remorse or sympathy. They would be free to walk among the people during the day as normal, natural humans; at night they would have the ability to shape-shift. The family killing would give them the supernatural powers they needed as a Skinwalker. And there would be no corner, no segment of their home territory safe from their evil. It was all up to them as to how their power would be used.

He shook his head slightly. The furred animal skull was heavy and hot, but it brought the maximum power to the wearer. The antelope skin draped over his arms exuded a musty smell of old fur. He used double walking sticks each covered with the antelope's hide and carved from its femurs. He moved hunched-over, leaning heavily on the sticks. Their pointed ends were the animal's original split-toed hooves. As he walked, he left a tracing of this distinct pattern in the sand. It was his calling card. His way of inciting fear, of giving warning that the individual being visited was being watched, possibly singled out for harm.

As a young man in school on the reservation, he had secretly stolen a National Geographic magazine from the classroom because there was an article on witchcraft. The author, a sociologist, referred to the practice as a way indigenous peoples controlled their environments, put restraints on what was considered right vs. wrong and punished those who ignored their prophecies. It also explained the unexplainable—the winds that scoured the earth, animals that leapt in front of cars causing accidents, epidemics of measles or chicken pox that marked its victims as it ravaged villages, fires from an overturned cooking pot, horses gone lame. The list was endless. Some pranks, some devastating. But all the evil intent of a Skinwalker.

Tonight his mission was different. He would appear to the gathering of people whose loved ones were dying as they gathered behind the tents of the white man. He would lend his powers to the medicine of the songs and stand to the right of the Shaman leading the ceremony. This scourge, which had befallen his people was a great evil—the power of many Skinwalkers across their land. It was only fitting that good and evil, the supernatural and the corporeal, must unite to establish balance and harmony to an upended universe.

Chapter 9

The bubbling cauldron of hot fat was in the center of the tent. Large wads of fragrant dough floated on the surface bouncing against each other and the sides of the pot before puffing up and turning a delicious toasty brown around the edges. The scent of baking bread permeated its surroundings, competing with the pungent odor coming from a skillet of diced lamb and onion on a Bunsen burner fed by a tank of propane tucked under the table. Plastic bowls of salad—chopped tomatoes and shredded lettuce—were cooling in chests of crushed ice along with cans of soft drinks and bottles of water. A metate still with a dusting of ground dried red chile, coriander, and garlic on the rim completed the open-air kitchen. Picnic tables, a discreet ten feet apart, stretched out from the tent's front opening allowing safe seating for up to thirty people at a time.

Zac was working on his second taco. "These are really good."

"What'd I tell you? They're my favorite," Nathan chimed in. "Is the kitchen going to stay here?"

"It's supposed to. I think they'll stay open for at least one meal a day. You guys may be relying on my ability to open a can of soup in the meantime—at least for lunch."

"Mind if I join you?" Dr. Henry had walked up to the end of their table. "I'd like to talk to Nathan for a minute."

"Please do. I see you were able to get a taco before these guys put the kitchen out of business."

"And I'm hoping I have room for a second, but the line's getting a little long. Nathan, I'd like to take you to visit your grandmother before the dancing starts. I believe that I can outfit you with protective gear that will keep you safe. Dr. Pecos, I want you in on this decision, too."

"If you feel he'll be safe, you have my vote."

"Will I be saying good-bye?" Nathan looked directly at Doctor Henry, who to his credit, Ben thought, didn't look away.

"I'm not seeing the improvement in her breathing that I'd like. I won't lie to you. Her heart just may not be strong enough to pull her through this time. By having her here, we're protecting her from the virus, but it may not be enough. She has too many challenges. I believe that she may pass soon. I think it's important for you to spend some time with her. I know she'll find it comforting."

Nathan nodded. "When?"

"Finish your dinner. I'll get the protective gear ready. Let's say, meet me at the entrance to the first hospital tent in twenty minutes?"

* * *

A plastic face screen, a surgical mask, a hood that covered his head and gathered via a draw-string to tie under his chin, latex gloves, a hospital gown that laced up the back above voluminous polyester blue scrub pants tucked into white, gauzy, shoe coverings—not an inch of his body was left unprotected. He would be safe from the rampant virus and keep his grandmother safe.

"Ready?" Doctor Henry was waiting by the door to the dressing area.

"Yeah."

The doctor led him to the hospital bed tucked into a cubicle at the very end of the tent. Screened from view by a curtain that could slide back and forth on a circular pole frame, his grandmother was dwarfed in a bed surrounded by the chugging machines and webbing of tubes that entered and exited her body. Doctor Henry pulled a chair close to the bed and motioned for Nathan to sit, then indicated that he was going to leave. There couldn't be any talking but gestures negated the need to communicate out loud.

Nathan sat and simply looked at his grandmother before reaching for her hand. He held it, smoothing the skin, feeling the parched, warm dryness even through his gloves. He sat that way for thirty minutes. Finally, Doctor Henry returned and Nathan stood pantomiming a heart by putting his two cupped hands together, fingers curved toward one another, thumbs touching, before covering his own heart with one hand and then palm up holding that hand out to his grandmother mouthing the words, "I love you."

The tears were streaming down his face, and the doctor left him in the dressing area to collect himself before rejoining Zac and his father.

* * *

At dusk a hundred or so people walked toward the leveled parking area now devoid of cars and took their places forming a large circle. Light was a huge bonfire in the center of the ring. A pile of burnable wood and scrap was literally falling off the back of a pickup parked some forty feet from the fire and tended by two men in ceremonial dress whose purpose would be to keep the fire roaring, sending sparks twenty feet into the air. The audience was quiet, lining up single-file but at a safe distance to allow ample space for those performing.

As Nathan had shared, almost all Native dances honored both the dancer and their community, giving thanks for their connection to the environment. One's surroundings were a gift to be treated with respect. This, Ben thought, was also the belief of Zac's Native family and not much different among all indigenous peoples. Once again, he was thankful Zac had Nathan as a friend and someone to bring him closer to his heritage.

Ben could not over emphasize the importance of the evening ahead of them. The world was out of kilter. And when this world would tilt, causing wide-spread calamity, if not disaster, dancing offered healing, putting things right again, and relieving the stress of facing the unknown. He felt an enormous pull to set things right, assure Mother Earth that her people would try harder, would practice what was right and shun the wrong. He sighed at the enormity of the task.

Tonight's Fire Dance was a good choice. The Fire Dance usually signified the culmination of eight days of celebration known as the Mountainway, and was performed on the ninth night. But dances could be tailored to fit the needs of the moment. Tonight would be both a christening of the hospitals and a blessing for the medicine and care being administered. And it was to be a cleansing. Chief Billie motioned for Ben and the boys to stand next to him in the front row.

The moon was high overhead, perfectly full and round. The crowd was quiet, a few murmured conversations here and there but most were staring at the fire. Ben was glad they were standing some forty feet from the heat; the evening was just too hot for this additional warmth. But there was something mesmerizing about a fire, even when the pine logs full of resin popped, scattering bits of smoldering bark into the air. Pine was a soft wood that burned fast, releasing a highly intense heat quickly. It wasn't optimum for stoves or hornos, but it was plentiful and usually free. In the Jemez mountains, members from his Pueblo would wait until the fully loaded logging trucks would come down the mountain before going up and picking cut-sites clean. It was a win/win—families had a year-round supply of wood and the forest floor was kept free of debris.

The people around him were clustered in groups. Not exactly social distancing, but families were staying together. Some had set up camp chairs for their elderly members, but most people stood. Not everyone wore a mask, but many did. There was an air of anticipation. Dances were special. In addition to blessings and the controlling of evil, a Shaman would often share important information—

sort of a town crier. Ben knew that tonight the Medicine Man would be lecturing on wearing masks and socially distancing and why it was important to close the borders of the reservation to outsiders. Deliveries would be handled by designated residents. It would be interesting to see how his requests would be received.

Suddenly six men appeared to Ben's right from around the back of the fire. Each carried a hoop drum consisting of an animal skin tightly stretched across a circular frame. The skins could be goat or deer and even horse pulled smooth across yellow pine or red cedar wood circles. The drums were maybe twelve to fourteen inches in diameter. Easy to hold but big enough for the sound to carry. Music was important to the Navajo and a part of every celebration. Rattles made from gourds, wooden flutes, whistles and rasps were just a few of the other instruments to be found among members of the group. Sometimes a large table drum that sat on the ground and had two and three men in attendance was added. But Ben didn't see one this evening.

Two men followed the drummers. One man moved closer to the audience. He had a bright red scarf rolled and tied around his head and several turquoise necklaces almost covered the front of his denim shirt. A turquoise-studded belt buckle held much-faded and worn jeans in place. This was the Shaman. And beside him was a man in crisp khakis with a western-cut jacket over a white shirt. A silver bolo tie glinted in the firelight. Ben recognized him as the President of the Navajo Nation—the man making the decisions about how to fight the virus and keep his people safe.

The President spoke first—a greeting in Navajo and one in English. He praised the work of IHS and the rapid response to a truly devastating illness. He congratulated those present for their diligence in following protocol and slowing the march of death. He reiterated the need to follow the rules of wearing masks, distancing, and hand-cleansing hygiene. He also made the announcement that the start of school for K through 12 would be delayed 2 weeks and possibly longer. He said he personally did not feel it was safe yet and there had been some delays on adding a filter-system to the school's heating and air conditioning unit that had recently been donated. He was also waiting on a donation of sanitizing products and face masks sized for younger children.

Ben took a sideways glance at Nathan and Zac as they smacked their hands together in a low-five and tried to hide their grins. Two students approved of the President's decision, Ben thought. It would give the boys extra time to pal around together. And that wasn't a bad thing. They had become inseparable in a short period of time. It didn't seem possible that they'd been on the reservation for not even four days. Yet, Ben would have to admit 'so far, so good'. Zac was doing especially well. He didn't seem to be homesick and was the first one up in the morning to feed the horses. Now, if Julie were only here, life would be complete.

The President continued to talk—praising first responders and the medical staff and hinting that the tent community might become a permanent fixture even after its immediate use had passed. Apparently, the well was coming along and the phone tower had become permanent. Next, there was talk of a store—groceries and other basics—and more housing, including a brick and mortar hospital sponsored by IHS and built by local craftsmen. The makeshift, pretend village was going to be a permanent one—with several amenities.

When the President finished, he walked to the edge of the group, giving center stage to the Shaman. Speaking in Navajo, the man began a chant and several dancers joined him. White buckskin skirts and leg coverings, eagle feathers, turquoise jewelry, brightly colored beading, silver bells sewn into skirts that reached the ground; it was mesmerizing as the ten dancers dipped and turned, some shaking gourd rattles, others brandishing rainsticks. Designed to mimic the sound of falling rain, the dry cacti branches were now tubes holding tiny shells or pebbles that would tumble against each other as the stick was turned downward then upward producing a melodic tinkling.

Ben watched as Nathan whispered answers to Zac's questions. The fire had burned down to glowing embers and the moon provided overhead light. There was an eeriness to the moon's soft illumination from above, making the dancers seem to appear in *bas relief* carved from some sandy desert tableau—moving outward, then stepping back into formation—all the while, moccasined feet tapped out the rhythm to the drums' beat.

And that's when Ben saw him. But Zac was the first to blurt out, "Dad, that's the dude, the one who ran beside us in the storm." And maybe it was. Ben wasn't one to cast doubt on the authenticity of a shape-shifter. The enormous head, bulbous eyes, and tall antlers of the Pronghorn Antelope was moving across the smoldering embers of the fire pit. Ben was pretty certain that the strips of sheep skin foot coverings wound tightly up past the ankle had soaked overnight in order to protect the feet of the Skinwalker. And he was reluctant to point out to Zac that this Pronghorn had on Levi's in addition to the skin of the antelope. But who was he to throw cold water on a legend as old as the indigenous tribe itself? Did he know for a fact that this animal couldn't become real—shift from human to Pronghorn on demand? No, he didn't, and he wanted to make certain that he allowed Zac to make up his own mind.

"Wow. Can I go see him? He's my friend."

Before Ben could answer, Chief Billie stepped in front of Zac turning his back to the Skinwalker. "Gotta be careful, Zac. The Skinwalker can do great harm. I don't want him to know who you are."

"He already knows." Zac edged around the chief to watch the Skinwalker step from the fire pit. Almost as one, the bystanders shrank back and the drummers stopped. A playful breeze seemed to tickle the feather headdresses of the dancers even though they remained frozen in place. Then the Skinwalker turned toward Zac and made eye contact.

"Oh no, this is bad. I don't want your son marked as evil. How did they meet before?"

In a whisper Ben filled the chief in—a sandstorm on their way here, the Pronghorn running alongside the truck. The chief merely nodded.

"Common Skinwalker tricks. You're lucky; they often cross in front of vehicles causing accidents. Just watch Zac. Note anything unusual—something outside his normal reactions to things. And keep communication open."

Ben nodded. "I'll do that. But why was the Skinwalker here at the dances?"

"The Shaman asked him to come and collect his evil." This from Nathan. "A Skinwalker can take away what he has put in place."

Ben glanced at Chief Billie just as he crossed himself. Ben must have looked surprised because the chief followed up with, "I'm just hedging my bets. My mother was Catholic."

The Skinwalker surveyed the crowd before he began to chant. No one in the crowd moved. He had their rapt attention. The song wasn't long and ended with his summoning the two men who had stoked the fire before. They approached the fire pit and with a few logs and what might have been accelerant, the flames once again shot skyward. The fire once again commanded attention. The Skinwalker disappeared behind it.

It was after ten by the time the ceremony ended. Individuals and families walked back to their trailers, mostly in silence. The outdoor concessions had closed, but both boys opted for a late-night PB&J before bed. After they had cleaned up the kitchen and their bedroom door was closed, Ben called Julie. She could tell he was tired; it had been a long day. But he caught her up on the start of school being delayed, how very sick Nathan's grandmother was, the Skinwalker, and Chief Billie's worry about Zac receiving some evil spell. She laughingly admonished him for having a much more interesting life than she was. It was past eleven when he hung up. It still seemed so crazy to be separated like this, with no idea of when they would be together. He stripped off his shirt and jeans and stretched out on the bed.

Chapter 10

Ben sat straight up in bed at the first sound of the owl. The distinct 'Hoo, Hoo' was loud and chilling. A Great Horned had to be sitting on the roof of the trailer. One-sixteen a.m. The digital clock flipped to one-seventeen as he watched. Then he heard the front door close. The boys must be up. Ben pulled on jeans and T-shirt and followed them outside. Nathan was standing barefoot at the edge of the porch with Zac beside him. Ben noticed the tears just as Zac put his arm around his friend.

"My grandmother died." Nathan turned toward Ben.

"How do you …?" Ben didn't finish. How *did* he know? The owl had come to deliver the message. The Pueblos and the Navajo believed the owl was a messenger of death. He'd seen it before, first hand. It was sometimes difficult to move from Anglo to Indian ways of thought. Ben admonished himself, but he needed to try harder.

Ben simply nodded and gave Nathan's shoulder a squeeze. What would follow next was a little more complicated. In fact, tears and human shows of sympathy— any inclination to mourn the person who had gone on was frowned upon by the Navajo. Too much display of sorrow and it might interrupt the dead one's journey to the next life. He or she might be lured back to walk among the living in an attempt to console the mourner. This return of the dead was feared and, at all cost, it was to be avoided.

"I see you know of your grandmother's passing." Dr. Henry stepped from the shadows at the end of the trailer. "I've sent word to her brother. Your uncle will be sending two individuals to prepare your grandmother's body. It is allowed to have a close family member sit with the deceased until they arrive. Would you be comfortable doing that?"

"Yes." Nathan walked down the steps to meet Dr. Henry.

"You know the risks?" Dr. Henry was looking at him closely.

Again, Nathan nodded, and murmured, "Yes."

Zac and Ben stood quietly at the top of the steps and watched as Nathan and Dr. Henry walked back toward the hospital tents.

"I'm not very tired. How about you?"

Zac shook his head. "No."

"Then I think a cup of hot chocolate might be in order."

Ben heated milk and mixed sugar and cocoa powder, dividing the mixture between two heavy, glazed clay mugs, pouring in the warm milk and stirring before putting them on the counter.

"There might be some Oreos in the cupboard." Ben paused before taking a seat.

But Zac shook his head. "This is great. I like cocoa."

Zac was quiet but after a couple sips asked, "What did Dr. Henry mean by risks? Does that mean that Nathan could get hurt?"

"Good question. All people have burial protocol."

"Like rules?"

"Yeah, exactly … rules. And the Navajo have very particular ones."

"What are they?"

"Well, only the closest family members—and then only two—are allowed to sit with the dying and stay with the body at the time of death. Sometimes a medicine man will be with the family members. Dr. Henry would be the medicine man in this instance. I'm sure he'll stay with Nathan and his grandmother. In some ways it's best that Nathan's grandmother was brought here to the hospital before she passed. Often the dying are taken out of their houses to a separate place to pass. If a Navajo dies within their hogan, the house must be destroyed, often burned along with all the person's belongings."

"Why?"

"Because of evil spirits. The living should never look at a dead person. The dead go to the underworld first. During this time of passage, precautions must be taken so that the deceased won't be tempted to return to the world of the living. Human ties must be broken. Their journey must not be interrupted."

Zac leaned on his elbows, chin resting on the palms of his hands, fingers doubled backwards pressing against his checks, and frowned. "It's just kinda weird."

"Then I'll tell you a story. Do you know why death even exists in the world?"

"Nope."

"Well, a Navajo legend explains it this way. One day the Navajo people were told to place an animal hide in a tank of water. If it floated and stayed perfectly flat on top of the water, there would never be death in the world again. But if it sank, death would be a part of life and dying would be something everyone must do. So, they stretched out the hide perfectly flat and floated it on top of the water. They went about their work planning to check on the hide later. In the meantime a coyote—you remember what a trickster he is—tossed stones on top of the hide. Of course, the hide sank."

"Why did he do that?"

"Well, the coyote said that if no one ever died, the world would run out of room and food. People would no longer be able to find places to live. He had to make a world where everyone had a chance at life."

Zac was quiet, then, "Do you believe things like that?"

"Legends have an important place in our lives. They explain things and are good teachers. The Bible has parables—stories meant to show us how to live better, be kinder to others. Other religions have equally important ways of guiding their members, usually through stories designed to illustrate the differences between right and wrong."

"Will they put Nathan's grandmother in the ground?"

"Yes, but not until her body has been properly prepared. "

"They do it really quick, don't they?" Zac looked confused.

"It's custom to bury the one who has passed within twenty-four hours."

"Wow. The body of our neighbor's wife was in our barn for over six months."

"When the ground stays frozen solid most of the year, rules vary."

"So, what happens next?"

"There's a strict ritual that must be followed. I'm sure her brother will send two men to complete that ritual. Again, it must be done according to tradition so that the person's spirit does not return to his or her home. Everything is done to steer the deceased toward their new home and make sure they have broken their ties with this one."

"What has to be done?"

"While a grave is being dug, two men attending the body will strip out of their clothing only leaving on their moccasins, and cover their bodies with ash which is thought to offer protection from evil spirits. The body is then washed and dressed. Finally, the body and its belongings will be carried by horseback to the final resting place. Only this time I bet the Bronco has wheels instead of hooves. People they pass along the way will be warned of their cargo. Remember, no one should look at the dead?"

"Will his grandmother be buried out by her house?"

"Probably. And more than likely sometime this morning. She may rest closer to her brother, Nathan's uncle—his hogan isn't that far from the camper-trailer. But only a couple people will know exactly. Once the body is placed in the ground, great care is taken to erase all footprints around the site. The ground around the site is brushed smooth and even the tools used to dig the grave are destroyed. Mourning is prohibited. One can feel sad but no outward show of emotion in case the dead might be enticed to return to earth. I doubt if Nathan will want to talk about his grandmother. I think he was able to say his goodbyes last night before the dance." Ben waited. Zac seemed to have run out of questions but still looked perplexed. "Anything else you have questions about?"

"I guess not."

"Then how about another cup of cocoa?"

"I think I'll just go to bed. But thanks, Dad."

Ben watched his son go into his bedroom and close the door. What a summer. To say it had become a true learning experience wouldn't even do it justice. And he wasn't just thinking about Zac.

Chapter 11

A pale peach glow spread along the horizon, highlighting the irregular shapes of the hills that marked the eastern boundary of the land he'd called home for over seventy years. This was his favorite time of day. He stood in the doorway of his hogan and surveyed the desert floor that gently sloped away from him. Good drainage for those brief and irregular rains that fell sporadically during the growing season. He always felt his own life renewed each morning as he watched the desert come alive. He idly watched a prairie dog pop up from its burrow, check its surroundings and then drop back into the hole it called home. Many of the desert's animals had symbiotic relationships. Burrowing owls, snakes, lizards—even the desert tortoise spent ninety-five per cent of its time underground away from heat and cold. Adaptation. The animals had done a better job of mastering their environment and helping each other than humans had.

Times had changed so much. When he was Nathan's age, he had stalked and killed a black panther. Now, if one was even sighted, it was cause for celebration. The complexion of the land had changed. The old ways were disappearing, forgotten, never to be passed from generation to generation. Even domestic animals were changing. Who kept horses or donkeys anymore?

Young men preferred the white man's transportation. And the grasslands to feed the sheep? Farther and farther away from the communities that owned the flocks.

Even the Navajo language was considered to be in an endangered status. Currently there were somewhere between one hundred twenty thousand and one hundred seventy thousand speakers remaining—thought to be all reservation dwellers. All too often he saw young people turn to adults for an explanation of a chant by elders. Or stumble over the correct words to reply to a grandmother or grandfather.

He looked up the road to the north, past the tin can that had passed for the home of his sister. An abomination— the white man's frivolous waste of money. Camping? Well, don't forget your memory foam mattress or your chemical toilet. And make sure you have enough propane to cook dinner on your gas range. He shook his head.

His ancestors must be laughing. And his sister had hated it, but it had been free, a gift from her nephew, his grandson, and did not require waiting to set up. As the elder in their family, he had warned her to be careful. But she was already aware of the spirits it embodied. Of consequence, she did no weaving inside, and even food preparation was mostly done outside. She had been a good woman, worthy of their clan. A model for young people. He gently moved the can of accelerant with his foot and stepped through the hogan's door.

Didn't he already know what he had to do? Hadn't he possibly made one mistake already? Put years of time into grooming someone to follow in his footsteps only to have that person make a mockery of the Witchery Way? Had he failed as a teacher? He had been tutored by his grandfather and then his father. He knew the requirements. Today's youth exhibited a lack of trust, of understanding. They relished the power but not if it required work to maintain.

There was time. He could right this error in judgement. He would entice a younger novice to join him. He would not let the line of Skinwalkers die out. And didn't he have the perfect young learner in mind? *K'e* or kinship, was all important. He would choose an acolyte from his own clan, adding strength to the journey ahead. He smiled. Yes, this was the path shown to him. He must honor the deities.

He leaned down and picked up the can of gasoline and tucked a box of kitchen matches in the cloth belt at his waist. Keeping the tin can in sight, he started up the road.

* * *

"Dr. Pecos, my apologies, I know it's not even six."

"Chief Billie, not a problem, what can I help you with?"

"I need to run something by you. I have a situation here that I hope you can help with. Nathan's grandmother's camper trailer was torched. Not unusual when there's a death but it leaves Nathan without a more permanent shelter. I really don't want him moving in with his uncle—I remember sharing my feelings on this with you before. Would you still consider letting Nathan continue to stay with you and your son?"

"Of course. That wouldn't be a problem at all."

"Good. One more thing. I'd like to promote you as temporary guardian for Nathan. Put a more legal spin on things. Would you consider that?"

"I'd be pleased to step in if I can help."

"Nathan needs the support that you and Zac can give him. This is a turning point in his life. He needs to be protected. I know I'm leaving you with a lot of questions, but I'll explain later. Right now, I really need you to come pick Nathan up. He's with me at his grandmother's house."

"I'm on my way."

"And Dr. Pecos? Thank you. This means a lot—I'll share the news with Nathan."

Ben slipped his phone into his jeans' pocket. Odd. Something was going on but he was glad to help Nathan. He pulled a T-shirt over his head and went to get Zac. Zac didn't need prodding—he was excited to finally see his friend. They were in the truck and on the road in under five minutes.

Chapter 12

"Do you think Nathan will want the top bunk?"

"Why don't you guys share? Every time you change the sheets, you switch. Would that work?"

"Yeah, I guess. I just want him to be happy living with us. I took the top bunk because I was here first. I never really offered the top bunk to him."

"I think it's great that you'd like to share. I'm sure Nathan will appreciate your offer."

"Is he going to be like my brother? I always wanted a brother."

"We'll see. I don't know how long my guardianship will last or just what the limitations are. We have some things to find out."

***

The smoke and the occasional tongue of fire dancing above what was left of the camper's blackened shell could be seen from two miles away. Torched. Probably by the uncle, Ben thought. But why would he risk pissing off J.C.? Hadn't J.C. threatened Nathan that he wouldn't have a home if his grandmother died? It had sounded like he was moving in. Family dynamics—always tough to figure out.

"There. There's Nathan." Zac lowered the truck's window and leaned out to wave.

Nathan was standing next to Chief Billie, holding a large paper bag. Ben pulled up to one side, making sure he wasn't downwind of the burning camper, and turned the truck off.

"Thanks, Dr. Pecos, I really appreciate the ride. And, thanks, too, for letting me stay with Zac."

"We're glad to have you with us. Can we help you put anything in the truck?"

"I wasn't supposed to, but I took a saddle blanket that my grandmother made for Apache. I think she'd want him to have it." Nathan patted the paper bag. "I don't think she'd come back for it, do you?"

"I think you're safe. It was a gift for your horse. I've always thought our dead honored animals. I'm certain she'd like Apache to have it. Now, I'd like to talk to Chief Billie here, if you boys could give us a few minutes."

"Sure." Nathan slung the paper straps on the bag over his shoulder and followed Zac to the truck.

"I dreamed of having a brother growing up. Did you have a sibling?" Ben turned to the chief.

"About five too many." The chief laughed, "All girls."

"Is it safe to just leave the trailer smoldering out here?"

"I've got a deputy coming out to babysit the fire. Probably would be okay but I won't take chances."

"I didn't think property was destroyed unless the owner actually died in the house."

"Well, mostly true but if a case can be made for the dead coming back, that is, if evil spirits are suspected of not wanting to leave their home, then whatever is attracting them must be destroyed and the area cleared so that no enticing remnant is left. This area will be planted in the spring. You won't recognize it next year. But, neither will the evil spirits."

Ben nodded. As always, so much to learn. Chief Billie motioned for Ben to follow him to the Bronco. Funny, before Ben got into the SUV, he looked around. He couldn't shake an oppressive, almost suffocating feeling. He'd never reacted negatively to a discussion of evil spirits before, but once the conversation had centered on the return of the dead, he'd felt he was being watched—and not in a good way. Out of nowhere a breeze ruffled his hair and tickled the skin under the collar of his shirt. It sent a shiver across his shoulders. He quickly opened the Bronco's door and stepped inside.

"I had some papers prepared giving you the guardianship of Nathan. Dr. Henry agrees with what we're doing here and has witnessed the agreement. I've told Trini that you would be returning the papers in the morning. Then we'll get them off to the tribal council. I don't see any difficulty. Being a Pueblo man will make this easy. I just need to know you understand what this entails."

"It's beginning to sound permanent."

"And if it turned out that way?"

"I'm going to say yes, but also point out that I need to talk to my wife."

"Understood."

"It just seems …"

"Sudden?"

"Yes."

The chief leaned against the steering wheel. "I'd do anything to make sure that Nathan does not end up living with J.C."

"But the uncle? Shouldn't he have a say?"

"There are things you don't need to know. Things that would put you in danger if you knew. Trust me on this. Nathan needs a chance at life—education, sports, siblings … a male model who is successful. Look on it as a sponsorship with maybe a few strings attached. I've seen too many bright young men rot on the reservation—drugs, domestic violence, high rate of high school dropouts, little or no job opportunities. I don't want Nathan set up to fail."

"I understand."

"I don't know your family situation. I believe Zac is a son by a woman other than your wife?"

"Yes."

"If Zac goes back to his home or school in the Pacific Northwest, and I could find the scholarship monies to support him, would it be possible for Nathan to attend a boarding school that would put him close to Zac?"

"That would be possible."

"Thank you for your trust. Someday when all this is past, I'll be able to share more—just not right now. Here's the application to become Nathan's guardian. Call me if you have questions and leave it with Trini. You're a good man, Dr. Pecos."

Chapter 13

Ben, you've known this child, Nathan, less than a week. And can you trust this Chief Billie? I mean, I don't understand why he's so involved."

"I sense that there's some underlying reason that the chief approached me. And frankly, Julie, I'm not sure I even want to know. Good and evil are honest-to-God real beings out here." Ben decided against any mention of Skinwalkers.

"You know I'll support you in whatever you decide. I just don't want you to get tangled up in something that is maybe a little more involved than what it seems on the surface."

"Wow, that's politically correct. Nice way of saying you think I might get screwed." Ben smiled.

"Ben, don't tease. I'm not there so it's difficult to really comment. I love you and I trust you. You know I'll support you—whatever your decision is."

* * *

Ben left the papers with Trini in the morning. Even Dr. Henry stopped by the office to thank him for getting involved. Yesterday evening over dinner, Ben asked Nathan for his honest opinion—would he want to stay with Zac? Maybe even go to school with Zac when he went back to the Pacific Northwest? And his answer sealed the deal— Nathan was so choked with emotion that he could only enthusiastically nod. After losing his grandmother and a place to live, Ben knew that he had just given Nathan's life a permanence and changed his future to one of hope. Ben didn't need any further affirmation to know that what he was doing was right.

"Dr. Pecos?" Trini's office intercom really just demanded a loud voice. "I forgot to mention that we're getting a good-sized shipment of PPE this afternoon. Chief Billie was hoping that you'd be around to help check it in—take inventory, make certain that the paperwork is in order. You know, that everything matches up."

Correctly filled out paperwork would be a first, Ben thought but bit his tongue and walked out to Trini's desk. "What's expected?"

"I've marked the catalogue we ordered from—thought it would help you identify some of the stuff. You know, product numbers and descriptions. Mostly it's gowns, gloves and masks. All government approved issue. Of course, Washington had to sign off on our list first. It's like we can't do anything on our own—but it is their nickel. The shipment is supposed to get here about lunch time. Not exactly timely—we needed everything yesterday. Did you see Dr. Henry this morning? He was actually wearing a garbage bag—there were no gowns. Can you believe working all morning in the OR in a black plastic bag?"

"Hard to believe the government couldn't do any better than this. Has anyone come out to see the conditions?"

Trini rolled her eyes. "I'm not sure we really exist, to their way of thinking. Out of sight, out of mind, you know?"

"I'm pleased that IHS is being supportive."

"To the best of their ability, being already underfunded and undermanned—and we're thankful. By the way, our new food source has a name and they put up a sign out by the road—Two Sisters With a Pot. Guess they're here to stay. Cute name, don't you think? Did you try their Navajo tacos the other night?"

"Best I've had in a long time."

The close-by blast of an emergency vehicle's siren rattled the office windows, interrupting any further discussion of lunch. Trini opened the blinds to look out. "Odd. I didn't think we were receiving any new patients this morning. Someone usually emails me a list and arrival times. Today was supposed to be spent restocking the triage tent and interviewing for overnight and weekend nurses. Oh dear, looks like the ambulance has an escort. That's the chief's Bronco leading the way. I wonder what happened?"

"I'll tell you in a minute." Ben walked out of the office and headed toward the triage tent just as Chief Billie and two EMTs were unloading a stretcher and wheeling it in Ben's direction. Ben quickly moved ahead to hold open the tent's door. As the stretcher passed, Ben realized that he knew the occupant—Charley Chase—the once-in-a-while delivery guy who was shot at the last time he tried to deliver supplies. The blood-soaked tourniquet around his forehead attested to a head injury that was serious. It was difficult to see under the sheet covering him, but it looked like his right arm was in a sling.

"Gonna need your help when I finish here." Chief Billie whispered as he pushed the stretcher past Ben and through the door. "Hope your afternoon's free."

Ben nodded. "Not a problem. I'll be in the office."

Ten minutes later Chief Billie stuck his head in Ben's office. "Is now a good time? I want to show you something. We're going to take a ride. I'll meet you at the Bronco; I need to talk with Trini before we go."

Ben nodded and walked out to the parking lot and leaned against the police SUV. He didn't have to wait long. The chief strode across the parking lot, mouth clamped in a tight, thin line. Ben thought the chief closed the Bronco's door a little too forcefully when he got behind the wheel. Disgusted? Frustrated? Angry? Something was eating at the man, Ben thought.

"Do we know what happened to Mr. Chase?"

"Rolled the delivery truck, just this side of the entrance to the reservation."

"What was he driving?"

"Transport—eighteen-wheeler."

"That's a pretty flat area out there—you can see for miles. Was he able to tell you what happened?"

"Supposedly a Pronghorn Antelope leaped across the road in front of him."

"You don't sound like you believe him."

"I'm not sure that I do. I think he might have been nudged off the road and then hit a patch of soft sand."

"So, why lie? That seems like an honest accident."

"Or maybe it wasn't. Maybe he fell asleep. I think the animal story is more for Mountain Transport. Lets him off the hook, insurance-wise."

"I see what you mean."

"And there's another thing. I've shared with you that I believe there's been an insider? Someone who alerts the thieves of what to expect and when. I've been meaning to take a closer look at our Mr. Chase."

"Do we know anything about him?"

"Civil Service worker out of Denver. I suspect he was hired by the Feds to drive. However, his paycheck actually comes from Mountain Transport Inc., or so it would seem. I think he's either a plant for the Feds or one of the bad guys. But that's not the worst."

"Which is?"

"You'll see."

The landscape flattened out as they left the reservation and followed the road east and south. The eighteen-wheeler was hard to miss—on its side, cab twisted with wheels tipped more skyward than horizontal, both back doors to the cargo area open wide with boxes strewn around and under the truck. A reservation deputy was standing by an SUV with tribal insignia motioning for them to pull in behind his vehicle.

"I would have thought there would be another truck to pick up the cargo. Has any of it been ruined?" Ben was curious. A hospital was waiting on, actually desperate for, everything in the transport.

"Come with me." Chief Billie turned off the Bronco.

"Seeing will explain more than my just talking about it."

And Ben quickly saw what the chief meant. The first box torn along the side was filled with masks. Masks that looked like they might fit a child of six. Ben leaned down to get a better look. "Ridiculous. Who could wear these?"

"Midgets, maybe." The chief didn't even crack a smile. "And not one of them the correct issue for use in surgery—even if they did fit. But look here." The chief picked up a battered box of gloves. "These are rejects. The box came this way; it wasn't ruined in the accident. And gowns? What do you think? Did the warehouse flood?"

The chief pushed a large cardboard box toward Ben. "Looks like the storage area had a fire-sale. This is water damage."

The box was falling apart and the gowns spilled out the split sides. All were badly stained and smelled of mold. And again, the size was x-small. The crates of gloves were all marked 'Latex'. No polyvinyl chloride or nitrile rubber. Again, of limited use to anyone, especially in a hospital.

"Someone has gone through this mess. But I don't think anything was taken. Gives credence to someone running him off the road to make a killer profit. Interesting, this stuff is too worthless to steal." The chief's mood wasn't improving, Ben could tell.

Ben started for the front of the truck, "I'm going to check the cab for paperwork. I want to see how the contents list reads." Ben left the chief to look through more boxes and climbed onto the cab, lowering himself through the window into the driver's seat. Everything he needed was on a clipboard hanging from the console. Ben grabbed the paperwork and, swinging his legs back through the open drivers-side window, carefully slipped to the ground.

Ben leaned against the Bronco and flipped through the pages. "Says here the shipment was received from China. Port of entry was fourteen days ago at San Diego. Cargo signed off by an Arthur Pierson. Not sure who this Pierson is affiliated with. No mention here of IHS, but there is a post script of sorts that lists the United States Government as procurer." Ben continued to read. "Who finds this stuff? I mean where do you go? Online? Are there catalogues? And who profits?"

"Cronies, friends with benefits—and I don't mean sex but somebody who's in bed with somebody in Washington. Say that someone receives ten million US dollars; eight million might be pocketed and supplies purchased with the rest. If the supplies are worthwhile, legit and not bogus, then often the same supplies can be stolen before they reach their destination and resold. That makes the entire eight million a win-win situation. There's a healthy black market just waiting for goods. If this crap had been worth stealing, it could have ended up in South America next week, who knows? There are lots of markets out there. But when the merchandise is defective, the second group of thieves loses out. I'm surprised this kind of double-cross is being tolerated. I've expected to find some dead bodies."

"Yeah, and the person delivering the bogus merchandise, such as bottles instead of test tubes, gets shot at. Do you think something like that happened here? Mr. Chase was beaten up after the shipment was inspected? Was he supposed to be one of your dead bodies?"

"Good question. Maybe the docs will have some clue as to how he sustained his injuries."

"I guess the real question is, what now?" Ben asked.

"It's a tough problem, but I have an idea. Maybe not

the best one but it will quickly get us what we need on the Rez. I've got a tentative okay from both hospital systems in Albuquerque—Presbyterian and Lovelace. They can put together a shipment close to this one in size and volume in under a week. They'll be sharing their stockpiled PPE and reordering immediately for themselves. And they're cutting me some slack when it comes to paying for it. I'm going to bypass the normal routes of transfer. I'll rent a twenty-foot box truck from U-Haul and keep everything under the radar. So, no telling anyone about the plan."

"You have my word."

"Secondly, I'd like you to be the driver."

"Because?"

"No one knows you. The word will be that you're picking up some of your stored furniture. I figure we'll be ready for you to pick up the loaded truck in Albuquerque on Thursday. I'm even having it parked at a storage center out on University Blvd. The U-Stor-It center's books will list you as renter of the unit it's parked in front of."

"Wow, good planning. Should throw off anyone who might hear about another potential shipment of supplies. Count me in."

"In the meantime we need to get some pictures of this fiasco to send to Washington."

Chapter 14

Ben spent the rest of the afternoon in the office firing off letters and pictures to his contacts in DC—especially to Indian Health Services leaders. He also copied Dr. Sandy Black in Albuquerque ending with the question--had he had any of the same problems? Circumvented deliveries? Inferior product? Ben refused to believe getting stuck with useless PPE and other supplies or simply missed delivery dates was only happening to Navajos. This whole thing had the smell of something organized and not just hit-or-miss happenchance—organized and aimed at indigenous people. At no other time in his life could he remember the failures of the US Government to be laid out so clearly—the failure to uphold treaties, legal trusts, tribal obligations—the list was endless. But the failure to help, to save lives by providing medical personnel and supplies, and the money to make certain that the help was ongoing simply shocked him.

Limited healthcare, above average rates of compromising underlying medical conditions, an infrastructure stretched beyond being even able to cope and meet needs, and it was a perfect stew of disasters. Hospitality and gaming enterprises were closed, adding another layer of hardship. Jobs on the reservation were fast becoming non-existent. But this wasn't the 1700s or 1800s. Hadn't America progressed past its initial bloodthirsty treatment of Natives? Weren't there monies to help? Unemployment checks? Safety precautions for schools, including PPE for students, maybe individual, plexiglass screens? Was a handful of FEMA trailers and a few hospital tents all that would be offered? There had been promises. And he knew the monies were late in being dispersed—promised, but then stalled within the government bodies who were supposedly appalled that many on the reservation had no running water or bathroom facilities. But still reluctant to help. There seemed to be a 'stick your head in the sand and maybe things will go away' approach.

He remembered the time he first heard about white settlers gifting the indigenous tribes with blankets taken from the sick beds of those with Small Pox. These contaminated gifts spread the virus like wildfire throughout the Indian communities, simply wiping out entire villages. Man's inhumanity to man. Had things changed? There was an overpowering, crushing futility to this catastrophe.

The knock on the office door startled him. "Come in."

"Just thought I'd tell you that you were right." Ben motioned to a chair and Chief Billie sat down. "Somebody beat the shit out of our delivery guy."

"Charley Chase? Have you talked to him?"

"Not yet. Just relying on Dr. Henry's expertise. His best guess is pistol-whipped, probably before the semi was rolled. Apparently, there's no body bruising. Nothing one would expect if he had been tossed around in the cab. And it appears that his arm was jerked backwards while being restrained—it's a 'pull' injury, not an impact one. He's still unresponsive, but I hope we can get an interview. I've left a deputy outside his cubicle. Not that I can spare anyone right now but I think his testimony will be invaluable. He's worth guarding."

* * *

Dinner that night was pizza—Navajo pizza, which meant pepperoni was replaced with chunks of mutton and the cheese came from goats. Two Sisters With a Pot gave him a taste before he picked up two medium pies to go. And the pizza was good. Had he become so anglicized that a little melted goat cheese had given him pause? It was probably the smell. Mozzarella had a good clean cow scent. This cheese brought the floor of the barn to mind. Maybe if he squeezed his nose shut while eating. That would get him laughed at by a couple pre-teen boys—and it might be impossible to live down.

But he seemed to be the only one who was squeamish about a little melted goat topping. One and a half pizzas had disappeared before anyone shared his day. Ben was careful to leave out the gory details of his but listened as the boys excitedly shared that Oscar and a couple friends were building them a round pen to exercise and train the horses. It was going up behind the stable and would be a great space to keep Apache and Rain during the day. So much bigger than just a corral. And Oscar had found a fifty-gallon, galvanized watering tank plus a hay rack. One end was designated as a covered shelter, roomy and wide enough for both horses to get out of the weather.

Dishes were done and the garbage bagged, then deposited in a closed container close to the road. Too many nocturnal animals, who probably wouldn't mind a bite or two of goat cheese, meandered through the camp at night. Ben wasn't sure but he thought the scent of goat cheese might be a Siren's call to the numerous, errant raccoons in the area—especially the one that lived under the porch of the office.

Nine o'clock and he was dead tired. He could hear the sounds of a video game coming from the front bedroom—excited squeals when one side or the other scored points or whatever they were playing for. There was a part of him that was glad he'd missed out on an electronic childhood. It had made him a reader and more reliant on his own problem-solving logic.

He closed the door to his bedroom and called Julie. A little over a week's separation already seemed like six months.

"You sound tired."

"Too much nightlife." There was a pause and Ben wasn't sure that Julie found his remark funny; so, he jumped in with tales of owls and Pronghorn Antelope and raccoons.

"I thought you lived on a reservation, not a game preserve." But she was laughing.

He would have liked to have told her about his new job as delivery person but it would only worry her—especially if he shared what had happened to Mr. Chase. Best to leave out some information.

He guided the conversation back to south Florida and asked how the house-hunting was coming. She was going to text photos of two possibilities. She had taken the afternoon off to meet with a realtor, and he'd found something at the edge of Hollywood, Florida with some acreage. She was guardedly excited about the find. She thought it would be perfect for when Zac visited.

After many repeated 'I love yous' Ben hung up, pulled off his T-shirt and jeans and crawled into bed.

"Dad, wake up." A strident whisper sounded at the bedroom door. The clock at his bedside said one forty-five. Wow. He wasn't even certain he remembered lying down.

"Zac?" Ben sat up and reached for his shirt.

"Shhhh. We gotta show you something. Be real quiet."

Ben slipped on jeans and eased through the cracked-open bedroom door before following Zac into the living room and out onto the porch. He could see Nathan already at the front of the trailer.

"Ghost Dust." Zac excitedly pointed at the ground. At the edge of the porch and down the steps was a fine coating of silt. It looked as though the fine particles had been sifted and placed there recently—after they had gone to bed. But it was the carefully etched silhouettes, prints of two pointed-toed hooves that made him catch his breath. The sign of a Skinwalker. And there were more animal footprints in fine sand under the boys' bedroom window—both leading up to the window and away.

"What does it mean, Dad?"

Ben noticed that Nathan was unusually quiet. "Are you okay?"

Nathan nodded but didn't offer anything more. Ben watched as the boy turned and walked back around the trailer to the front porch. Nathan was frightened. He knew this was the sign of a Skinwalker. But Ben was at a loss—what did it mean? That they were being watched? Yes, but that wasn't exactly evil in itself—or was it? Maybe a warning, but why? And for whom? Then Ben felt it again, that prickly cool breeze that left his exposed skin tingling. A breeze that wasn't moving anything else in the yard—not a leaf on a tree, not a blade of scruffy grass.

Chapter 15

No one slept the rest of the night—maybe some intermittent dozing at best. The boys were up at six and joined Ben at the breakfast bar.

"How about an omelet?" Ben poured two glasses of orange juice and set them on the counter. "Any takers?"

"Yeah, I want extra ham." Zac already was refilling his glass of juice.

"Nothing for me. I'm not hungry." Nathan wasn't even drinking his juice, just wiping the frosted sides of the glass and looking preoccupied.

"What's on the agenda for you guys?" Ben was hoping to get Nathan to engage, but it was Zac who spoke up.

"We might be able to finish the round pen today. Oscar said he was picking up extra nails and some corrugated plastic roof material in Gallup."

"Sounds like a full day's work. Want to meet at Two Sisters With a Pot for lunch—maybe twelve-thirty?"

Both boys nodded this time.

* * *

"Chief Billie was looking for you." Trini barely looked up from her computer as Ben stepped into the office.

"Do you know what he wanted?"

"Nope. Didn't say a thing to me. Sorry, end-of-the-month reports are due in a week; I don't mean to be antisocial."

"Not a problem. I'll see if I can catch up with him at the hospital."

It had been a couple days since Ben had visited the tent area. Of course, he couldn't go in. But he could leave a note on the windshield of the Bronco—at least let the man know he was sorry to have missed him. It was just eight now. It looked as though more than one person around the compound had an early morning.

The place was bustling—equipment being carried between tents, nurses and doctors in full PPE gear, more garbage bags than hospital issue, unfortunately, followed closely behind; Ben vowed that he'd help change that by the end of the week. He watched as ten individuals, shedding PPE as they walked to the parking lot, stopped to talk before getting into their cars. Must be the last of the seven a.m. shift change. He was just getting ready to go back to his office when he heard his name.

"Glad I caught up with you. Coffee? The Two Sisters café is open. My treat." The chief looked as tired as Ben felt. Coffee might be considered medicinal this morning.

"Sure. Sounds good."

A side tent of ten strategically placed tables-for-two adhering to social distancing had been erected over the weekend. It was a great place to get out of the sun and hold a private conversation.

"Any change in Mr. Chase's condition?

"None. The head wound is severe, lots of swelling. I'm leaving a guard there, but it looks less and less likely that he'll regain consciousness anytime soon. He's still our best bet though to put a name or a face to the hijackers." The chief paused to put extra cream in his latte. "Boy, you two are a godsend." The chief commented to the waitress/owner behind the makeshift counter. "I'm going to break down and have two of those doughnuts. Those two at the back." He turned to Ben as the woman lifted the glass cover on the display and picked out the two chocolate frosted doughnuts with sprinkles. "I didn't have time for breakfast this morning. Anything for you?"

"I'm good. Took time for an omelet before I came to work."

They settled into a corner table partly obscured by the tent's entrance flap that doubled for a door. The chief stirred three packets of sugar into his latte before putting his spoon down. "I've gotten word that we're ready to go Thursday. The storage unit and U-Haul truck are taken care of. We just need to get you to Albuquerque that morning. I think I have a lab tech going back to IHS the night before that you could ride with." He took a sip of coffee and put his cup down. "I think I know what the answer's going to be but do you own a gun?"

"No."

"I want you to have one with you. It's only a precaution. I'll give a package to the tech with a letter from me authorizing your carry. That'll be good on the reservation, but may or may not be sufficient in New Mexico, and it's too late to get you a permit."

"You really think this is necessary?"

"I do. It worries me to possibly put you in danger. I cannot impress upon you enough that you can tell no one about the true reason for the trip. Not Trini, Dr. Henry, the boys … do you understand? You're bringing office furniture from the Indian hospital to use here at the compound plus some boxes of household goods for yourself. The truck will be packed to show tightly loaded and stacked items at the back totally covering the real reason for your trip. If anyone inspects the contents, I doubt they will dig deep enough to uncover the PPE. I want you to check the personal items and make certain they didn't get mixed in with the PPE. It's just pots and pans, linens, and then things like shampoo and soap. Stuff you'd be expected to bring to wherever you were living."

"Sounds well disguised."

"The truck will be loaded and waiting for you. At most you will be away a single overnight and back on the reservation the following afternoon." He paused. "I know what you're going to say, but I think those boys will be fine with roughly twenty-four hours on their own. At eleven and twelve, trusting them to be on their own builds character. Makes them believe in themselves when someone they admire believes in them."

"I hope so. Any chance I wouldn't be overstepping boundaries if I asked you to keep an eye on them?"

"Not at all. I'll be around here most of the day per

usual. No problem."

"Then I need to run something by you." Ben told him about the Ghost Dust and Pronghorn hoofprints from the night before. The chief pushed his chair back, index finger tapping on the table in front of him, eyes averted before meeting Ben's gaze.

"You know what this means? Who's behind it?" the chief asked.

"A good example of a Skinwalker. But I have no idea of the meaning."

"A safe bet is that the message simply means you're being watched. It's a straightforward warning, but I'm at a loss as to why you might be singled out. I was disturbed when Zac seemed so eager to interact with the Skinwalker at the dance on Saturday. I feel I'm missing something but for the life of me, I don't have a clue as to what it might be. In the meantime, impress upon Zac the importance of being careful. And be vigilant; don't be reluctant to run even the simplest thing past me—if it's unusual, I need to know. Forewarning is often guaranteed safety out here."

"I'm not sure I understand all I know about Skinwalkers."

"I'll share what I can. If you weren't a Pueblo man, I couldn't say anything. The white man is usually a non-believer and any discussion of tribal ways is strongly discouraged. But I imagine you've been exposed to witchery growing up."

Ben smiled. "My favorite story concerned one of my grandmother's friends. Her husband was driven mad by witches—stones skittering across his roof at night, the innards of freshly butchered animals left on the doorstep, old friends who had died would come up from the underworld and leave snakes in his bed. His wife finally couldn't take it and had to leave him. They'd had so many problems over the years that everyone suspected it was the wife who drove him mad just to get out of the marriage."

The chief smiled. "We have stories like that, too. But the Navajo, especially the elders, have deeply rooted—unshakeable—beliefs in evil and the ones who deliver it. Sociologists would say it's a control mechanism. Keeps the kids in line at least. But if I had to describe Skinwalkers to the outside world, I'd compare them to the European concept of werewolves. Just maybe a little more evil. But being a Skinwalker is desired—in its own way, it's an honor. It's a show of power. And nobody has to get bitten to join the cursed."

"So, an ordinary human somehow discovers that he can turn himself into an animal?"

"Not just men, women can be Skinwalkers, too."

"But why? What was the driving factor—the reason for wanting to shapeshift?"

"One theory that makes the most sense is that it was an escape ploy to outdistance persecution and forced relocation. Have you read of Kit Carson's troops driving the Navajo far into Canyon de Chelly? Cornering them and later forcing them to relocate to Bosque de Redondo? It was disastrous."

"I vaguely remember that now, from comments handed down—but it's nothing we learned in school."

"There's a lot we don't teach in our schools. One time my youngest son's teacher assigned the class a short story to read about Indians, only they lived in teepees. Not one Navajo child had even a clue what that was." The chief took a moment to sip his coffee and finish off the second doughnut. "My favorite legend involves the Anasazi, which makes sense because of where we're located—so close to the ruins. This has been Indian country for a really long time."

"But the Anasazi disappeared—nine hundred? A thousand years ago? I always thought it was because of a famine."

The chief shrugged. "No one knows for sure. But the Navajo believe in the Anasazi curse. They also think that Skinwalkers gained a lot of their powers from the grave sites of the ancients and brought witchcraft back to flourish among the Navajo. One particular Navajo witch is the *'ant'jjhnii,* or *ayee naaldlooshii.'* The translation literally means *'with it, he goes on all fours.'* This person can be a high-ranking priest or medicine man within the tribe. It's believed that he gains supernatural powers by going against a taboo. For example, he crosses the cultural barrier by being willing to do a despicable deed, possibly the murder or the ruination of a family member. Membership comes with a high price."

"It surprises me that the Skinwalker appeared at the dance the other night."

"The evil that has currently befallen the people has spread too far. It takes evil to know evil. I think the idea was that the Skinwalker could stem the tide, so to speak. Would know how to keep the evil in check—maybe with counter evil, we'll have to see. Oh, look at the time. I need to be in Gallup before noon."

Ben thanked him for the coffee and advice and promised to meet the tech late Wednesday afternoon at the triage tent. He was apprehensive but what he was going to do had to be done. He was there to help in whatever way he could. He just wished he felt better about it.

Chapter 16

The old man coughed and spat on the ground. It was time for action. Hadn't he made his decision? Hadn't he already started the ball rolling? What a funny Anglo term. But then wasn't most of the white man's language full of strange-sounding words with stranger meanings? A language that can be written down loses its power. A language spoken from one person to another is not open to interpretation and misunderstanding. But, it should be noted, a language written down lives on forever; it doesn't die with the speaker. Wasn't that important?

Yet, the printed page can't gesture, or yell, or show anger. It can't really intimidate or induce rage. But do the young people today really care? Do they study their heritage by listening to the stories of the elders? Will they pass those stories onto their children? Perpetuate history in the only true way practiced for centuries? An oral tradition must have participation if it is to continue in truth. The printed page can lie.

But these musings weren't getting him closer to a plan. He must anoint a follower, the one to take his place someday. What had been passed from his great-grandfather, grandfather, and father to him must stay in the family. He had been groomed from an early age; the parameters laid out, the secrets shared. Tested, again and again. He hadn't disappointed. But now, a stumbling block after a long life of service.

He had trusted but hadn't picked carefully the one to inherit his powers. He excused the brashness of youth, the inattention to detail, as things that would improve with age. But that wasn't happening. Repeated visits by tribal police gave rise to suspicion and distrust. Drinking, sex with underage girls, unchecked advantage taken against the less fortunate—these were the traits of a weak leader. Or no leader at all.

A Skinwalker could never be laughed at—never, and retain his powers. He must be feared, not because of baseless threats but because of supernatural powers that gave him an understanding of human need, and the ability to command fealty. He had to make decisions, wield evil, not to receive personal gain but to mold a tribe of peoples to stay within their boundaries and adhere to rules.

As painlessly as possible, he would demote his appointed, take away the promise of greatness but leave him in a position of deputy, a faithful follower. The lesson would be a stern one, life-altering and not soon forgotten. And not appreciated. His replacement? Young, malleable, bright, a superior understanding and talent when working with animals. Originally, he'd thought the supreme sacrifice and rite of passage into the brotherhood of Skinwalkers for the young man would be the challenge of killing his horse. With a lack of sibling or other family, he knew this animal was his support. It would have been an acceptable substitution.

But now a young friend had entered the picture. Someone his chosen had grown fond of and treated like a brother. This would be the ultimate sacrifice. His protégé would kill this pretend-sibling. It was the right decision.

He had looked into the eyes of this newcomer and saw a purity, a naivete, that qualified him for a mercy killing without malice. But his death would elevate his friend to a position of power and service. An honorable death, one his spirit would be proud of.

But first, he must figure out how to lure the young men away from their home. It could not arouse suspicion—cause the father to suspect foul play. Ah, if the deities were listening, a path would be shown to him. He only had to wait and be patient. For the first time in a very long time, he felt right about this choice. He had a clear vision of the future and knew a long tradition was in safe-keeping. The Skinwalkers from his family line would continue.

Chapter 17

Trini was just hanging up the phone when Ben walked into the office. Landlines. Soon they would all be museum artifacts. But out here he guessed he should be glad that there was any workable link to civilization.

"Oh, there you are. You've been chosen for a new job."

"New job?"

"Lucky you, you get to deliver water this morning. There are three families roughly seventy-five miles from here that missed their delivery last week. It'll take two trucks; Oscar will be driving the tanker and lead the way. Both are loaded and waiting in back." Trini motioned out the window.

Ben walked out to the parking lot just as Oscar was getting out of the truck.

"Hey, Doc Pecos, do I have time to grab me something to eat?"

"Sure, not a problem." Ben watched Oscar head toward the Two Sisters café. He sat down on the back steps to wait. He knew what he would be doing that day was tantamount to saving lives.

To have missed a water delivery put a family in dire need. It was difficult for the outside world to realize that forty percent of the households on the reservation had to rely on water being hauled to them—water for cooking, bathing, cleaning; not to mention drinking. Drawing a clean, clear glass of water from a tap just wasn't a part of their lives. Ben knew dropping in a few ice cubes to make that glass more palatable wasn't even a possibility in their wildest dreams. Yet, that was something he'd taken for granted all his life.

If the hogan was home to the infirm or elderly, it was not melodramatic to view a water shortage as a life or death matter. Deliveries had to be consistent, no dates missed. At least the trucks were filled from onsite wells. A well in this part of New Mexico and Arizona could be four hundred to five hundred feet deep. Often near the foot hills, a well partially dug through rock, tapped into an underground aquifer. Water was usually high-grade and limitless. One well provided water for up to two hundred residences within a fifty-mile radius. Many families had given up their fifty-five-gallon storage barrels and installed twelve-hundred-gallon cistern tanks, usually with their own wooden, well-shaded, lean-to sheds beside their hogan to protect the containers from the relentless sun.

Ben was always amazed at how people adapted. Ingenuity helped the Navajo live widely spread out over the rugged land they called their own. No longer did villages have to cluster around sources of water to exist. Yet, with stock to water and access to grasslands limited by federal regulations to keep animals from overgrazing, the *bi'iiná*, or 'lifeway' was always precarious and fraught with obstacles.

When he was young, his grandmother took him to see a herd of Churro, the sacred sheep of the Navajo, which the white man thought was inferior. Probably brought to the Southwest by the Spanish conquistadores in the 1500s, it was westward expansion that almost eliminated them. Kit Carson's troops were ordered to destroy them when the Navajo were relocated. Much later the tribe carefully brought them back when they were allowed to return to their ancestral lands. Yes, they were smaller than other breeds, but the long, wavy, beautifully lustrous wool was a gift to Navajo weavers. They were an integral part of the *bi'iiná* Ben remembered his grandmother saying sheep were the backbone, the lifeline of the Navajo. For centuries they provided fleece for weaving clothing and blankets, sinew for thread, and, of course, meat for sustenance.

But it wasn't until 1972 that the Churro made a strong and permanent comeback. Thinking it knew best, the United States government first introduced other breeds of sheep, forcing the Navajo to tend to them. It was not unusual to see the black-faced Suffolk roaming the reservation. But they were a poor substitute for the Churro. It was with unfailing dedication and scouring the hidden canyons on the reservation before enough Churro were discovered to form the nucleus of a breeding program. But the result meant that a way of life was preserved.

"Sorry I took so long. Sure you don't want to share some fry bread?" Oscar held out a greased-stained sack with the scent of warm yeast dough.

"Thanks, Oscar, I'm fine."

"Then let's hit the road. We've got five stops and that will probably take us until late this afternoon. Did Dr. Henry talk to you? He wants you to keep an eye out for anyone who might be ill. He was going to leave a bag of supplies—thermometer, wipes, hand sanitizer—plus a box of hand soap to give away. We need to drop off some of these supplies at the school. Don't know when it will open, but they'll be prepared. I'll run over to the triage tent and pick the stuff up."

Ben could have done that instead of sitting around. Seemed like the waste of half the morning but he was feeling peevish and more than a little worried about his upcoming trip to Albuquerque. Ben climbed into the cab and pulled the truck he was driving in behind Oscar's. Finally, they were off.

Chapter 18

The schoolhouse had a new bright blue metal roof, a corral constructed of saplings, six outhouses, three on each side of the building, a maintenance barn, a flag pole sans flag, and a wall of freshly washed windows. In fact, as they got closer, Ben could see that the person wielding the hose and a long-handled scrub brush was Miss Otter. Ben followed Oscar and pulled in next to the maintenance barn as the teacher opened the storage unit's double doors.

"I know you're going to think window-washing is a terrible waste of water, but it's only done once a year. Just a part of the welcome back. We were lucky to get a new roof earlier in the summer before all the travel restrictions."

"Any idea of when you'll be back in business?" Oscar handed the teacher a clipboard with some papers to sign.

"Oh, I wish I knew. Tentatively we're hoping September 1—less than two weeks away—and we all know a lot can happen in that time frame."

"You still got that fifty-five-gallon barrel on the side porch?" Oscar was pulling hoses off his truck.

"Yes, that's drinking water for the month. That and a hundred cases of bottled water that were donated by the First Episcopal Church in Albuquerque. The donations of water and toilet paper are going to help us meet the suggested opening date."

"I saw the stack of toilet paper. Aren't you worried someone might break in and take it? It's better than legal tender now." Ben laughed, but strangely enough, he was actually telling the truth. He'd read where someone had been shot wrestling a carton of the stuff off a delivery truck in Espanola earlier in the month.

"There are some good things to be said about isolation. I honestly don't think the school has ever been broken into or even vandalized. We're too far out to even have an outhouse tipped over." She laughed. "Come with me. I'll show you my second home."

Ben turned to Oscar. "What do you need me to do?"

"Nothing here—I got it covered. Go see where that son of yours is going to do some learning."

Ben turned to Miss Otter. "I'll get the medical supplies out of my truck. Do you want them inside or in the barn?"

"I'll store the wipes and masks and sanitizer in the classroom. Let me help you."

Walking back to the truck meant walking around an open field that appeared to be the playground. Swings, a see-saw, and a slide sat next to a homemade round-about. At the other end of the field were two basketball stands—

one missing a hoop and the other had a hoop but no net.

"Before I forget, I'd like to offer my help in providing some physical education—maybe workshops after school. I noticed two basketball hoops—at least the stands are there. I'd like to contribute an upgrade—new nets, two new backboards and balls if you need them. Plus, I'd like to add soccer equipment. There's room to mark out a decent-sized playing field. Do you think there'd be any interest?"

"Oh, Dr. Pecos, you have no idea--the kids would be thrilled. I don't know how to thank you. There's a lot to be learned from competitive sports. Things that can't be taught in the classroom."

"I'll order equipment in the morning, but I'll need an address off the Rez in order to get it delivered."

"You can send it to me in Shiprock. I'll give you my address before you leave today. Believe me, anything will be so appreciated, and I love the idea of after school PE. Your son's name is Zac, isn't it? Chief Billie mentioned that Nathan Yazzie is living with the two of you now. I'm so glad he's found a home. His life hasn't been easy and he's such a good student with a lot to offer."

"The boys have bonded. I couldn't ask for a better situation. I was worried about my working all day and having to leave Zac on his own."

"Well, here we are." She held open the back door and pointed to a corner in what was a kitchen. At least a stove, a disconnected fridge, and several cabinets qualified it as such.

"Now, come with me."

The kitchen opened onto one huge room—not divided into smaller sections by walls or partitions. The only divisions or boundaries that might indicate different grades were marked by small tables and chairs in one corner and actual flip-top desk/chair units in other corners. Only the two differing sizes marked a difference in ages of the learners.

"I'm sure this wasn't what you were expecting. But here it is—an old fashioned, one-room school house, which isn't a bad thing. Remember, there's only one of me and I have students ranging in age from six to twelve. This year I'll welcome six new first graders, a combined class of ten second and third graders, nine fourth, fifth and sixth graders and another five seventh and eighth graders. Oh my, I honestly didn't realize the total was thirty students in all, and I wasn't counting Zac. I usually don't have so many beginners—that's upped the tally for this year. But I can call on help from nearby families. I often have a volunteer mother or two when I need them."

"Seems challenging." Ben noted the walls covered with blackboards and low shelves holding a globe, stacks of construction paper, boxes of scissors, and jars of paste, next to a collection of watercolor trays. Taller shelving held books, a reference series and rows of texts.

"It does look like something out of the last century, doesn't it? I was supposed to have delivery of forty tablets, iPads, before school started. The pandemic slowed that down. But we are getting Wi-Fi. I've seen the work on the tower. That will make all the difference in preparedness. From here most students continue to high school in Gallup or Shiprock. It's tough to catch up when they haven't been exposed to electronics."

"Finished. What can we help you with in here?" Oscar offered each of them a bottle of water. "They're cold, straight from the cooler in the truck."

"If you had the time, could you help me arrange the chairs six feet apart?"

"Sure. You tell me how you'd like them placed."

"I drew this diagram." Miss Otter went to the desk at the front of the room. "I think this would work."

Ben and Oscar moved tables and chairs, dividing sections by dragging shelves to act as borders. An hour later they were finished and satisfied that the classroom would meet any virus requirements for distancing.

"I can't thank you enough. This would have been a full day's work for me by myself." And then as Ben was going out the back door, she handed him a slip of paper with her address and put a hand on his sleeve, "I don't want to alarm you, but be aware of what goes on around Nathan, protect him. There are rumors about his uncle. Nathan has so much promise, I want to see him fulfill that promise."

Ben immediately thought of the hoof prints in the ghost dust. Had that been a message for Nathan?

* * *

By the end of the day, all water had been delivered and Ben was tired. He hated to admit it, but it was more work that he'd done in a while. They serviced eighteen houses, topping up tanks or filling them from scratch. All the residences were within a fifty-mile radius of the hospital.

Ben was careful to keep his mask on and in interviewing families, he found four people who had been exposed to the virus through their jobs outside the reservation. Testing. There was a need and it wasn't being met. He took the individuals' names and would submit them to the traveling nurses who tried to check outlying areas on a bi-weekly basis. But everything had a too-little, too-late feel to it. This was such a 'sitting duck' population—isolated, spread out over miles, scanty health care, many older members of the tribe already struggling with diabetes, dementia, alcoholism. Once again, Ben applauded the Navajo Nation president's quick action in shutting down the roads in and out. Keeping outsiders from coming in was literally life-saving.

* * *

Ben didn't get back to the trailer until after six. A long day. He was already planning what he would order in the way of PE equipment for Miss Otter's school. But first, he had a couple hungry boys to feed. It would be the easiest to just go to the Two Sisters café but when he went by, there was a line outside waiting to be served, which would put their meal another hour in waiting. No, Ben thought he could come up with something from their kitchen.

"Mac and cheese?" Ben got an immediate and enthusiastic "yes" from both boys. "And it's not going to make a difference if there's a side dish of broccoli?"

"Ahh, I don't want broccoli." Zac literally scrunched up his nose.

"No broccoli, no mac." Ben knew that wasn't going to get him any popularity points. "But the broccoli is going to have cheese sauce."

"Okay."

"Nathan, how about you? Are you okay with broccoli?"

"Yeah, I'm good."

"Then I'll get things started if you two will set the table."

"Can we go to the movie tonight?" Zac asked.

"Where's a movie?"

"Here, in the parking lot. They've put up a big screen and you can sit in your car or bring a chair." Zac added, "I think it's a Disney."

"Sounds good. I'll turn the truck around so you guys can sit on the tailgate."

By eight-thirty the trailer was quiet. By nine Ben had finished his order to Amazon for playground equipment. He could hear the movie in the background, muffled other than a chorus of honking horns every once in a while. Must be a comedy with the occasional audience participation—horn honking approval instead of laughter. Adaptation was everything nowadays.

It was too early to go to bed but a walk sounded good. Maybe even catch a little of the movie. Desert air was always invigorating in the evening. He couldn't believe the contrast, living in Florida where the difference between day and night temps might be a whole ten or twelve degrees. Twenty or thirty degrees was much more like it here—and no humidity. Would he ever get back to New Mexico? He wondered. No matter where he lived, it would always be home. Before he left the house, he cut an apple into slices and tucked them into a zip-lock bag. He had a feeling that there were two horses who might enjoy a treat.

He took the path that wound around the office, finally dead-ending at the corral. He was almost squarely in front of Trini's office window when movement caught his eye. Ben stepped back into the shadows of the building but kept an eye on the window. And there it was again. Decidedly human, not a bear, anyway. But wouldn't a human pull the blinds? The figure was standing, moving first right, pause, and then left, pause, which didn't make sense. But wait, maybe it did. The figure was moving from one file cabinet to the other.

Trini? No, much too tall for her. This was someone who most likely had broken in. But before Ben could even think about what to do, a figure clad all in black including a hood rushed from the trailer, cleared the back steps in a leap before taking off for the stables. Ben sprinted after the person but was stopped by a blood-curdling scream and the sound of splintering wood.

Ben knew exactly what had happened. Apache had lived up to his red ribbon and stomped the shit out of someone.

"That son-of-a-bitch needs to be shot."

"Wrong call, J.C. It's a horse, not a dog." Ben was pretty sure his attempt at a joke was lost. The man was obviously in pain, clutching his arm close to his body. "Maybe the question should be why were you in Trini's office?"

"My arm's fucking broken."

"I don't think that's answering the question. I think there's proof of breaking and entering."

"Oh yeah, prove it."

"My word places you in the office."

"The door was unlocked and a light was on. I was just being a good citizen. We can't afford to waste power out here. I walked in to turn the light off."

"Sure. That's believable." It sounded too sarcastic but Ben didn't care.

"Hey, search me." J.C. started to hold his arms out, then grimaced and clutched his left arm to his chest. "I need to see a doctor."

"Guess you've come to the right place. I'll walk you over to triage."

The nurse on duty pronounced the arm badly bruised with the possibility of a sprained wrist. A soft cast of taped together tongue depressors and a tightly wound gauze wrapping would immobilize it. That and a sling and J.C. was ready to go.

"Better report this to the cop-man. Maybe he'll make you a deputy seeing as how you're so good at sneaking around and accusing the innocent." A derisive snort and J.C. walked out the door. Ben let him go. Yes, he'd tell the chief and check with Trini to make certain nothing had been taken from her files. But there was no reason to detain him even if he could. He watched J.C. walk to the road. Ben would bet that the Camaro was parked just out of sight. He texted a brief message to Chief Billie, from *shrinkwrap*, before sitting down on the front steps of the office to watch the last of the movie.

Chapter 19

Ben almost missed the soft knock on his front door. The boys had just gone to bed chattering away, still talking about the movie. Anything with Ninjas and swords had to be exciting—at least to them. So, the movie wasn't a comedy after all, and the horn-honking was just to cheer on the heroes. It seemed the camp organizers had hit upon a popular family-oriented pastime.

"Iced tea? Soft drink?" Ben offered Chief Billie a chair at the counter. "Too late for coffee?"

"I'll take you up on a soda. And that information you promised."

Ben filled him in on seeing J.C. in Trini's office. J.C. getting kicked by Apache brought a smile to the chief's face.

"Couldn't have happened to a more deserving guy—but guess I shouldn't disparage the unfortunate. Have you talked to Trini? Made certain that nothing's missing from her files?"

"I didn't want to worry her. I pulled the front door shut and locked it. I really wanted you to be making these decisions about how much to say and when."

"I appreciate that. How 'bout meeting me at her office at eight?"

* * *

"This file is out of order—unless Q now comes before M. Looks like he pulled out several and then poked them back in. I wonder what he was looking for." She moved to the file cabinet on her right and pulled the top drawer open. "Odd. I had slipped last month's calendar in front of the files. It's gone. Now who would want an outdated wall calendar?"

"What was on it?" Chief Billie asked.

"I had it on my desk when I first moved in—before I even had a computer or there was wi-fi for my phone. I jotted down phone numbers, names of contacts within IHS, contractors from FEMA—we were just setting up here; so, anything and everything having to do with getting this place in order. It was a pretty good overview of who all was involved."

"Dates of PPE delivery?" Chief Billie was taking notes.

"No deliveries in July but several dates of when the supplies were ordered."

"I'm not sure I see how that would be helpful," Ben offered.

"Nor do I. I can only wonder if Ben didn't scare him off before he got what he wanted. But it's a lesson for me not to get complacent. I have a safe under my desk. I often have cash to pay for deliveries. I'll make sure anything that might be of interest to the wrong parties is kept out of sight."

"Well, just make sure you lock up at night. I wouldn't have thought there would be a need, not out here and under these circumstances, but I was wrong. Let me know if you run across anything else missing."

"Believe me, Chief, I won't be leaving any doors unlocked again."

Chief Billie walked Ben out. "Ready for tonight? I haven't heard from Albuquerque yet, but I'm assuming everything's on schedule—truck should be loaded and waiting for you."

"I'll be out front of the triage tent at four-thirty. Any change in Mr. Chase's condition?"

"None. Still in an induced coma. He's got a lot of mending to do before we can talk."

Ben waved good-bye and walked to his trailer. He'd discussed the overnight with Zac and Nathan that would put the boys on their own. He'd ordered pizza for that evening and a six-pack of Mountain Dew. Otherwise, the fridge was stocked—breakfast and lunch tomorrow were covered. He told himself not to be heavy-handed with rules and regulations. He needed to trust the boys. This was a small community structured around a hospital and family needs. And it was the Rez. It would be difficult to find a safer place. He would not remind them to lock the back door, make sure burners were off on the stove, scrape their dishes, wash them, carry out the trash—the list could be exhausting and daunting if you were eleven and twelve and eager to be accepted as trusted almost-adults.

Ben was prompt at four-thirty, but his ride was already waiting on him in front of the triage tent. He knew very little about his driver for the afternoon other than he was a bull rider. Ben wasn't sure that instilled confidence, and he soon found out that the country/western radio station blasting in the cramped cab was probably his worst fault. That was before he found out the guy chewed. Ben didn't know if he should be relieved or upset by the fact that his driver was spitting into a can down by his feet. At least he wasn't opening the window and taking a chance on a tobacco-laced wad of phlegm getting blown back into the cab. It was a little upsetting that chewing seemed to negate wearing a mask. The radio and the man's off-tune singing along with every song kept any conversation to a minimum. That was a plus. Still, this was going to be a long trip.

The package that the chief promised would be waiting for him was on the front seat. Ben slipped it into his duffle. He still wished the chief hadn't felt a gun was necessary.

* * *

Finally, he was waving good-bye to his ride and walking up the steps of the IHS hospital. It was a few minutes after eight, but Dr. Black was in his office.

"Good to see you, Ben. Glad to know you made it here safely. Give me five or ten more minutes to finish up some paperwork, and I'll give you a ride to the motel. The U-Haul is being delivered here mid-morning so that the used office furniture will be loaded last. Should be all packed and ready to go by noon. I still can't believe we have to go to all this trouble just to safeguard hospital supplies."

The evening was uneventful. Ben called Zac, but the call went to voicemail. He left a message and then called Julie. More voicemail. His mouth was watering for crab cakes from the Artichoke Café but luckily he called first—temporarily closed due to indoor dining restrictions. He walked to a Blake's Lotaburger and had a green chile cheeseburger instead.

He hadn't realized how tired he was until he awoke at six stretched out on the bed, still wearing street clothes. A quick shower and a cup of motel coffee from the lobby and he was ready when Sandy Black picked him up.

"Sure you don't want to stop for breakfast?"

"No, I'm fine, thanks."

"I set aside a carton of gloves for you to take. With the Navajo Nation shut down and nearby Pueblos not traveling into Albuquerque, we've got a pretty good stockpile in place. Might as well share when we can."

The five desks and matching chairs were stored behind the hospital in the garage reserved for government vehicles and groundskeeping equipment. According to schedule, the U-Haul was delivered right at ten. Before the furniture was loaded, Ben checked the row of boxes marked personal. In the kitchen box was a complete set of copper pans. Nice ones. Ben wondered where they were going to end up. Maybe with the Two Sisters? Next, the linens—flowered sheets that he'd never choose, but nice. Something Trini might like. The personal toiletries were complete—several bottles of shampoo and conditioner, air freshener, antibacterial soap and salve, and lastly, a red leather case of manicure tools. Expensive and a somewhat odd addition because of their obvious value, but it fit in with the other personal items.

Ben made sure all the boxes were closed and added some extra tape to a couple. There were no boxes of PPE mixed in with his 'pretend' household items. Those valued items were at the front of the truck, next to the cab, and safely hidden behind all the rest. Finally, they were ready to add the furniture. He had the help of a couple maintenance men and the loading went quickly. He was on his way a half hour early.

The speed-limit was seventy-five, but the older model truck seemed to labor a little if he pushed it over seventy. He wasn't going to make good time, but he guessed it didn't matter. He'd just be glad to have the PPE safely in the hands of those who needed it in the camp. He'd forgotten that truckers pretty much dominated Interstate 40. And now with travel restrictions in place for anyone other than intrastate commerce, eighteen-wheelers were about the only vehicles on the road.

He was just settling in when the truck began losing power in general—no lights, low battery warning came on, no power windows, no air-conditioning. And then it just quit altogether. He coasted to the side of the highway and pulled the big truck completely off the road. Now what?

The rental paperwork was in the glove compartment and he called the U-Haul agency in Albuquerque. He gave them his exact location and was assured that they could send help his way when their mechanic returned from lunch. Nothing to do but wait, and think. Could it even be possible that this was planned? Someone set him up to have the truck break down? No, he couldn't give into that; he'd be looking over his shoulder all the time if he let himself suspect sabotage. But he pulled his duffle up onto the seat next to him and patted the side that held the gun, then slipped it out and placed the .38 under the driver's seat.

* * *

It was four before the U-Haul was towed back to the garage adjacent to the rental agency. A faulty alternator, its serpentine belt in tatters, had drained the battery, even causing some bearings to fail in the engine. It wasn't going to be an easy fix. In fact, there was no way it was going to be fixed in the agency's shop. The manager was apologetic and said he had calls into shops in surrounding communities hoping to find a twenty-foot, box truck replacement. It was another hour before he walked out into the waiting area to tell Ben the good news and the bad.

The good news? He'd finally found a truck of the necessary size. The bad news? The truck wasn't due to be returned to Santa Fe U-Haul until the following day. By the time they got it loaded, it wouldn't be ready to roll before late afternoon.

Ben called Chief Billie and then Trini. The chief was sorry he'd volunteered Ben for the job and once again admonished him to be careful and not advertise the cargo unless he had to declare it for some reason.

Trini assured him the boys were fine. They had taken the horses up to the north pasture and she expected them back in time for supper. Ben left a message for Zac just the same explaining what had happened. And then it was back to the hospital and another night in the motel.

Chapter 20

Nathan cooked the eggs that morning. He'd talked the Sisters out of some green chile, potatoes, and cheese and a half dozen flour tortillas. It was a skillet dish that his grandmother used to make and Zac loved it.

"This is better than Dad makes. You'll have to fix it for him."

"It's easy. Want more juice?" He passed the carton to Zac. "I have an idea for today. There are three pastures about five miles north. Sheep graze the grass too close and need to be rotated to keep the pastures alive. I always take Apache and Rain up to whatever pasture is being used at least once a week. But I haven't been able to treat them lately. Fresh food is good for them. Let's take them up today. We may not have a lot of extra time after school starts."

Nathan suggested they pack lunches. He promised Zac a surprise after they situated the horses. Two PB&Js each, chips, and bottled water were placed in a canvas bag and hung over the pommel of Nathan's saddle. By now Zac could saddle Rain without help or even being checked. Rain stood still while being saddled, bowing his head to take the bit. Zac had won the horse's trust by bringing him apple slices every day, and Zac was already wondering how he could leave his new friend when he returned to Alaska. A horse wasn't exactly like a dog who would just jump in the back seat of a car and go wherever you went.

Today the horses were frisky—too much standing around in a small space. Zac told himself that from now on, he'd ride Rain every day even if only around the camp. But now, it didn't take extra urging to bring Rain to a trot as they headed across the road. Nathan had taught Zac to post and this technique of rising up out of the saddle on every other stride made the normally teeth-jarring trot much smoother. But both horses wanted to stretch out into a gallop.

Rain with his shorter, stocky, pony legs couldn't pass Apache; but he could keep up, nose to tail. Again, Nathan's riding lessons came in handy. Zac relaxed, pressed his thighs against Rain's sides, leaned slightly forward holding the reins somewhat loosely and enjoyed how quickly the pony could cover ground. Finally, Nathan reined Apache in somewhat against the horse's will. But with only a little head-tossing, the horse settled into a walk.

"That was fun." The wind in his face had felt good. Zac wished he'd grown up around horses. There was something so special about them.

"You're getting good. I was afraid I'd have to scrape

you up off the ground back there." Nathan laughed as Zac made a face.

"How much farther till we get to the pasture?"

"You're on pasture land now. There are over three million acres of open range on the Navajo Nation. "

"How many sheep do the Navajo have?"

"Over a hundred thousand. Probably closer to a hundred and fifty thousand, maybe two."

"Sheep? How do you know all this?" Zac couldn't believe what he was hearing.

"Last year our class project for Miss Otter was on the Navajo Nation. We studied our history—from the time of the Spanish to today. It was the Spanish who brought cattle and horses as well as sheep. A lot of families still keep sheep. My grandmother kept fifty Churro just for their fleece. Most of the year they were mixed in with my uncle's flock. Some men in the community do nothing but tend to them year-round. People who have stock can get a grazing permit. But the land has caretakers, those who make certain that the land stays in balance. For example, it's not overgrazed. You know, the BIA pretty much has control."

"We have the Bureau of Indian Affairs in Alaska, but they don't oversee sheep."

"What do they do?"

"Make sure villages have supplies—like heating oil, building materials, fuel for highway equipment to fix the roads every year. A bunch of the villages that are right on the ocean need to be moved. They're getting flooded by the ocean. Even the graveyards have to be moved before everything falls off into the water."

"Wow. Your home is a different place than mine is. "

"Were the Navajo warriors?"

"When we had to be. We fought the Spanish but we also raided your dad's tribe."

"Pueblos?"

"Yeah, this was a pretty wild place to live. And the horse made us good at surprising the enemy. Did your people fight?"

"Maybe bears. It's too cold to travel much. They spent time setting up villages and staking out fishing territory."

"I'd like to visit someday."

"Will you come with me when I go back to school in Washington?"

Nathan was quiet. "I don't know. I think I'd like to. Do you like your school?"

"Oh, yeah. It's really neat. You'll like playing soccer and basketball. We were regional champs last year in the middle-school tournaments in basketball. I know you'd make the team."

"Someday I want to work on computers—design games. I'd have to go to college to do that, I think. There's probably some good colleges in Alaska or Washington. But no sheep? Not anywhere in Alaska?"

Zac was laughing. "No sheep, no horses, but lots of dogs." He shared his mother's experience racing in the Iditarod earlier that year and how his grandfather had been a well-known musher. "Think about it. We could have a lot of fun."

"I will."

"Promise?"

"I promise."

"Then I want you to wear this." Zac slipped a braided sinew bracelet from his wrist and handed it to Nathan.

"This is *ivalu,* caribou tendons used to sew together the sealskin boats of whalers. They hunt the bowhead whales. Strong tendons, properly cured, will bring the boats home safely. My Auntie threaded these tiny shells into the braids saying the sea would always call to me no matter where I am. I would always be pulled back to the sea and my home. So, now maybe it will call to you."

Nathan slipped it on his wrist, tightened it and looked at Zac. "I will visit your home someday. I think you're right. This will make it happen." He held out his arm and admired the white braiding and tiny white shells.

"How close are we to the upper pasture?"

"Maybe another two miles. We passed the first pasture and that kinda blends into the second pasture, and I don't see any signs that a flock of sheep have even been through here. This pasture is half grown back. So, I guess we'll need to go to the high pasture. It's the best. It includes the foothills, not far from some ruins. There's a swimming hole and caves—that was my surprise. We can have lunch and go swimming."

The sun was almost straight overhead when they came to the high pasture. The upper grassland made up several thousand acres of its own and stretched in all directions with huge flocks of sheep busily grazing in the distance. Zac was amazed at the amount of land that Nathan called home. And everywhere he looked, it was green. Zac watched Nathan strip off his shirt and tie it around his waist. It was hot. The horses had broken out in a film of light sweat glistening on their necks with a dark, wet smear across their chests. Nathan urged Apache forward, expertly guiding the horse between two boulders and urging him up a slight incline. It was beginning to dawn on Zac that maybe Nathan wouldn't like Alaska—the cold, the dark. But they could stay in Bellingham, at school. That would be better, but it was hard to imagine Nathan spearing salmon or skinning a seal. Still, it felt right to give him the bracelet. It might just work its magic on him.

"Let's stay close to that stand of trees. We can put the saddles and tack in the shade and just let the horses run free. They won't go far. Eating is all they want to do, and Apache will always come when I call."

Nathan was right. The horses knew the drill. The minute they were free of saddles and blankets, they turned and trotted to a foot-high patch of grass and simply put their heads down and started munching.

"Horses are so picky."

"What do you mean?" It looked to Zac like they were doing a good job of eating everything in sight.

"See all those weeds at the edge of the grass? A horse won't touch them. Takes a goat to really clean up an area."

"Do Navajo people have goats, too?"

"My grandmother did for a while. She even owned two milk cows."

"We don't have cows where I live either."

Nathan laughed. "Maybe you should move down here with me."

Zac didn't say anything. He was missing his mom and he was really missing his friends from school. By now he should be having soccer practice with his teammates. But, most of all, he was missing Romo. The Alaskan Husky puppy was his best friend, and he looked forward to training him to sled. His mom was thinking of moving to Seattle and working in the city. She'd promised to rent a house with a yard for Romo so Zac could visit him on weekends. Besides, his father wouldn't be staying in New Mexico after the pandemic was over. He'd be going back to Florida and Zac knew he wasn't going to be ready for alligators and pythons.

"Hungry? Grab a sandwich." Nathan handed him a bottle of water and motioned to the saddlebags.

"Thought I was going to starve." Zac pulled out a bag of chips and a PB&J.

"After lunch we can go swimming and take a look at the ruins."

* * *

He couldn't believe his luck. Hidden in an outcropping of rock above the boys, he watched them eat lunch. They were alone. Wasn't this exactly what he'd wished for? What he needed? The boys, separated from others, would in all likelihood fall into his trap. He could lure them there. It was time. The initiation into the Witchery Way must happen now. He felt his ancestors looking down. They approved. By the end of the day, the honor of becoming a Skinwalker would be bestowed on someone worthy of his family's tradition.

Chapter 21

"Finished?" Nathan was putting his empty sandwich wrapper and water bottle in his saddlebag. "I want to go swimming."

"Yeah, me too." Zac picked up his trash and added it to Nathan's. "Is the place very far from here?"

"No. It'll take some climbing and that's why we can't take the horses. But you'll like it. This is a good place to leave the saddles. Nobody's going to take them."

The afternoon had turned hot, but when they reached the hidden pool tucked in between several boulders, there was a nice breeze. The pool was the receptacle for water that cascaded over a piling of rocks some twenty-feet high. There, it defied collection by spilling in a stream, leaving the pond and following a gravitational pull to the pasture below. Zac could see that someone had built a trough to catch water for grazing animals near the bottom of the hill.

Zac and Nathan stripped to their shorts, and Zac didn't wait for encouragement. He clambered up on a rock overhang and jumped into the water. The shock of the seventy-something degree pool took his breath away and by the time he'd scrambled up onto the opposite bank, his teeth were chattering.

"Hey, that's cold."

"Stretch out in the sun, you'll thaw out." Nathan was trying to keep from laughing. "It's good for the blood, my grandmother always said. Aren't you the one from cold country?"

Nathan jumped in, floated on his back and even dove, swimming under water back and forth across the width of the natural pool before pulling himself out at the water's edge. Zac ignored him and sat down on a rock, letting his feet barely touch the water. He didn't care that Nathan was showing off by swimming and pretending that the water wasn't cold. He was comfortable out of the water. The breeze dried him off and he laid back against the warm granite and closed his eyes. Peaceful. The sun felt good. But that didn't last long.

"Hey, sleepy-head. Watch this."

Zac rubbed his eyes, then leaned up on one elbow as he saw Nathan walk right into the waterfall above the pond and disappear. Now *that* had Zac's attention. He stood up, waiting for Nathan to return. What was he doing? Why hadn't he come back out? He slipped his sneakers on and, trying not to slip on the wet rocks at the base of the falls, Zac followed.

When he got close enough to touch the waterfall, he

could see there was nothing behind it. A five-foot wide wall of water fell straight down into the pool, foaming and splashing outward as it hit the rocks. Tentatively, Zac stuck his arm through the foot-thick torrent. There was no rock on the other side, only air. He stepped through.

"Hey, you're okay. That took some guts." Nathan was standing in the middle of a room which, over centuries, had been hollowed out by the elements and maybe the help of indigenous tribes.

"This place is great. It's sure not easy to find. How'd you know it was here?"

"My grandmother used to bring me to the pool. She told me about the rooms but warned me never to walk through the water."

"But, of course, you did."

Nathan grinned. "Of course."

"Where's the light coming from?" It wasn't bright by any means but certainly more distinct than mere shadows.

"Look above you. Sun tunnels—holes cut in the ceiling of the cave to the ground surface above it."

Zac looked and sure enough, five, foot-wide round openings were allowing light to filter down into the room. "That's cool."

"But I'll show you the best part. Back here, come with me."

Zac hadn't realized that the cave had more than one room, but a dome-like curve to the ceiling stretched above him and continued toward the back. The astounding thing was the ceiling was filled with pictographs. Wall to wall across the ceiling barely fleshed-out stick figures went about daily life.

"Nathan, wait. Look at these." Zac pointed above his

head. The drawings weren't realistic but easy to interpret. The one that had caught his attention showed two hunters running a deer to ground. Another showed several men fighting with spears. Zac was mesmerized. "Wow. This place is really old."

"You haven't seen anything. The best part is back here." Nathan disappeared into another room. Zac followed, stepped across the threshold, and quickly sucked in his breath. It was all he could do to keep from crying out. He wanted to run. His breath came out in short gasps as he looked around the walls and his stomach was doing some kind of bouncy thing that made him feel sick. But he couldn't look away.

All around the room there were eight-foot spikes, saplings whittled to points on one end, the other anchored to the floor, and each holding the head of a wild animal. But they weren't just heads, they were masks with eyes made of glass or some material that made them glow. And every one had its natural teeth, incisors and canines intact and threatening. A bear, a five-point buck, cougar, fox, coyote—their skins hanging slack against the posts, paws and hooves attached. All with mouths open, as if to emit some primal scream before an attack. Zac could almost hear the snarling, howling, growling sounds as each head stared down at him. He wasn't sure he trusted his legs to stay standing.

"Where are we?" It came out as a strangled whisper.

"This is a part of the Anasazi burial grounds. We're not far from the ruins."

"We need to leave. We're not supposed to be here."

"Scaredy cat. They can't hurt you."

"This place is evil."

Zac turned to go, but the door was blocked. The Pronghorn Antelope loomed above him, its head tipped downward so the enormous horns were aimed right at his head. But it wasn't moving. The figure was bent slightly over two canes, femurs ending in hooves, animal skin covering the arms and torso, a tan chamois-like skin hiding its throat and dipping down to drape over the chest.

Zac turned to Nathan and saw the shock. He hadn't meant to endanger his friend. Zac felt sure of that. What had been a fun exploration of sharing with a pal had just turned possibly deadly.

The Pronghorn stepped into the room and right behind him was a wolf. Slightly smaller in stature and frame, but nonetheless threatening; this creature circled to stand behind Zac. His teeth were yellowed with one incisor chipped, and his eyes glowed red. He wore hairy gloves with long nails and his legs were bound with strips of wolf hide, hair intact.

Instinctively, Zac moved away from the creature's hot breath only to have a clawed hand grasp his shoulder, holding him in place by pinching the skin.

"Let him go." Nathan stepped toward the wolf. "I said, let him go."

The Pronghorn motioned with a hoof to the back of the cave and the wolf twisted Zac's arm up between his shoulders, moving him forward and pushing past Nathan. And then Zac saw something he hadn't noticed before—a cage. Iron bars marked a five-foot by five-foot enclosure in the farthest corner of the room. Floor to ceiling, the bars maybe six inches apart and the door three-feet wide. The wolf kept one hand on Zac and opened the cage with the other, then pushed him inside. The clanging of the cage door sounded deafening in the closed space of the cave.

Zac turned to look at Nathan. Zac felt totally at a loss, but he knew that Nathan understood what was happening. Was that why he wasn't doing anything? He might have called Zac a scaredy cat before, but now it was Nathan's turn to look traumatized.

The next thing to happen mystified Zac. The Pronghorn got down on his knees—slowly and carefully, like an old man, before turning and dragging several pots and tightly woven baskets from along the wall toward the center of the room. And then he started. The small containers held crushed sandstone, pollen, red minerals, blue and white crystals. Using his hand as a funnel, the Pronghorn began to outline, blend, and scatter pigment as a pattern started to emerge.

It was a sand painting. Zac's father had said there might have been one at the dance last weekend. They were used as medicine, to heal, but to also seek out spirits and commune with those who had passed before. The Pronghorn was methodical as he slowly chose colors and began to lay out the design. Zac watched as several figures began to form—Skinwalkers. And the Pronghorn chanted as he worked.

Did Nathan know that this cave was home to Skinwalkers? He remained frozen in place.

Zac couldn't see the sand painting clearly, but it seemed that the figures were circling another figure on the ground in front of them—a person, someone not in animal dress. He watched as a spear was being formed in the hand of the painted cougar. A sacrifice? Yes. That was exactly what the painting represented. Zac didn't need to ask someone, even he could figure out what was depicted. It had taken almost an hour to form the tableau on the floor, but the sand painting meant the Skinwalkers were making an offering—of a live human being.

Suddenly, his attention was diverted from the painting as he realized that the Wolf in front of him had a spear. And he was handing that spear to Nathan. In a language that he couldn't understand, Zac knew that the wolf was telling Nathan to kill him. The chanting from the painter on the floor had risen to a crescendo. A drum had materialized and the painter was rhythmically beating out a cadence that was getting louder and louder.

Nathan pulled open the cage door. The wolf was standing right behind him, almost touching. Zac couldn't have cried out if he'd wanted to. He opened his mouth, but there was no sound. He just stood, arms at his sides, and faced his friend. Whatever was meant to happen, would happen. Nathan raised the spear and then using his height, swung in a half-circle away from Zac to face the wolf—with both hands on the spear's shaft, he thrust upward and buried the sharp point in the wolf's neck.

There was no chamois covering to deflect it. Nathan's aim was spot on. The point of the spear hit the carotid artery. The wolf grabbed his neck as blood bubbled through his fingers. Then, lightning fast, Nathan jerked the spear head back out and thrust it into the wolf's neck a second time. Blood sprayed three feet away to the cave's walls. The wolf fell backward, still clutching his neck and making gurgling noises before falling silent. Nathan stood over him until he knew the Skinwalker was dying and wouldn't threaten them. He then turned to Zac.

"Run! Go to the road, and follow it to camp. Do not tell anyone what you've seen here. Your life and your father's life depend upon you keeping this secret."

"Come with me." Zac found his voice.

"I cannot go with you. This is my destiny. I belong here. When you can, leave this land—go back to your home. But know you always have a brother." Nathan placed his closed fist over his heart.

Zac nodded, stepped out of the cage, and bolted for the cave's opening beneath the waterfall. He slipped and fell twice in his frenzy to get away. And he never looked back but just kept running.

The sand painter stayed hunched over his painted circle on the cave's floor. He let the Native boy go. There was no need for him anymore. It took the spirits to show the old man the perfect ending—an outcome better than he could have imagined.

Nathan belonged to him now and his mistake, the grandson who mocked the ways of the ancients and diminished the powers of the spirits, was dead. The one who would inherit, who proved he had the strength to kill a family member, stood tall in front of him—ready to put on the mantle, to learn the secrets of the past and carry them into the future.

Tonight, there would be a meeting of The Witchery here in the cave. He would present the initiate. He knew his nephew would be accepted openly and without question. Welcoming him into the society strengthened the *K'e* or kinship of the group and guaranteed a future. But *K'e* was more than just the mark of togetherness, it was a unifying thought process among his people. *K'e* was a gift from the deities. The way a fine rug is woven without a stitch out of place.

The deity who created the Navajo people, Changing Woman, divided them into four clans—Towering House clan, One-Who-Walks-Around clan, Bitter Water clan, and Mud clan. This was her gift to his peoples before the deity went back to the West.

From those four original clans, his tribe formed many clans, each with its own meaning and story. A clan became more than a name; it was a history, an identity and offered a sense of belonging. As a society, The Witchery Way would offer all those things to Nathan. It would become his family.

Chapter 22

Dammit. Ben hadn't planned on a second night on the road. Should he have checked the truck before he took off? But check for what? Would he have caught a frayed serpentine belt? He doubted it. And when you rented one of these trucks, couldn't you count on it coming recently serviced and trustworthy? More than just tread on the tires and all fully inflated. Obviously not. At least someone had filled the tank but that didn't mean anything now. And could he be absolutely certain that he hadn't been set up to fail? Have the truck break down? He had to stop thinking this way, questioning every little thing that happened. He took a deep breath and dialed Sandy Black's number only to find he was on his way to a conference in Dallas.

Ben was thinking maybe he could borrow a car, drive

to the Rez, and return after the new truck was secured and ready to go. A waste of time and energy but he worried about the boys. He didn't have a Plan B other than to stay the night in Albuquerque. So, he made arrangements for another night at the motel he'd stayed at last night and called a cab. It was another Lotaburger chile cheeseburger dinner. Which actually he wasn't complaining about. He knew between the reservation, and Florida, he wouldn't get another one for a while.

He tossed his duffle on the bed, turned on the TV and flipped to a station that looped the current news for twenty-four hours when it hit him. He'd left the borrowed gun that the chief had given him under the driver's seat in the U-Haul's cab. Originally, he'd tucked it in his duffle, he wished he'd left it there.

Well, there was no way he was going to take a chance on someone else finding it and helping themselves to a nice little .38 with leather holster. He felt foolish. He just wasn't used to having a gun. But that was no excuse for not taking care of it. He called a cab and went back down Central to the rental agency.

It was almost nine. Did he expect someone to be there? He guessed he had hoped a mechanic was putting in a little overtime, but the office was locked up tight with only a couple lights on—both illuminating U-Haul advertising hanging in the front window. The agency bordered on an alley with a good-sized fenced area securing other rentals. The twenty-foot box truck was the largest vehicle on the lot. He could see it in the far corner as he rounded the corner of the building.

Instantly, he knew something was wrong. Very wrong. The office furniture, desks, chairs, white board, were all scattered in the yard. It looked as if they had been thrown there. And the back doors to the truck were wide open. The 'holding pen' as the manager had referred to it behind the office was surrounded by six-foot, chain-link fencing with a razor-wire top. Double gates facing the ally were wide open. Ben didn't think twice but entered the yard and sprinted toward the truck and the open cargo doors. The truck was empty. Not one box. Not even the cartons containing his household goods.

Ben pulled out his phone and dialed 911 as he walked to the cab to see if the gun was still there. It didn't look as if the cab had been touched. He pulled a Kleenex out of his jeans pocket and opened the door. He reached under the seat. The gun was there. But what happened next was a blur of activity. At the very exact time the 911 operator came on the phone line with, "What's your emergency?" three patrol cars screeched to a halt at the gate, with four cops leaping out and running toward him.

"Hold it right there. Hands in the air." The lead officer came through the gate motioning the others to fan out covering all sides of the truck.

"He's got a gun!" The yell ended with two cops hitting the ground, their own weapons drawn.

Another cop came up behind Ben, knocked the gun out of his hand and slammed him against the truck. "Okay, Red—on the ground, hands behind your back." The cop kicked Ben's feet out from under him and fell on top of him, a knee planted in the middle of his back before grabbing Ben's hands at the wrist and slapping cuffs in place. It took two cops to drag all of Ben's six-foot-two frame upright, once again bending him back-side first against the truck.

"Why don't you assholes stay on the reservation. We

don't need you here causing trouble. Whose gun did you steal? Betcha we'll find this one listed as missing from someone's home. Breaking and entering looks like your speed. What'd ya get out of this truck?"

"I'd like you to pick up my phone and slip it in my pocket." Ben was pissed but also knew he needed to be careful. He kept his voice steady, and willed himself to be polite. This was the kind of situation that could escalate in a heartbeat and he wouldn't be on the winning side.

"Oh, you would, would you? Just step and fetch it. That's me, let some Indian order me around. Hey, Dirk, take this asshole's phone." The cop scooped up the phone and tossed it to the cop beside him. "If you're nice, you just might get it back. But, oh, I just remembered, you'll be under arrest—no phones where you're going."

"You might want to hear my side of the story—what I'm doing here."

"I doubt it. You probably wouldn't even recognize the truth if it bit you in the ass. Dirk, take our guy downtown. There's plenty of time for your side of the story. Then run down the manager of the U-Haul agency and get him out here. We need to know what's missing."

* * *

There wasn't even an apology—at least not from the cop who had cuffed him. The sergeant on duty that evening turned himself inside out trying to circumvent what he anticipated as Ben filing a complaint. But that wasn't going to happen. Ben wasn't sure complaints didn't do more harm than good. There was no changing the cop's attitude by singling him out for punishment.

It was after midnight before Ben walked out the front door of the station. He'd spent two hours locked up before Chief Billie and IHS could verify his credentials and why he was in Albuquerque, corroborated by the U-Haul manager. He was allowed a phone call around ten-thirty to check on the boys and Trini assured him all was well.

"I just looked out my window and one of the boys must have been in the kitchen because someone turned the light out. After taking the horses up to the north pasture to graze this morning, I bet they're tired. Don't worry Dr. Pecos, I'll make certain they get a good breakfast. I'm so sorry you're having all this trouble."

That was a relief. It was good to know the boys were safe. Yeah, they complicated life but in a good way. It would be impossible to imagine life without Zac.

He couldn't get a ride back to the reservation before morning and that was going to be with the same tech who had brought him to Albuquerque. He doubted he'd get much sleep, but one of the cops gave him a ride back to the motel.

* * *

Ben's longest phone conversation was with Chief Billie. Who could have known what the U-Haul held? Could it have been just a lucky score? No. That wasn't even a possibility. Not when the cargo was so specialized. Only someone who could fence a few hundred thousand dollars in PPE—had buyers lined up and waiting—would be interested. But who? This was a best-kept secret. Ben had been careful to tell Trini about office furniture, nothing else, and Dr. Black was well aware of the need to keep quiet.

No, the way the heist was done—early in the evening when adjoining businesses were all closed for the day; the building cameras disconnected along with yard lights; maybe another U-Haul was used to transfer goods, something that wouldn't raise suspicion but could get in and out of the yard and down the alley hardly noticed—these were all marks of a professional operation. Or at least one that had been carefully thought out, been done before. There was no way that Ben thought this was anyone's first rodeo. He had been right, but there was no joy in knowing he had been set up.

But how had they known? Nothing had been written down. Nothing outlining the truck's contents, or giving destinations. At least, not that he'd known about. Unless there were some pretty adept mind-readers, there was just no way anyone could have known about the shipment. But the shocking thing? The mechanic from the U-Haul agency told him that the alternator belt had been sliced—a cut difficult to detect but guaranteed to unravel and do exactly what it did, strand the driver and render the truck undriveable. Now *that* had taken some planning.

Chapter 23

Seven o'clock. Would the boys even be up? Trini had asked the Two Sisters to prepare waffles that could be quickly warmed up for a good, hot breakfast. True to their word, a box of the goodies along with butter and syrup waited for her to pick up. She was just going up the steps of Ben's trailer when Oscar ran up.

"You talked to the boys?"

"No. I'm just taking them breakfast now."

"Well, something's wrong. The horses showed up sometime last night without saddles or tack, and Apache's got some pretty nasty-looking scratches on his shoulder. Looked like they'd been running for awhile. I rubbed 'em down and fed and watered 'em. But those boys would never leave their horses in that condition. You sure they're all right?"

"Oscar, I just said I'm here to see them now." She knew she sounded short, but he could be exasperating—not always paying attention. And maybe, if she were being truthful, he struggled to understand even the simplest things. Trini turned and knocked on the door. She knocked again and the door, apparently unlatched, pushed open. "Oh, I don't like that. They know better than to leave the door unlocked. Nathan? Zac?" No answer.

"Let me get by. I'm going in." Oscar pushed the door fully open and entered the living room.

"What do you see?" Trini called from the doorway. Not getting an answer, she entered the trailer.

"I could be wrong, but I'd bet they haven't been here for a day or so. Look at the beds here in the front bedroom. Now what two boys are going to make their beds when their dad isn't here to tell them to. And nobody's eaten anything in that kitchen recently."

"I talked to them yesterday morning when they were taking the horses to the north pasture. And last night I assumed they were in the trailer because I saw the light go out."

"Betcha it wasn't one of the boys."

"Oh, this couldn't be more awful. I have no idea when Dr. Pecos will get back. I assured the doctor that I'd keep an eye on them. I'm going to call Chief Billie. But I have no idea where to start to look for them."

* * *

The faint gray light of dawn brought Zac back to consciousness and he knew he must make his way back to the trailer.

He'd gotten away. And no one had chased after him. No animal or spirit. Follow the road. Wasn't that what Nathan had told him to do? Good advice if he could find it. It was easier to know directions back home; the ocean was on the west and there were mountains to the east. Everything out here was pretty open—lots of grass, some pretty tall cactus and that was about it.

The night had been moonless and that didn't help. No moon and no stars, only a dense cloud-cover. The result was an inky blackness that acted like a blanket over everything. He couldn't really see to move forward. Wouldn't it be best to just stop? What if he *was* being tailed by cougars, or wolves, or bears—the real kind. That was a scary thought. That's when Zac had decided to just wait until dawn. He'd probably run a couple miles—far enough away that he felt safe from the Skinwalkers. But he could still close his eyes and see the Skinwalkers and the sandpainting that foretold his death. He shivered and swallowed hard. He had to be careful.

It was almost dusk but still light when he'd started out. He'd looked for the horses, but he couldn't even find the place in the trees where they had eaten lunch. Were the horses still grazing? Or had they found their way back to the camp? Would wolves and cougars stalk them? Attack them? Would they even be safe? And where could he go to be safe? Maybe he'd find a sheepherders' camp. But there was no being able to find anything at night.

When he was just about ready to give up, he'd stumbled upon a lean-to—poles laced with sinew holding several tattered hides together to form a roof. It looked used but not for a long time. Now, it sat all by itself. He must be in one of the two secondary pastures—one that currently wasn't used. He imagined it took pastures a good amount of time to recover after being grazed.

The blankets inside were filthy, half buried in sand. The structure wasn't new, but it had a door—another hide that could be draped shut across the opening from the inside making it, at least, warm by keeping the wind out.

Zac shook out the blankets and discovered some animal had made a nest at the back. The big bundle of twigs and dried grass could have just been tinder for fire building and might not have anything to do with wildlife. If it was a nest, Zac hoped the animal was long gone. If he'd thought he wouldn't be able to go to sleep, he hadn't counted on how tired he was. The afternoon had literally sapped his energy. The minute he stretched out on the dusty bedding, not even the dirt and musty smell could keep him awake.

* * *

Ben realized he should be thankful for small favors—it appeared that his driver didn't chew in the mornings. The maintenance guy who had brought him to Albuquerque was also taking him back to the compound on the reservation. The country music was still a couple decibels too high, but it kept conversation to a minimum. And that was a good thing. Talking about how hard it was to learn to line dance seemed to be the limit of challenging things the driver had done lately. That and whether he'd try to ride the bull, Smokey Mountain, at the Bernalillo county fair next month—if they even had a fair, due to the virus.

There probably wasn't any topic of interest to Ben. He wasn't up to chatting. In addition to the failure of the PPE mission, he was worried. In more than two days, he hadn't been able to reach the boys. He tried to stave off any panic—there could be a dozen completely reasonable explanations for it. They could have taken the horses to pasture and decided to spend an overnight camping out. He remembered that Nathan had brought a tent from the camper he'd shared with his grandmother. And Ben had to admit that would be a fun thing for a couple boys to do.

But it didn't feel right. Zac would have let him know. He was smart enough to leave a message on his phone saying where he was. No, Ben's sixth sense was screaming an alarm. He'd tried twice more to reach Zac before they left the city and again only voice mail. He stopped leaving messages.

The three-hour drive to the reservation seemed like an eternity, and seeing Chief Billie's SUV parked outside the trailer when they turned down the road to the hospital tents just about made his heart stop. The minute Ben hopped out of his ride's vehicle, Trini ran to meet him.

"Dr. Pecos, I'm so sorry. I meant to be better at watching the boys, but they're gone."

"Gone?"

Chief Billie came out of Ben's trailer. "Not sure what's going on, but I don't think there's a need to panic. Not yet, anyway. I'm just getting ready to drive up to the north pasture. We know that's where they took the horses. My guess is they turned the horses loose to graze and something spooked them. I think we're going to find a couple kids with saddles and tack by the side of the road trying to lug all that stuff home."

"Are you saying the horses returned?"

"Yeah. According to Oscar, it looked like they'd been running hard. That's why I'm guessing they were spooked—

doesn't take much, a coyote or bobcat, and those horses will take off. Fight or flight is truly the choice."

Just then the two-way radio in the Bronco squawked. "Damn, I need to get that." Chief Billie hurried down the steps and reached through the SUV's open window to grab the receiver. Ben couldn't hear what he was saying, but it was a short conversation.

"Problems?"

Chief Billie motioned for Ben to get in the Bronco.

"We need to take a detour before we check the upper pasture. Report just came in of a car fire out on old Highway 666 just before it turns toward Gallup. Somebody called it in after passing it on the side of the road. Says it looks like there's someone still in the car—driver's side. An emergency vehicle is on the way."

Ben and the chief took off with lights on and siren wailing. Forty-five minutes later the smoldering ruins of a car came into view. A tank truck with New Mexico Highway insignia on the side was hosing the car and surrounding area.

"Didn't get here in time to save the driver. But not sure he was feeling any pain before the fire started. Woman who reported smoke coming out from underneath the hood said the driver was slumped over the wheel. Said she was alone and was afraid to get involved."

"Drugs." Chief Billie said it more as a statement than a question. "Wish I had a nickel for every time I'm called out on a suspected overdose."

"And I think we know the driver," Ben added.

The back end of the silver and black Camaro was a giveaway. Blackened but not destroyed, there was only one car like that on the reservation. And J.C.? Not a lot left to identify.

"I'm just glad he was alone—didn't have some young sweetie with him."

"Who'll do the autopsy?"

"Not allowed. That is, if he's on the reservation our rules will win out. The question is, was he on state road land? That would make a difference. I'll get a deputy out here and then we need to visit his grandfather. I feel badly for the old man. I think J.C. was a big help to him. It won't be easy being alone out here."

Another forty-five minutes before they could leave, but only fifteen minutes to the road that led past where Nathan and his grandmother had lived and on up the road behind the windmill to a large hogan. And standing in the doorway was Nathan. His uncle was sitting in a folding chair with his leg propped up on a log.

Ben barely waited until the Bronco had stopped before jumping out. "Nathan, is Zac with you?"

"No. My uncle twisted his ankle. He was helping us with the horses. A couple cousins gave us a ride home. I needed to help him, so Zac offered to take the horses back to the compound. You mean he didn't get there?"

Ben shook his head. "The horses made it, but he didn't. When was this?"

"Yesterday afternoon. He just got lost. I'm sure he's okay."

Chief Billie had squatted down beside the old man and was saying something to him in Navajo. Nathan turned to listen, then kind of shrugged.

"Do you want a ride back to the compound?" Ben asked.

"I need to stay here with my uncle. He won't be able to walk for a while. He needs somebody to cook and take care of the stock. I'll catch a ride with a neighbor down the way and come get the horses. Probably tomorrow."

"I understand. I hope you're right about Zac just being lost."

Nathan nodded. "It probably got dark before he found the road and he stopped for the night."

* * *

Chief Billie backed the Bronco away from the hogan and onto the dirt road, then turned toward the compound before finally breaking the silence.

"Something was wrong. The old man didn't even flinch when I said J.C. was dead. No questions, no comment—no surprise. He just said he'd have someone take care of the body."

"Yeah. More or less the same thing with Nathan. He overheard and just shrugged—also like it was no biggie. I know Nathan didn't like J.C., but that was just callous. And no questions about how it happened."

"Looks like the kid is staying out here, too. I was hoping that wouldn't happen. Nathan needs a better life."

"Told me he needed to help his uncle—which I guess is the truth. It looked like the old man had suffered a nasty sprain."

"Let's go find Zac. If Nathan is telling the truth, it makes sense that he's just lost."

"I wonder if the boys had a falling out. Some of this isn't adding up." Ben said.

Chapter 24

The flap covering the door had slipped down during the night and when the sun came up it sought out every crevice within the lean-to, flooding the makeshift dwelling with light. Zac startled awake. Where was he? And then he remembered. He swallowed hard but couldn't keep the images of wolves and Pronghorn Antelope from dancing across his memory. But he was alive thanks to his friend. And the quicker he forgot what he'd seen, the better.

He stepped outside. The desert was beautiful in the morning—still, nothing moving, not even a breeze, the songs of birds all around him. But he was hungry and thirsty and lost. He saw two desert scorpions scurry past before he realized standing barefoot might not be the best thing to do. He hurriedly pulled on his sneakers. Decision time. Should he just stay put and hope someone would come his way? Or continue to walk knowing sooner or later he had to come to a road?

Walking won out. He couldn't see any bit of civilization around him. He turned in a complete circle, but the landscape didn't change. He tried not to think about Nathan. He knew he might not ever see him again. And he knew that Nathan had sacrificed the chance of a new life to stay with his uncle and become a part of the old ways of his tribe.

Zac's people in Alaska wouldn't make the same demands on him. He didn't have to live in a village. His mother had opened a tattoo parlor in Anchorage and lived in that city for many years. But out here in the desert, one's strength and identity came from a strange and demanding brotherhood like the one for witches. Nathan would become a witch, a Skinwalker. One who would do evil. But he had saved Zac's life at the cost of his own. No one could ask that even of a true, blood brother.

* * *

It was eleven-thirty before Ben and the chief spotted Zac about a hundred feet from the road.

"There he is." Ben had been scouring the landscape using the chief's binoculars. "To your right."

The chief gunned the Bronco up and over the slightly banked lip on the dirt road and took off in the direction of a solitary figure walking slowly toward them.

Ben jumped from the Bronco and ran to Zac, leaving Chief Billie to stay in the SUV while Ben hugged Zac and didn't try to hold back his joy and relief. "Are you okay?"

Zac barely had the energy to hug Ben back. "Yeah, just tired. I got turned around."

"Nathan said he told you to go to the road, but it's tough to tell where the road starts and the desert stops. It all looks alike out here."

"You saw Nathan?"

"Yeah, at his uncle's house. That must have been a nasty fall the old man took. It was lucky that the herders found you guys and could get his uncle back to his house. I hope he's checked with a doctor."

Zac had stepped back and was staring at Ben. "Yeah, that was lucky," he said slowly.

"I'm sorry about J.C.—sorry for the grandfather—without his grandson to help him, it's good that Nathan could step in."

"What happened to J.C.?" Zac hesitantly asked, "Is he okay?"

"J.C. is dead. We'll probably never know for sure, but it looks like he lost his life when his car caught fire."

Zac turned away, took a breath, turned back and met Ben's gaze. "Was it drugs?" Just to be on the safe side, Zac crossed his fingers after sticking a hand in the pocket of his jean jacket. Any lie that he might have to tell wouldn't count if he crossed his fingers. But this was unbelievable; it was as if yesterday afternoon never happened.

"Chief Billie thinks so. J.C. had the reputation of partying. You know that. Woman passing the Camaro on the road phoned in the fire, said someone was passed out behind the wheel. She didn't stop, and help didn't get there in time to make a difference. I know J.C. caused a lot of trouble, but a life lost at such a young age is always sad."

Zac nodded. Wow. Just like that, everything was

covered up. Just like magic. In fact, maybe it was magic.

"A penny for your thoughts." Zac had grown quiet and was looking at the ground. A reaction to J.C.'s death, Ben supposed.

"I'm glad Nathan will be able to help his uncle." Zac pushed his left hand in an opposite pocket and crossed the fingers on that hand, too. "But I don't think he'll want to leave and go back to school with me."

"That might not be possible now. But later, maybe."

"Yeah, maybe for high school."

"Let's get going. I don't want to keep Chief Billie waiting any longer."

* * *

The horses were already gone when they got back to the camp. Neighbors of the old man with one driving a pickup, had collected the horses' food and even loaded up the galvanized watering tub Oscar had provided. Trini came out to say that two herders had found the saddles the boys had left in the trees and brought them in. And then she fussed over Zac as though he'd been lost a month. Finally, they were back in their own trailer. Chief Billie was going to the hospital tent to check on Charley Chase, so the two of them were alone.

"Hungry? There's some ham and Swiss unless you guys made more omelets."

"I'm not hungry."

"Really?" Odd. "Well, then, how about a ride out to see Nathan—maybe take them a treat from the Two Sisters."

"I don't want to."

"Zac, what's wrong? Nathan's your best friend."

"We had a fight." Zac stuffed both hands into his pockets to hide his crossed fingers and added a silent prayer.

"What about?"

"He said Alaskan Natives aren't real Indians. Not like the Navajo, anyway. He said it was a lie that the Alaskan Natives were the first indigenous tribe. That they were lying when they said they were already here when the others came. And he didn't think we were real men because we didn't have to fight anybody. Not like the Spaniards who had horses. And nobody forced us to leave our land and killed hundreds of us."

Ben listened quietly. "You don't think you can make up? Maybe text him some articles?"

"No. It's okay. I want to go home."

"There's been talk about the airlines reopening for domestic travel by this weekend. Do you want to go that soon?"

"Yeah. That'd be perfect. Can you find out? And get me a ticket? I'll call Mom and tell her. The guys have been texting me. They're already practicing on the city's soccer field. I need to be there." With that, Zac hurried to his bedroom and shut the door.

Ben admitted to being a little hurt. But wasn't this the timeframe he'd originally hoped for? A couple weeks, not more than three, before Zac's rejoining his mother? And the spat probably wasn't that serious. It didn't sound like it. Maybe Zac was just homesick. After all, according to his mom he'd been quite the star of his school's team. Getting stuck in the desert of New Mexico had probably lost its mystique. Sheep vs. a walrus … probably no comparison.

He pulled out his phone and googled Southwest

Airlines—Albuquerque to Seattle.

And then his phone rang.

"Do you believe it? I'll be on a flight to Albuquerque this Saturday. I got the first flight out once they lifted the restrictions." Julie sounded ecstatic. "I can't wait."

Chapter 25

In three days he would put Zac on a plane to Seattle at one end of Albuquerque's airport, then wait two hours and meet Julie at the other end. Zac's mother was so thrilled that her son would be coming home, she was even nice.

But maybe Ben was overreacting to Raven's usually caustic demands. Not that he blamed her. An entirely new family dynamic had presented itself over the past year—one completely out of her control. Going from being a single parent to sharing with the other parent was a shock to everyone's system, with lives changed forever. Still, in seven months Ben had grown to like being called 'dad'; he wasn't about to go back to his life the way it was before. And on the trip in to Albuquerque's airport, Zac had seemed like his old self—laughing, telling Ben stories about his friends at school in Bellingham. And he thanked Ben for bringing him to New Mexico—showing him the Pueblo of his relatives. They were still on the reservation, almost to the highway when suddenly Zac yelled for Ben to pull over.

"What's wrong?" Ben coasted to a stop along the side of the road as Zac quickly jumped out.

"There. Do you see them?" Zac pointed a little to the left about fifty-feet away.

And then Ben did see them. Two Pronghorn Antelope, one large, the other smaller, stood staring back at Zac. They remained motionless as Zac walked about twenty feet in their direction. They didn't move. He said something, but Ben didn't catch it. Then he saw Zac make a fist and press it over his heart. Almost in acknowledgement, the two antelope tossed their heads, turned and trotted away from the road, unhurried, seeming almost reluctant to break the spell of contact with a human being.

Zac turned back and climbed into the cab of the truck. "We can go now." He was looking out the window, but Ben could see that he was smiling. Ben couldn't help but think of the Pronghorn that ran along beside the pickup when they first came to the reservation. There was only one animal then. This meeting had a feeling of goodbye to it. But without sadness.

"Dad, can I tell you something and you'll promise not to tell anyone."

"Sure, Zac, I can keep a secret."

"Well, Nathan and I didn't have a fight. Nathan saved my life but had to kill someone to do it."

Ben glanced sideways at Zac who was still staring out the window watching the Pronghorn disappear in the distance.

He didn't start the truck but waited until Zac had told him everything—the waterfall, the cave, the Skinwalkers, the sandpainting, the test that would make Nathan a follower of the Witchery Way. And the killing--a spear to the neck of J.C.

* * *

The hug was a long one before he boarded. When Zac stepped back, Ben reminded him to ask his mother to take videos of some of his soccer games. And then to think of another time to visit. Zac assured him he would. He asked Ben to say hello to Julie for him. Then an attendant scanned his boarding pass and he was walking through the door with one quick wave before disappearing into the plane.

Ben walked to a window facing the tarmac and watched the plane push back from the gate and turn down the runway. Bittersweet. Families seemed to perpetually evolve. It was difficult to describe what was normal anymore. But he wasn't going to let Zac forget that he had a father.

Julie's plane was late, and packed. Stranded vacationers from the Miami area probably. An unplanned two or more extra weeks had been tacked onto an already expensive time away for a number of people. And there was no social distancing when she saw Ben. He didn't care but held her and ignored the stares when she took her mask off for the first of several long kisses as they made their way through baggage claim and out to the parking garage.

"I can't believe we're together. Has it only been three weeks?" She leaned over the console in the pickup just to hug him. "Did Zac get away okay?"

"Yeah, and he said to say hello."

"He's a good kid. I'm sorry I couldn't spend time with him while he was here. Are you thinking of seeing him at Christmas?"

"We left the next visit TBA. Not sure what will be happening by the holidays. A lot depends on the virus and also where we'll be."

He exited the parking garage, paid at the kiosk, and headed toward the interstate for the trip back to the reservation.

"Wherever we end up, I want you to be there to help me pick out a place to live. I don't like choosing for two all by myself. But we don't have to worry about that for a while. The *Herald* gave me a leave of absence—put me out on assignment. I'll be doing a series of articles spotlighting the inequities between the reservation and the outside world, as has been starkly defined by the pandemic. The average American just has no idea of the problems facing the tribes in this country."

"Good topic. I have a who's who meeting with the powers that be tomorrow afternoon— everyone from the President of the Navajo Nation to the Chief of Police. Get tested. If everything's okay, sit in. It'll give you a good idea of what we're up against. And you'll make some valuable contacts."

By the time Ben had emptied the pickup of Julie's three suitcases, carried everything inside, and waited while she took a quick shower and put on fresh clothes, it was time to go back to the office. He needed to check in with Trini and finish up some loose ends as needed. If he'd had other activities in mind for the afternoon, he'd have to shelve them in favor of work. He glanced at Julie, who was reading her email. Guess he could put off the reacquainting time until later in the evening. She looked up.

"Did you say something?"

"Nope. Just enjoying some lecherous thoughts."

She laughed. "Save those 'til later when I can share."

Chapter 26

Julie, I'm so glad to be meeting you finally. I feel I should know you. I look at your picture on Dr. Pecos's desk every day." Trini handed out bottles of cold water. "And wait 'til you see what I found." She dragged two cardboard cartons from behind her desk. "We finally got a partial shipment of the PPE we had ordered weeks ago, and mixed up in the medical supplies were these two boxes of household items. How 'bout some really screaming loud colored sheets? I think the fuchsia flowers are supposed to be daisies. And here, check out this cookware—it's all Rachel Ray stuff--not bad if you like lime green enamel on copper. I'm sure it's better than the hospital issue I loaned you. It's all brand new. When you no longer need it, I'll be able to find a home for it all here, I'm sure."

Ben stepped around Trini's desk and picked up the package of sheets. "Where did you say this came from?" The household items not only looked familiar, he'd seen them before—the exact same ones. They'd been a part of the shipment stolen from the U-Haul in Albuquerque— the shipment he was supposed to have brought to the reservation.

"AMSA—American Medical Supply Association. It's some new group that Dr. Henry suggested. We've been bombarded with companies wanting to sell to us. Several are foreign—including some from China and one from Taiwan. AMSA is out of California, I think. With the US government picking up the tab, we have to go with the lowest bidder, but they're all expensive. I had to have a check cut for over two-hundred thousand dollars for what was delivered yesterday. And then we only got a portion of what was originally ordered."

Interesting. Had the cargo been paid for twice? It would seem that way. First, when the order was put together and secondly, when it was delivered to camp. Not a bad grift and worth some big money.

Ben didn't believe in coincidence. The fact that it ended up back here would seem to point a finger at someone from the camp being involved. It was still a mystery how anyone knew what he had in the U-Haul. This might be information that he best kept to himself.

"Thanks for thinking of us. These are certainly brighter than hospital linens."

Julie added, "I rather like them."

Trini laughed. "Thanks for making me think I did the right thing by swiping them for you. And before I forget, the meeting tomorrow afternoon is set for four, here in the office."

* * *

Julie's test was negative which was a sigh of relief. Oscar and three helpers had moved the couch and two side tables from the office waiting room into a back room and set up ten folding chairs—more or less in a circle—adhering to the six-foot distancing rule by staggering the line whenever possible. The meeting got started a little late due to the Navajo Nation's president requesting a tour of the hospital tents. Finally, everyone was present. In all, ten people plus Julie helped themselves to apple empanadas and cold drinks before the discussion started. Trini sat in the doorway to her office with notepad and pen.

Dr. Henry cleared his throat. "Some of you know each other, others are strangers to this group. We'll take time for introductions later. President Nez's time is limited and I'm going to let him go first—catch us up to date and give us some much-needed background information on just where we are now. And where we need to be. President Nez."

"Thank you, Dr. Henry. Let me start by thanking all of you for taking this time to meet. Especially Dr. Black from Indian Health Services in Albuquerque, who traveled the longest distance to share his expertise. I will be sharing some facts about the way we live on the reservation for those of you new to our culture—the nurses and technicians who have volunteered to help us.

"I want to start by putting the pandemic, as it has ravaged the reservation, into perspective and why that has made this meeting a top priority. Our current infection rate is 3.4%. By way of comparison, New York state has a rate today of 1.9%. We've made strides to control the virus, closed the highways that cross our land, brought the sick to a safe place to be nursed back to health—but there's lots of work left to do. Logistically, a reservation is a nightmare to contain—especially to police. I think Chief Billie would agree with me there." Chief Billie nodded.

"Families live in clusters separated by sometimes long distances—many miles. Stores for food, especially fresh food like fruit and vegetables, and necessities like milk are not readily available, making staying in place impossible. The Navajo are social. We have pow wows, rodeos, church services—many opportunities for people to gather. It's not just families getting together but clans. Far-reaching groups of people travel to feast days and other group activities, and these are an important part of our culture. We need them to remain who we are. So, to tell our people to quarantine, not to join others in tending their stock, or getting their kids in school, let alone attend life's celebrations, is wasted breath."

"Is there an answer?" Dr. Henry spoke up.

"Not one that I promise will work. I want us to concentrate on smaller pieces of the bigger puzzle—not try to tackle everything at once. For example, when we open the highways on Monday, there will be limited access and more than one check point. I have accepted the services of a small independent trucking firm who has offered refrigerated trucks to carry food to the doors of those living many miles from any commerce. There will be eight trucks carrying life-supporting food to those in outlying areas five days a week. I'd like to make certain that there is no need to leave one's home. Quarantine will be supported. And help assured. Our camp here with six hospital tents has reached capacity. We will be constructing three additional treatment tents in the coming week."

"But personnel? We're way understaffed." Again, Dr. Henry interrupted.

"IHS out of Albuquerque will send five permanent nurses and three lab techs who will live on site. I'll get a list of names to you, Trini, and to Chief Billie. It's not a lot, but it's an important start, and I thank Dr. Black once again for depleting his workforce to add to ours. IHS did a surge projection in July, and we are falling in line with their worst case scenario. We need to act now."

"Where is the funding coming from? Most of what you've mentioned will be huge expenditures," Ben asked.

"Really good question. IHS, operated by the US Department of Health and Human Services, provides services to five hundred and seventy-four tribes across the US. I think it's a well-known fact that Native health has never been a priority. IHS gets funded at one-third the amount of money per capita as Medicare or the VA."

"That's criminal." This from a nurse in the back.

"Calling it names won't change the situation that we're in now—but I agree." Dr. Black spoke up. "It just makes our jobs harder to perform."

"With the money that we do have coming in—we've been promised eight million dollars from the federal government to be shared by tribes, in order of need—I am appointing a task force made up of many of the people in this room to oversee the way it's dispersed. Yes, I expect there to be a lot of paperwork, Trini. The government demands a paper trail."

"I'd like to volunteer. I could help with the reporting if needed." Julie offered.

"Oh, I think my life has just been saved. Thank you so much." Trini looked relieved, and Ben was pleased that

Julie had jumped in to help.

"We'll be adding two new doctors, and Dr. Black will add the Navajo reservation to his rotation one week out of every month. With extra volunteer nurses, we'll have twelve on duty. Adding staff has been number one on the list of needs and I think we've made a dent in that. Let's take a break and then I'll ask those new to the group to introduce themselves."

"Before you get away today, I want to share something." Ben leaned close to Chief Billie and lowered his voice. "I think it might be a clue as to what happened to the shipment in the U-Haul."

"Why don't we step out on the porch now?"

Closing the door behind them, Ben shared the fact that at least two items from his supposed 'personal items' from the ill-fated U-Haul shipment had turned up here and were actually handed back to him by a thoughtful Trini who had no idea how they were connected to him in the first place.

Ben added, "I just think the coincidence is too much. My instinct says someone here was involved with stealing that shipment. And I think it was paid for twice. I'm thinking of having Julie find out everything she can about AMSA—where they're headquartered, the CEO, other contracts—that sort of thing."

"Good idea. Sounds like buyers were lined up for that shipment from the start. So, we're back to learning who knew where it was going to be and when. By the way, I'm glad your wife could join you. She sounds like she's not afraid of a little work. That's great; we need her."

"She'll be writing articles on what's happening on the reservation for her employer, but I know she's excited about working with our project."

"Speaking of which, we may have seen the last of any hijacked shipments this close to the reservation. Charley Chase was able to give a description of the man who forced him off the road and pistol-whipped him. If you're thinking J.C., you're exactly right. Without J.C. no more thefts, I'm hoping. Of course, it doesn't tell us who he was working for, but I think it significantly changes things."

"I hope you're right."

"We'll know soon enough. With the expansion of the camp, there will be all kinds of equipment slated to come in here. I just wish I had the manpower to put some extra deputies out here."

"Keep me posted. If there's anything I can do, let me know."

"Will do. Sounds like we need to get back inside." Chief Billie held the office door open.

After the break, the president also mentioned that the Two Sisters With a Pot would be getting a more permanent structure with a modern kitchen which would include a new pizza oven and an enlarged indoor/outdoor seating area. That brought a cheer from his audience.

Next, several task groups were formed. Groups of three would be going out to interview families and check on their health, offering tests for the virus in strategic, easy to reach places—schools, two grocery stores, and a church. Plans were under way to evaluate the need for another tent city of hospitals on the other side of the reservation. Dr. Black was heading up that effort.

The drilling of a second well and the laying of additional electrical cable were both scheduled to be completed within a month. Lobbyists for the Navajo reservation would be meeting with various groups in Washington DC, and the senators and representatives from both Arizona and New Mexico were also helping to push funding. After another forty-five minutes of questions, the meeting adjourned.

* * *

It was dusk before Ben and Julie returned to their trailer. An intended quick meal at the Two Sisters with Dr. Black had turned into over an hour of discussion of additional needs and services that might be provided. Julie stayed late to discuss a possible work schedule with Trini, and Ben walked back to the trailer by himself. The second night they had been together and sleep had ruined any thoughts of a true reconciliation the first night. He wasn't taking any chances of being turned down two nights in a row.

Finally, alone time. Ben uncorked a bottle of red and turned the lights off. He lit a few of the strategically placed candles he'd left around the living room earlier. He was glad they were alone—just the two of them. He had to admit there were times when children sort of got in the way. It was tough to make an evening special in a trailer, on a reservation, out in nowhere—but he was going to give it a try. Somehow Julie's just being there made his world right. And thoughts of christening those fuchsia-colored daisy sheets made him smile.

* * *

There was no better way to wake up in the morning than to open your eyes to find someone curled into your body with a bare leg casually thrown over your own—after a night that almost made him forget they'd been apart for three weeks. Ben smiled. He couldn't even remember snuffing out the candles last night, but he must have—at least the place hadn't burned down. Not that it hadn't gotten hot enough for some type of combustion in the bedroom ...

He had taken the day off under the pretext of showing Julie her surroundings, but in all truthfulness, he just wanted to be with her. Three weeks had seemed like a year. After breakfast and coffee at the Two Sisters, he had them pack two hoagies and two bags of chips for their lunch. It was odd to buy hoagies from Navajos on their reservation—Italian meats and cheeses, sweet dills, pickled onions. He'd just eaten two waffles, and his mouth still watered for a hoagie. He threw a couple extra bottles of water in the ice chest. If they did any hiking, the water would be appreciated.

New Mexico was hot this time of year. But that wasn't a surprise for Julie—this region was home for her—close to where they were, but the more civilized, citified part far from what they were going to see today. Ben had planned on an hour's drive along the edge of the reservation—home to the ancients. The Navajo were fortunate to still live on ancestral lands. They hadn't been permanently displaced. Even after the catastrophe of attempted resettlement and the 'Long Walk' home to return to their origins, the hardships seemed to only make the nation more cohesive. The land within their four sacred mountains was theirs—forever and always, as the elders would say.

It was tough finding shade on land level enough to park the truck. But a stand of aspen just at the edge of rangeland offered a chance to get out of the sun.

"I see why they're called quaking aspen." Julie stood

looking up at the silvery leaves, some just barely turning gold, that jiggled and bounced in the wind and the white bark with black etching that made the trees stand out from their less dapper neighbors. "They really are unique. We're not going to find anything like that in Florida."

"We probably need to talk about Florida." Ben had lowered the tailgate and hopped up to sit at the edge of the truck-bed.

"As I said, I know that I don't want to house-hunt without you. Too many choices—a townhouse? Condo? Three-bedroom house on an acre or two? Then there's how close-in do we want to be. It's going to be difficult for at least one of us not to have to commute for an hour. Adding two hours to a workday gets tiresome. I've done that before. And the whole area is so congested."

"Sounds like the project has lost its appeal."

"Yes and no. It's a great job, one that my colleagues would fight over. But when I'm out here like this, it's tough not to fall in love with the natural beauty of open spaces. I think there's still some Southwest in me."

"I don't mind a commute; I just want a permanent position. I'm flattered to be chosen as a fixer—a fill-in of sorts—but I'm not able to activate any programs of my own for IHS, let alone see results. And, my top priority is our being together. I'm really tired of having a long-distance relationship. So, a couple extra hours a day on the road doesn't sound all that bad. I think I could look at it as an investment in a future together."

"Two careers suck."

"Two careers just mean extra challenges." Ben added, "We both knew what we were getting into. And as far as housing in the Everglades? Let's keep Zac in mind and find something with a little room—a place for animals and maybe on the water."

"Might take a little extra time to find, but it's doable. All I know is how much I want to be with you."

Ben stood and drew her to him. The kiss was long and intimate, then he pulled back. "Hey, much more of this and we'll never make it up to the ruins. Tuck this bottle of water in your pocket, and let's go."

The hike was almost straight up—over boulders and around loose rock. There was a path of sorts but covered like it was in gravel, the going was treacherous—sometimes two steps forward and up, then slipping three backwards and down. But, it was worth it. Julie was enthralled by the cutouts in the cliff above. Crumbling walls of chiseled rock indicated rooms, living arrangements for families of a different time. Doorways in walls without ceilings or roofs stood in stark relief, no longer keeping anything out.

As she entered one of the rooms, the indentation of a long-ago used fire pit dominated the center. Had this been a kitchen? Maybe. It was the room closest to the steps up the side of the cliff. She stepped back through the doorway and looked out across the rangeland, stretching as far as she could see. What a protected place to live. No one could sneak up on you. With the posting of a sentry at night, 24/7 safety was assured.

"Amazing, isn't it?" Ben walked up to stand behind her. "Tough to think this place has a reputation for being evil. But I think that has been perpetuated to keep people from walking away with souvenirs. There used to be pot shards everywhere. But those are gone now." Ben was digging in his backpack for the hoagies and chips. "Let's sit on the stone steps over here."

"There's no way I can finish this." Julie was staring at the foot-long roll loaded with filling.

"Eat what you can. I'll probably be able to help you with the rest." Ben laughed, "I think I used extra calories climbing up here."

Fifteen minutes later she gave up and handed Ben the remains of her sandwich. "Makes me glad we have two salaries coming in. These sandwiches were huge. I can't believe you're still hungry."

"Fortification for the hike back down," he said, polishing off hers with three bites. "Hand me your garbage and we'll get started back."

Julie could have easily spent the rest of the day among the ruins. She'd brought her camera but had left it in the truck, having no idea how unique the ancient buildings were. This meant a trip back, and soon.

She was following Ben and trying to stay upright. It quickly became apparent that going down was more difficult than climbing up. She skidded, losing her footing and sitting down. Ben reached level ground first, turning to pick her up and carry her the last twenty feet.

"There's not any mountain goat in you, is there?"

"You sound disappointed. I'd like to think that's a good thing." Ben put her down. They both turned toward the truck and saw the problem at the same time. Both of the truck's rear tires were flat or, at least, nearly so.

"Damn it." Ben sprinted ahead to the truck and knelt by the tailgate to inspect the tires.

"We must have run over something." Julie walked up to stand beside him.

"Nothing apparent." He ran his hand up and around each tire; the tread and the sidewalls. "No nails, sharp rocks … nothing; they're just flat." He pulled his phone out. "And, of course, no service out here. I have one spare but not two. I'm going to hike up to the road and hope I get phone service before too long. I'll give the chief a call and have one of his guys bring another tire. I'm assuming somebody could at least loan me his spare until I can get these repaired. Stay here with the truck. I don't have a good feeling about leaving it. And you'll be here if the chief has someone in the area that he can send before I get picked up. With any luck I won't be too long."

* * *

Julie watched Ben take off at a jog through the edge of the aspen, around the last tree and onto the flat grassland. He turned to wave and blow a kiss, then he was up and over the road and out of sight on the other side. Julie opened the truck's passenger-side door, reached in and rummaged a moment in the console for her trusty Nikon. It was a COOLPIX Digital Point and Shoot, one she had used for years before phone cameras got good and she'd gotten tired of carrying so much equipment around. Times like this she was really glad she hadn't tossed it. Today it was going to come in handy. The article for the *Herald* that was beginning to form in her mind cried out for candid close-ups of the ruins she'd just visited.

She put the camera strap around her neck and started back up the rock steps. This time she could move a little faster remembering where she'd have sure-footing. The afternoon sun was now behind the ruins, leaving her path mostly in shadows. The boulders on each side of the path towered above her head, blocking a lot of the sun's light.

She stopped to stare upward. Something had caught her attention.

She would never know for certain what happened first. Was it the scraping sound above her, making her think some animal was wiggling out from between two large rocks? Maybe the hunched-over shadow of a two-legged animal bounding across the tops of the rocks to her right and then out of sight? Or was it the complete blocking of light as a four-foot wide boulder broke loose and began its crashing descent from some thirty feet above her directly into her path. No, the mystery would be what happened next.

First, she froze. Her mouth was open but there was simply no sound. A voice in her head was screaming 'jump' but before she could move, she was hit with a force from the side that threw her off the path, occurring almost simultaneously with the explosion of the boulder ricocheting dangerously close, brushing her pant leg as it crushed everything in its trajectory down the steep steps.

She hit her head and felt the camera bounce up to glance off her chin; she was hurt, but she was alive. Something had saved her life—pushed her body forward, out of the path of the runaway killer. She tried to sit up but was too dizzy; she slumped back against the rock. And that's when she realized she wasn't alone.

She blinked. She had to be seeing things. She was staring into the red, glowing eyes of a fox—long, pointy nose, ears erect, with mottled red fur, clawed feet hanging down.

Moments later she couldn't remember getting back down the steps to slide down the side of the truck, and to sit on the ground holding a washcloth of ice cubes against the side of her head. She knew she hadn't done these things for herself.

No, Ben wasn't there, but the fox was. Rocking forward, sitting on his haunches, watching her, holding out a bottle of water in a hand bound at the wrist with a braided bracelet of sinew and shells.

Chapter 27

I can't leave you for five minutes before you get into trouble." Ben was leaning over her with Chief Billie at his shoulder. He was smiling but not hiding his concern very well. His hands were shaking as he took the bottle of water from her and set it on the ground.

"Looks like a boulder broke loose. Must have had some rain up here recently. A little wet ground, things shift, and this sort of thing is a given. We try to keep these ruins off limits because the area is unpredictable—unstable, as you found out." The chief was examining the truck's tires. "I'll get my spare out of the Bronco."

"Is the fox still here?" Julie struggled to sit up straighter. She was still holding the washcloth, but the ice had melted.

"Fox? What fox?"

"I saw one when I was climbing. It followed me to the truck." There was no way she could tell him more and not have him be scared to death that she'd knocked herself silly. Who would believe her? A human fox who pushed her out of the way of the boulder, half carried her down the path to the truck, made an ice pack, and gave her a bottle of water. She wasn't so sure herself that she wasn't hallucinating.

With the two men working on changing the tires, they were on their way back to camp in forty-five minutes. Chief Billie put Ben's flat tires in the Bronco to be dropped off at Tire Kingdom in Gallup. He even offered to wait while they were repaired and bring them back.

"That would be great. I'd like one of the docs to look at Julie. I'm guessing she's going to get by with only an impressively large goose-egg on her forehead, and some bruising. Still, I'd like her checked. I'm thinking we might need to ask for something a little bit stronger than aspirin."

"Good idea."

* * *

Ben had been right. Nothing broken. Swelling, tenderness, a really impressive black and blue bruise but otherwise, Julie was good to go. A few days of eight-hundred mg Ibuprofen when needed, and everyone admitted she'd dodged a truly life-threatening accident. Trini was appalled and felt responsible for not telling them of the dangers of the ruins. Ben pretty much figured he'd learned his lesson about exploring areas he knew nothing about and could assure Trini that it wouldn't happen again.

"Did the chief reach you?"

"No, I forgot and left my phone in the truck." Ben had settled Julie on the couch in their trailer before going back to the office. Between the clinic visit and making Julie comfortable, his phone wasn't a priority. But he turned and went back out to the parking lot. He could hear the phone ringing before he reached the pickup.

"You sitting down?" The chief didn't waste time with 'hello'.

"No, should I be?"

"Up to you, but try this on for size. Your tires were cut and it was done where the truck was parked. We're not talking accident here, run over something sharp and air is expelled slowly. No, this much more fits a slash and run MO. Know anyone with a switchblade? Maybe someone you've pissed off?"

"C'mon, you've got to be kidding. There wasn't anyone around. Maybe the truck wasn't in view all the time, but I swear we would have seen something. Or heard something. I can't imagine someone was on foot skipping over the rocks, running through the aspen just hoping to find a vehicle to vandalize."

The chief's sigh was audible. "You know this fits the description of something a Skinwalker would think up. And I might throw in Julie's accident, which I'm beginning to believe wasn't one. I think she might have been targeted."

Now it was Ben's turn to be speechless. He'd never understood evil. And why would it be aimed at them? Was there an explanation? Did he believe in witches? He'd said once to the chief that he didn't rule out witchcraft. But believe in it? He wasn't sure. Was what happened today really some sort of retribution with crazy supernatural overtones? Had he done something, wronged someone, or was it just a matter of being in the wrong place at the wrong time?

Later, when he shared the chief's suspicions with Julie, he thought she reacted strangely to the chief's theory of blaming Skinwalkers. And she asked him about his own beliefs. Was she having second thoughts about their marriage? Maybe thinking an Anglo and part Pueblo Indian match wasn't a good one? No, he knew Julie too well. She honestly wanted his take on Chief Billie's assumption that her accident could have been planned—no secret agenda just the need for getting at the truth.

"Do you believe in witches, Ben? Shape-shifters? I mean your people, Pueblo people."

"All the Southwest tribes have some sort of boogie-man. And the dead can be particularly problematic. There's a story that one Pueblo stopped buying woven woolen clothing from another Pueblo when it was rumored that the dresses and shirts were stolen from the graves of the dead. But water spouts, dust devils, fireballs caused by lightning—these are all thought to be the work of witches."

"None of that is necessarily evil. At least, no one is being killed."

"I'd agree. Pueblo witches are a bit less evil than Navajo ones. They can cause windstorms, upsetting a dance. They are often believed responsible for a couple's affection to sour, even to providing temptations that cause one person to stray. Floods, crop damage caused by insects like grasshoppers, mental illness in the young--these are all manifestations of a darker, blacker world. But you're right; no one is targeted for death."

"Have you ever seen a Skinwalker?"

Ben briefly told her about the Shaman calling upon a

Skinwalker to appear with him at the dance to honor the president of the Navajo Nation a couple weeks back, when he first visited the camp. "It seemed to be the hope of the local tribal leaders that one evil would understand another evil and would be able to make the contagion disappear."

"Actually, that makes sense. One could block the other."

"Most tribes' witches live in caves, rock outcroppings, or the base of cliffs. I should have been more aware of the sacredness of the cliff dwellings I chose to show you. We were viewed as trespassers. It's easy to see why we weren't welcome."

"So, Skinwalkers might have been behind what happened?"

"Might have been."

"And I think that's as close to an answer about whether you're a believer that I'm going to get. Right?" Julie was smiling.

"Could be." Ben smiled back.

Chapter 28

W ell, today's the day we'll find out if J.C. being out of the picture makes a difference in whether we get our delivery."

"What's scheduled?" Ben was in Trini's office reviewing the balance sheet before emailing it to IHS. The tribe had received the first of the promised federal monies and the accounting had begun.

"Ten ventilators supposedly supplied by a company on the west coast and shipped through AMSA in Denver. It's only half of what we requested but something is better than nothing." Trini answered. "We're also expecting two additional hospital tents to be erected today or tomorrow."

"How many patients so far?"

"Fifty-six. And that's in only three weeks. And we've

lost an additional five. Dr. Henry estimates up to two hundred are in need, ill but have no way of seeking help. As far as the number of possibly exposed individuals? That could be up in the hundreds. Has anyone talked with you about taking some daily scouting tours? Going to outlying clusters of families to do a wellness interview?"

"No, but it sounds like that's needed."

"Yeah, like as of yesterday. We're so behind on what needs to be done. We need to start with more testing— daily, and accurate with quick turnaround for results. There's talk of setting up a lab out here. The reservation really needs to be divided into sections with each receiving the exact type of help they need, but the manpower to do that and to staff another clinic with docs and techs just isn't going to happen."

"Do we know when the ventilators are supposed to get here?" Ben had volunteered to check in supplies as they arrived and keep a record of serial numbers where applicable, as with any machinery.

"They said mid-morning which would put them here about now."

"I'm going to run over to Two Sisters for a latte before I get busy. Can I bring you something?"

"I'm addicted to pumpkin lattes."

"I'm on it."

But Ben didn't reach the bottom of the office's front steps before almost running into Dr. Henry.

"That's it. I've had it. You want to see something criminal? Follow me." The doc abruptly turned and headed toward a white van parked outside the triage tent. He opened the van's back doors and pointed inside. "There, and there, and there. Water stains on the crates. Ten ventilators and not one in working condition. See the rust? And this one with parts obviously missing? Three crates have been opened and the machines are on their sides. Who's playing with us? Sending this crap. I want tracers put on this shipment. I want to know every stop, every time these crates have been touched." His voice rose until finally he slammed the cargo doors of the van, walked to the triage tent, and turned at the door, "I want the report by tomorrow morning." Then, slamming the door behind him, Dr. Henry disappeared into the tent, and Ben was left standing next to a dumbfounded driver.

"I work for a transport company. I'm assigned a route and cargo; I just pick up the van and take off. I had no idea …" The driver shook his head.

"I never thought that you did." Ben added. "It's just not the first time we've received sub-standard equipment, *if* we've gotten our order at all."

"What happens now?"

"I'm going to make a list of all the serial numbers and begin a trace. It's probably futile to think I can get to the bottom of what happened to the original order or if this was what was intended from the start. But I'm going to have to try."

"Do you want me to unload these?"

"Let me make some phone calls. I'll let you know. If you're hungry or just want a good cup of coffee, I can recommend the Two Sisters. It's a little early, but have lunch. Uncle Sam's buying." Ben pointed to the café.

"That's great. Yeah, I left pretty early; lunch sounds good."

Ben went back to the office, told Trini what had happened, picked up his iPad and walked back to the van.

And then he remembered the pumpkin latte, made a trip to the cafeteria tent, had them put extra brown sugar and cinnamon packets along with a stir-stick in a sack before delivering one pumpkin latte to Trini.

"You are the sweetest man. I wouldn't have blamed you for forgetting. It's so time consuming and such a lot of extra work to trace serial numbers on damaged equipment that you may find out is salvage anyway. I'm sure Dr. Henry didn't mean to be ordering you around. He's just as frustrated as we all are—maybe more so since it interrupts patient care."

Ben nodded. But he honestly had better things to do with his time. He thought of Julie. She was transcribing patient records—transferring everything handwritten into computer files.

Another one of those tedious jobs that needed to be done. And nobody available to do it. The entire pandemic and the reservation's reaction to it depended upon good, concise, clear record keeping. At least the two of them were needed and could be helpful. But Ben was missing Zac. He hadn't anticipated that the much-cherished vacation to New Mexico would end the way it did.

Raven had picked up their son in Seattle and taken him straight to Bellingham. School had started and so had soccer practice. She had packed clothes and school supplies ahead of time and there was no need to take a side trip to their home in Moose Flats, Alaska. Besides, she'd just rented a house in the outskirts of Seattle and had Romo with her. According to Raven, if Zac had thought the puppy would have forgotten him, he shouldn't have worried. Raven sent a video of boy and dog getting reacquainted. Romo was so excited he finally just sat down and howled. Every other day, Zac texted with a Romo update that usually included pictures.

Eleven-thirty. Maybe he'd be able to pry Julie out from behind the computer in the office and take her to lunch. It might be the only down-time they'd have for the rest of the day.

* * *

They took their two Navajo tacos outside to one of the tables in the shade of the café tent. The weather was desert-perfect—warm but not yet hot--with a breeze that made sitting in the open comfortable.

"I'm so hooked on these. Is this a good enough reason not to move to Florida?"

"And miss out on some really great seafood?"

"Okay, you have a point." Julie took a bite and the two sat in silence, finishing their lunch. The camp was quiet for lunch time with most eating inside. "Let me do the tracing for you. Give me the serial numbers of the units originally purchased—Trini should have those on the advance paperwork sent out. Then let me have the serial numbers from what was delivered this morning. I should be able to come up with some answers."

"Sure you don't mind? I need to meet with Chief Billie. I have an idea that I need to run by him."

"I don't mind at all. It makes a nice break for me, and I'm almost caught up with record transfers."

* * *

Ben let his message for the chief go to voicemail. It

wasn't as if the man really had an office. He was more of a roving protector even though spotty phone service often put him out of range. In the meantime, Ben helped the driver of the ill-fated ventilators unload them and stack the crates behind the office. At least the driver was free to go.

The machines were in even worse condition than he'd thought at first. Rust meant cleaning them first before he could get an accurate reading of serial numbers. There was something almost diabolical about sending equipment in this shape when it was necessary to save lives. And to think it had been paid for—probably twice. It would be interesting to know if new, workable machines had even left the warehouse, and, if so, where and how had they been replaced by these. He hoped Julie would be able to come up with answers.

He'd just handed Julie the list of serial numbers when his phone buzzed—a text from Chief Billie. He was on his way to the camp; would Ben have time to meet around three?

* * *

More lattes, but Ben could think of worse ways to spend an afternoon. The chief was late and it was more like three-thirty before he pulled into camp.

"New problems?"

"Same old ones. I need to organize a search and rescue team but it's going to mean more manpower than I have at the moment. I'm meeting with Dr. Black and several members of the All Indian Pueblo Council in the morning in Albuquerque. Health and Human Services promised halfway decent salaries for anyone wanting to join our team. Volunteers will need their own transportation but will get reimbursed at government rates as part of a *per diem*.

"I'm hoping to come up with seventy-five to a hundred men and women to cover every corner of the Navajo and Hopi reservations. That's the only way we'll have accurate numbers as to how many are affected by the virus and what kind of care is needed."

"Count me in."

"I thought I'd put you in charge of what I'm calling Territory One. It includes the Hopi and I think I can count on getting some volunteers from the tribe."

"Actually, before I sign my life away, let me run this by you first. We have to get PPE and hospital equipment into camp—already inspected and functioning. As you know for every step forward, we're pushed two backward by unusable supplies, or just plain hijacked deliveries. I'm still not over what happened in Albuquerque with the U-Haul. I'm angry. I'm tired of begging for supplies and then not receiving them. In addition, at least wherever possible, I'd like new equipment. But the priority is just getting serviceable PPE in quantity to stock this camp and possibly additional ones."

Ben quickly filled the chief in on the shipment of faulty ventilators. "I want to concentrate on just getting equipment here—not catching thieves, but simply safeguarding what we so desperately need. I'm going to suggest we order everything to be flown in. Set up a contract with the government, and not just ask for a month's worth but enough PPE to stock this camp for several months and possibly provide supplies for another hospital camp if your teams identify the need for another is warranted. I can pretty much bet that it will be."

"I agree. I think additional camps are a given. I would be shocked if my search and rescue teams didn't uncover a tremendous need across the reservation."

"If the right strings were pulled, a government cargo plane could be made available. We'd collect everything and keep it in a guarded hangar until we could move it. I think we could use the National Guard here. I'd like to have everything in Albuquerque, ready to be loaded and delivered to the reservation in ten days' time. I think Dr. Black has enough clout with IHS headquarters to put this plan in place."

"I think you're right."

"Then, with everything in place, I believe there are enough car dealerships in Albuquerque to come up with trucks and vans to form a convoy and again with the Guard helping out, make certain our shipment gets here safely and exactly as ordered."

"I like the plan. Can you organize it?"

"I'd be glad to. But I need to get the Navajo Nation president to request assignment of the New Mexico National Guard—that has to come from the reservation's highest official. If he agrees with the plan, I'll have him contact New Mexico's governor. I'd like to hand-deliver the request letter keeping the plan as much of a secret as possible. And I'd be able to answer any questions the governor might have."

"Then ride into Albuquerque with me in the morning. You could get things going with Dr. Black. A meeting with AIPC won't go past lunch and we could both meet with Dr. Black if you don't mind my tagging along."

"I'm counting on you."

* * *

Ben spent the afternoon on the phone. His plan was met with enthusiasm by the tribal council. President Nez's office promised a formal vote among council members in the morning and a call to Ben with their decision before noon. The president was squarely behind Chief Billie's search and rescue plan and Ben's convoy delivery of enough PPE to stockpile. He asked Ben to meet with Dr. Black and report any problems that IHS might anticipate. Everyone agreed that speed was of the essence. The need was simply teetering on the edge of catastrophe.

Chapter 29

It had been wrong, and he expected to be punished. But locked in the cage at the back of the waterfall cave wasn't something he expected. He hadn't eaten since yesterday. Had someone forgotten him? Was his uncle so mad that he wanted him to die? No, he couldn't believe that. He had been a disappointment, but the old man needed him. He was the last of his family's line rooted in the secret society of witches. He had proved his worth by killing his uncle's grandchild and relieving his uncle of having to live with a bad choice. But the stepmother of his friend, the wife of the man who had befriended him, offered to pay for him to have a new life; he couldn't let her die.

But hadn't it been a test? To see if he possessed the evil that was necessary to carry out orders? Hadn't one of the

Skinwalkers, maybe even his uncle, pried loose the boulder sending it down the woman's path? Set up the murder to see what he would do? And to them, he had failed the test.

He pulled his sneakers out from under a low bench. He'd hidden a corn cake in one of the shoes. It wasn't much but it would give him some energy. He sucked on the hard, nutty, coarse bread, finding it difficult to swallow without water. But he would force it down. He had to be prepared to escape, and he would need sustenance to go far.

He didn't trust the men of the society. He only half believed that his uncle would protect him. His family's association with witchery was more than just a way of life; it was a pledge, as well as an inheritance. And once you took that pledge, there was no turning back. You were prepared to carry out any heinous crime dictated by the group that owned your soul. In an oral tradition, he had grown up hearing about the escapades of Skinwalkers. Some stories so bloody and gruesome, and meant to scare, that he remembered losing sleep—afraid to even close his eyes, knowing that a monster could come for him at any moment.

Was this the life he wanted? He knew he was expected to step into his uncle's shoes when he passed. But then what? Life would never be normal. He would be robbed of any family, any schooling, travel—any life that wouldn't be loaded with danger, death-defying feats meant to maim or kill human beings or things that they loved most. He thought of how he would feel if someone killed Apache or Rain. Or Zac. The newfound friend had almost become his brother. Was it too late? Was there time to join Zac? Play soccer? Skin a walrus? He laughed out loud at this last part.

Could he leave the only home he'd ever known? But, if he stayed, could he become the embodiment of evil? A killer? Someone whom everyone would fear? He had no parents or siblings. His grandmother had died. He had killed the child her brother had raised, and this man, his uncle, was elderly. He wouldn't be on earth that much longer. In many ways there was probably nothing to lose and so very much more to gain. But he was Navajo, a member of an indigenous tribe. Not an immigrant or second-generation implant from some European country that he'd read about in his school books. This was his land, his religion, his past, as well as his future. It said as much about who he was as his name. Could one just walk into another world and fit in? Belong in a meaningful way? And he was not quite thirteen. Was he old enough to know what he wanted? To take a chance on a life that would give him friends his own age?

He hadn't heard the three old men approach the cave until one of them was approaching the cage. His uncle needed him. He was ill and only a family member could tend to him. He must come with them. One old man shuffled to the front of the others, put a key in the lock and opened the door, moving to one side, and beckoning him to follow.

He stood, looked around him and, in that moment, vowed that he wouldn't return. He would not be locked up to die or, at the very least, be pressured to become what he was beginning to think wasn't meant to be. Hadn't the deities shown him his true self in allowing him to save Zac's stepmother? Proved that he wasn't evil? He followed his three visitors, taking one last look at the pictographs before stepping through the waterfall and into the sunshine.

<h1>Chapter 30</h1>

Ben checked Zac's text once more. Second pre-season soccer game and another two-nil win. Zac ended the text wishing his dad could be there to cheer the team. That part meant the world. As a post script Zac had included a picture of Romo; the puppy was growing quickly and now weighed fifty-five pounds. Boy and dog both looked happy. Ben closed his phone and slipped it into his jacket pocket before climbing into the Bronco next to Chief Billie.

"Good news?" The chief started the Bronco and headed up to the road.

Ben filled him in on how Zac was doing, even showing him the picture of Romo. School had just started and Raven had shared that the pandemic restrictions had taken some getting used to, but all of the students seemed to be accepting the wearing of masks and distancing. No wonder the freedom of being outdoors on a soccer field meant so much. It wasn't confining, yet was probably safe, and offered a chance to interact with friends. Ben was glad Zac was happy—a dog, friends, soccer—no wonder life seemed pretty good.

A couple hours on the road gave Ben the opportunity to bounce some ideas off of the chief and, likewise, give him feedback on his plan. Coordination and communication were of utmost importance. Choosing the right people as team leaders would make or break the chief's proposal. Ben was flattered to be asked to head up one of the allotted areas.

In Albuquerque, they left the freeway and took Twelfth Street north to the Indian Cultural Center in the North Valley section of the city. North Valley, South Valley, the Heights—it was a city of sections. In what natives called 'the close-in North Valley', the museum with an A1 rated restaurant was a showplace for the nineteen New Mexico Pueblos. Over the years it had become a major tourist attraction offering year-long special events—dances, art exhibits, and workshops.

The chief pulled into the parking lot. A few cars but nothing like it would normally be. At least most of the people getting out of their cars were wearing masks. But the Center's conference room was less than a quarter full with marks on the floor as to where to stand to maintain proper distance. Signs in the entry advertised several workshops and lectures with an art exhibit featuring Pueblo women artists taking place that morning. Judging by the few people in attendance, the virus had interrupted the art show featuring women. There was going to be a lot of catching up to be done once the virus was over.

Dr. Black had saved two seats next to his at the large conference table in a room adjoining the Center's business office. The chairs were six feet apart. What a strange new normal, Ben thought. But normalcy was in the center of the table where a huge platter of nachos sat next to paper plates and napkins.

"Better help yourselves, these are disappearing fast." Dr. Black's mask hung from one ear as he spooned a dollop of sour cream onto a paper plate before also scooping up more of the bean, beef, and cheese concoction. "This is going to be my lunch. I highly recommend it."

"Looks good." Chief Billie loaded a plate of his own; only Ben said he'd wait a while.

Three of the principal Pueblo representatives were forty-five minutes late. Usually people just nodded and said, 'Indian time'. It was a local joke of sorts that Indian and Anglo time differed. Ben could remember more than one meeting at the Indian hospital that didn't start at the time advertised. It was just something a person got used to.

Finally, representatives from fifteen of the nineteen Pueblos were seated in the room, scattered safely with distance between them, and Dr. Black called the meeting to order.

"I want to point out that what we decide today—the extent of your contributions—will not just benefit the Hopi and Navajo. The guidelines as to how we want to set up what Chief Billie calls a search and rescue mission will also be available for any help you might need with your own support in identifying those with the virus on your respective reservations. So, keep in mind what your own needs might be and how your own Pueblo might be best served. Chief Billie, fill in a few details for us."

"Thanks, Doc. I think all of you know distance is the enemy of the Navajo. We are working against an immovable barrier in providing timely, sometimes life-saving, help. You can't get around an area the size of New Jersey in a day—or even two or three—and do a good job of discerning need. Now, we're relying on word of mouth, not reliable first-person cries for help. And we're missing a lot of the elderly who are in dire need. When it comes to testing, that can be impossible if individuals have no means to travel, let alone receive the test results after they have returned home. Wherever possible we need to take help to the people and follow through with checking back."

"How is the hospital camp that I've heard so much about coping with these problems?" the Laguna governor asked.

"Surprisingly well seeing that we're understaffed and have far from adequate supplies. As of tomorrow, we will have eight hospital tents, a triage tent, and living facilities to house fifty families or personnel. We are tentatively looking at two additional hospital tent camps strategically placed on the reservation depending in part on what we learn from a search and rescue operation."

"I'm not sure I understand how your Pueblo neighbors can help," the governor from Zia commented.

Chief Billie then mapped out how with seventy-five men and women divided into teams of three, they could cover all corners of the reservation in two weeks or less, assessing problem areas, administering tests, contacting backup for anyone needing hospitalization. A team could order a food or water truck if an area was in need of service. He ended with a dire warning.

"We have people dying because they have no access

to help. We must do everything possible to save lives. If you feel that you could provide some manpower to help us, please leave your contact information with Dr. Black. There will be a meeting at the Indian Health Hospital this Friday. Anyone interested in volunteering should attend. Volunteers will be paid a per diem, plus mileage if you are using your own vehicle, and provided a place to stay—room and board paid for—at the hospital camp."

Another forty-five minutes was taken up with more questions before the group broke up.

"Let's get a cup of coffee." Dr. Black pointed down the hall to the restaurant. "I think Ben needs some of my time."

All three men agreed that the meeting had been positive. They would know more on Friday. If seventy-five plus individuals showed up, then the morning would have been productive. Everyone there appeared to agree on the need and moving quickly. But acknowledgement and action could be miles apart. Still, the three men were congratulating one another.

"Now, let's see if we can solve another problem." Dr. Black slipped into a red Naugahyde booth. "I don't know when times have been this challenging. Ben, what do you need?"

"I hate to lean on you any more, but safely getting supplies to camp is going to require your help. Shamelessly, I need to beg some of your cronies in Washington for a piece of that forty million dollars of virus money allocated to IHS. I'm asking for five million—every penny to be spent on PPE plus some one hundred ventilators, and all to be sent to the hospital camp on the Navajo reservation."

Ben continued to lay out his plan of airlifted supplies,

stockpiled in Albuquerque, and then via convoy taken to the reservation. The minute he had a letter of introduction from president Nez, he would be back in Santa Fe to plead his case with the governor to make use of the New Mexico National Guard.

Finally, Ben sat back and waited for Dr. Black's comments. "It's doable. I don't think you'll have any problem borrowing the Guard. If you need additional backup, I'll volunteer to go to Santa Fe with you."

"I'll take you up on that. I see the current camp as a depository for the bulk of PPE and a place to allow us to stay ahead of ordering supplies and restocking the outlying areas. We'll be able to set up our own testing lab and establish contact tracing in addition to treatment."

Chief Billie replied, "I'm investing in a hangar-style metal building to be erected behind the hospital tents by borrowing from my own building fund for this year. Once this virus has passed us by, I'll be able to store police vehicles and parts, especially tires, closer to where they are used. Having the fleet located in Shiprock puts a strain on the force. Makes it impossible to handle vehicle repairs in a timely fashion."

"We already have a second community well going in, two new Wi-Fi provider towers, along with underground cable—plans for a small commercial center are also on the table. A gas station, grocery store, and the Two Sisters restaurant would all be welcome, permanent additions to this area of the reservation. The trailers may or may not stay. Six more closed septic tanks are going in, banking on the area housing becoming permanent whether it's trailers or cement block homes. I think any investment in this area will be rewarded by tribal interest and support. In the meantime, the health care provided is lifesaving." Ben added.

"So, let me get this straight. IHS will provide protective equipment in bulk in addition to whatever hospital mechanical equipment is needed, such as ventilators, using federal monies already approved by Congress. The hangar will act as a storage receptacle and, under supervision, orders for supplies will be filled from this stockpile. We can use the garages at the Indian Hospital to collect and hold everything until the convoy is ready to load it and proceed to the reservation."

"Exactly. Do you see any stumbling blocks? Anyone refusing to use funds in this way, for example?" Ben asked.

"I think the plan is pretty straightforward. Let me make some calls and get back to you no later than tomorrow afternoon. I think we'll get the support."

Chapter 31

Shaking the droplets of water from his hair, Nathan stood for a moment in front of the waterfall, breathing deeply and looking out at the range land below. In some ways it felt as if he was seeing his home for the last time. Perhaps, he was. But for now he let his eyes take in his surroundings.

Lush grass dotted the land to his right, indicating the edge of the second pasture. Flocks of sheep roamed freely, watched over from a distance by men whose entire life revolved around tending livestock. Were those his grandmother's Churro sheep? His grandmother and his uncle both had some of the fleece-rich animals. Maybe one of the old men who came to get him was a herder. Many of the old people were. But as a vocation it was dying out.

What teen or twenty-something would want to get stuck out here? Maybe, if there were enough drugs.

To be fair, there was something calming about watching the flocks methodically eat their way across the valley floor. But who would want to sit out here contemplating … what? A future that might not exist? He wanted more; even if it meant losing his identity, becoming more than all this or maybe just in addition to all this.

In that moment he knew his mind was made up. He took a deep breath, relaxed, and pushed the long side of his mohawk haircut behind his ear. The man standing directly behind him gave him a nudge, a sign that they needed to get going. There were four horses tied to the brush below— and one of them was Apache. The horse looked his way as he started down the path from the cave and whinnied loudly, pawing the hard-packed clay and pulling back on the lead rope that tethered him to a small bush.

The other horses carried saddles. But that was okay. Nathan had ridden bareback since he was a child. He'd used a saddle when he was teaching Zac to ride Rain, worried that someone not used to riding might struggle with balance. Otherwise, Nathan preferred feeling the horse beneath him, able to guide it expertly with his legs, without the constricting stiffness of leather and a blanket.

He quickly untied Apache, who nickered softly pushing his head into Nathan's shoulder. After a hug and a few rubs behind his ears, Nathan jumped to land mid-section first across the horse's back before swinging a leg up and over, scrambling quickly to sit upright. Apache did a fancy little two-step, kicking up dust, happy to have his owner aboard.

It was six miles to his uncle's house, a hogan with two corrals, its own well, a summer stick house and a sweat lodge. Nathan knew, compared to others, he was rich—a landowner, with several houses, and several hundred sheep. No doubt some of these riches resulted from his position in the society of witches. His uncle held immense power in the tribe, mostly garnered out of fear. When he was younger, his uncle had been a Shaman; only in later life did he weave evil into his practice of good. Nathan always wondered how two complete opposites could join to make a whole. How could you make people well only to possibly kill them?

His uncle had seen many changes on the reservation in his lifetime, yet still represented the old ways. Even when others brought in trailers like the one Nathan had lived in with his grandmother, or built block houses, his uncle remained traditional—an eight-sided hogan built out of logs, saplings, and covered with weeds, grass, and bark before a layer of mud was applied. There was a hole in the center for the smoke from a cook fire to escape and the doorway opened to the east to welcome the morning sun and receive good blessings.

Nathan had a friend who bragged about how much money his family made by renting out their traditional house during the summer. There were people who wanted 'an authentic experience', he used to say—would pay big money to sleep on a mattress on the dirt floor and cook outside, grinding condiments in a metate. He wasn't sure his friend was telling the truth.

Nathan turned Apache loose in the corral farthest from the hogan after a quick brushing and making certain the horse had fresh water. And then, just in case the horse hadn't eaten that morning, he tossed a flake of grass/hay mix into the feed trough. Then he carefully rolled the lead rope into a circle and looped it over a post not visible from the hogan. Before he walked back to the hogan, he moved Rain to the same corral and tossed out another flake. The horses had been together since they were foals and were seldom separated now.

The day was warm and someone had moved his uncle to the summer stick house to lie on a pallet of mattresses where he could be fanned by a natural breeze. His skin had shrunk to cling to the bones of his face and hands, outlining the cavities that had once been plump cheeks and a pencil thinness that had once been fleshy fingers. These were the only parts of his body not covered by a light wool blanket. There were dark patches of skin beneath his eyes and his body seemed brittle and small beneath the covering. His eyes were closed and every fourth or fifth breath seemed to stick in his throat causing a gurgling sound before escaping. Nathan sat in the dirt beside his uncle's makeshift cot. The old men who had brought Nathan here stayed in the background out of respect for the dying and a fear of contamination. Any death was to be shunned.

There was no doubt his uncle was dying. As the only living family member, Nathan would have to choose the two or three men who would dig the grave and carry his uncle to his final place of rest. As part of the Witchery Way ritual, the grave would remain a secret but his uncle would probably join others from the society who had passed before him, and more than likely would end up in an area close to the caves of his ancestors. In death the Anasazi were not a threat.

In fact, it was believed that the newly dead added their power to the graves of the ancients, feeding the evil of the Witchery Way, making certain that Skinwalkers could draw upon this power by always having access to it.

Growing up, Nathan heard stories about how Skinwalkers who died of natural causes—like old age—would not be buried but left naked in a sacred place so that they could more easily return to their animal form. Would this be how his uncle's body was prepared for an afterlife? Would a Pronghorn Antelope take on his spirit, the old man melding into the very flesh of something so alive?

To continue his evil?

From his perch within the stick house, Nathan watched the sun slide lower in the west. His uncle's condition hadn't changed, but his labored breathing had slowed and become more of a rattle. The minute his uncle passed, and after he had helped tie the body to a horse for its last journey, Nathan would have a narrow window to seize his own freedom. As the afternoon hours crept on, the boy knew exactly what he would do. He felt a blip of excitement, knowing that a new life was almost within reach.

Chapter 32

All in all, an extremely satisfying trip into Albuquerque. That is, Ben admitted, if the Pueblo representatives in attendance were successful in convincing their people to get involved. They would know Friday. If a healthy number of men and women showed up in their pickups or on horseback, ready to scour the reservation for those who needed help, then the plan would have been a winner.

Ben really felt that the Pueblo Governors he met at the meeting had been persuaded to help, but could they persuade others, the members of their Pueblos? In the meantime his own plan was becoming challenging. He'd spent most of the morning on the phone, working to make certain that transferring PPE and other hospital equipment could be done safely—collected first in Albuquerque then brought to the reservation to be stored and handed out as needed. There was something so very wrong, when life-saving equipment needed to be controlled, as well as guarded.

He wished his own plan didn't depend on a letter from the Navajo Nation's president and a supportive New Mexico governor, high-powered, busy people who might not give his plan their full attention. But he had to have faith. Now the only thing left was the waiting. He hoped to have a yea or nay answer by noon tomorrow. And the minute the request letter was ready to be delivered, Ben would be off to Santa Fe.

"There doesn't seem to be any animosity between Pueblo tribes and the Navajo." Julie was standing at the stove stirring a pot of green chile stew. Picking up something from the Two Sisters and not having to cook in the evenings made life easy. Three large pieces of fry bread were wrapped in foil and warming in the oven.

"Not any more. A few hundred years ago the Navajo raided the Pueblos. The Pueblos really didn't become war-like until after the Spanish arrived. The tribes are different—Pueblos farm and Navajo raise livestock. Their ways of life are not in direct competition. In many ways they're complimentary. I'd like to think that the key to getting the Pueblos to help the Navajo identify those in need here on this reservation is the promise of returning the favor. Plus, it's money. Jobs have dried up and travel is limited. This opportunity comes at the right time. I think it's going to be attractive to a lot of people."

"So, what's on the agenda for tonight? Make it something enticing so I won't be tempted to go back to the office."

"Well, how about a couple beers, a bowl of popcorn, and a movie? I'm afraid that means squinting at my computer screen."

"You have a date."

*　*　*

One movie led to the additional viewing of a documentary and a second beer. It was after one in the morning when Ben closed his laptop and shut off the living room lights.

"Coming to bed?" Ben paused by the bedroom door.

"I need to put the stew away. I'll be there in a minute." Finding a plastic container the right size was going to be a problem. It was great that the trailer came stocked with something so simple, and so helpful, but it appeared that several freezer-safe boxes had just been tossed under the counter. With her head in the cupboard, rummaging through a stack of mismatched containers and lids, the knock at the door was muffled.

"Ben, someone's at the door." But the bedroom door was closed. He couldn't hear her. "Okay, I'm coming."

Julie didn't even think to turn on the porch light; she simply opened the door. The young teen standing in front of her looked like he'd traveled a long way—and quickly, judging from the sweat on his horse.

"I'm Nathan." He held out his hand, inviting her to shake it. But it wasn't the gesture that caught her attention; it was the white, braided sinew bracelet dotted with tiny shells circling his wrist. The same bracelet had been on the arm that pushed her out of the way of the boulder and saved her life.

"Come in, Nathan, I've been wanting to say thank you."

The answer was a shy smile and a nod as he stepped inside.

"Nathan." Ben walked into the living room. "Is something wrong?"

"My uncle died. If you meant it, about sending me to go to school with Zac, I want to go."

"Of course, I meant it. Let's tackle this in the morning. You can have your old room for the night. But first, let's get Apache over to the corral and bedded down."

"I brought Rain, too."

"Then we'll get both of them ready for bed." Ben put a shirt on and, with an arm around Nathan's shoulders, the two of them went back outside.

* * *

In the morning Ben let Nathan sleep in. He fed and watered both horses and had barely checked in with Trini and poured his second cup of coffee, when the call came. It was a go. The president's office had made an appointment for him at three that afternoon with the New Mexico Governor in Santa Fe. The Navajo Nation would send the formal, written request to him by courier and he should have the letter within an hour.

Now, Ben had some work to do—come up with his convoy. Melloy Dodge, Larry Miller Chrysler Jeep, Galles Chevrolet, Rich Ford, and a half dozen other Albuquerque car dealerships didn't even ask to think about it. Once Ben talked to the managers, there were instant offers of help. Ben was looking for twelve vehicles, pickup trucks of varying sizes, and he ended up with twenty. The pandemic was bringing out the best in people and this offered a way to help—a way to be part of the solution and help the state. So, now the only thing left to do was wait as the pieces of the puzzle came together. Wait, and also put the plan to get Nathan to Bellingham in motion.

Ben reached Raven on the first try and she was thrilled. Apparently, she'd heard nothing but good things about Nathan and knew how much Zac wanted him there. Ben was going to transfer money for clothes and school supplies immediately; and later, set up a fund for other necessities with whatever bank she recommended. He'd pay school fees and monthly room and board and pick up air fare for a couple trips home during the year, if Nathan wanted.

He explained to Raven that Nathan had no family any more on the Navajo reservation and that Ben was asking the Navajo Nation Council to grant him guardianship. He would get the official paperwork probably within a couple weeks and send her a copy. Enrolling Nathan in the Indian school in Bellingham had already been agreed to by the council. He didn't say so out loud, but as quickly and smoothly as Nathan's quasi-adoption was being pushed through, more than one person seemed to think they were saving a life. And Ben agreed. The human identity of Skinwalkers was always a best-kept secret, but many knew the families whose history could be traced to the Witchery Way.

Ben pulled his phone out of his pocket. Next was an airline ticket on Delta for tomorrow morning—one passenger, one-way to Seattle.

Chapter 33

It promised to be a crazy, busy day. Ben had checked his itinerary at least three times while eating breakfast. It was five-thirty in the morning. He had to be in Albuquerque by eight-thirty in order to get Nathan to the airport by nine for an eleven o'clock flight. Then, lunch at noon at the Indian Hospital—a catered affair of tacos with all the trimmings. Every indication was that they could easily expect seventy-five to a hundred Pueblo volunteers to show up and offer their services to help with Chief Billie's search and rescue plan for the Navajo reservation. They just might run out of tacos.

Then, allowing extra time to get to Santa Fe, Ben would be back on I-25 by one-thirty for the three o'clock meeting with Governor Lujan. It would be tight but he'd allowed a spare half-hour here and there for the unforeseen—which usually meant traffic problems.

"Ben, look." Nathan had just opened the front door after dragging a stuffed suitcase from the bedroom. Everything and anything that Zac had left behind, from a catcher's mitt and several t-shirts, to a relatively new down jacket was on its way to being returned.

"There." Nathan was pointing to the light dusting of silt that covered half of the porch. Right in the center was the imprint of two pointed-toed hooves.

"You know what Zac would call this?"

Nathan nodded. "Yeah, ghost dust. And he's sort of right. The Pronghorn Antelope is the mark of my uncle. I think he's saying goodbye. I think he's saying it's okay for me to go."

"He wants you to have a good life."

Ben felt a moment of relief. Had another Skinwalker taken over the persona of Nathan's uncle? Maybe. Still, the ghostly imprint seemed positive. More than one person wanted Nathan to succeed. Now Ben wouldn't worry about Nathan leaving his home, this last symbol of the break made things easier, positive and hopeful.

Once he started his new life, there would be no looking back, Ben believed that. Both Raven and Zac would be meeting Nathan's flight about the time Ben would be taking off for Santa Fe. Zac had been beside himself. He must have called Nathan five times since he'd found out that his friend would be joining him.

"I'll be right back. I want to say good-bye to Trini. I think her grandsons might like Apache and Rain. I want them to have a good home."

Ben had wondered what he would do with two horses,

but giving them to Trini was a great idea. He picked up Nathan's suitcase and headed toward the truck.

* * *

Ben relaxed for an hour at the airport with Nathan and a third cup of coffee to wash down a sugary pastry. In a weird sort of way, Ben was envious of Nathan's situation—a new life, a family to give him support, schooling that would prepare him for college if he chose to go. Ben hoped he'd assured Nathan that he was always welcome to visit him and Julie wherever they might be. Any sustained conversation was interrupted by more calls from Zac, who simply couldn't contain his excitement. Finally, it was time for Ben to head to the Indian Hospital. A handshake turned into a hug and a heartfelt "thank you." Nathan adjusted his mask, pretending like something had fallen in his eye and it wasn't tears threatening to spill over his lower lids. A last wave and Ben turned to go.

* * *

The moment Ben turned off of Central and onto Vassar Street, he knew the chief's project was going to be a success—the hospital parking lot was overflowing. No one had talked about maybe having to turn people away, and he doubted that would happen. They could probably use as many able bodies as volunteered. The lack of tacos would be their only problem.

The chief had set up five, six-foot long tables for signing up—each line correctly spaced, both at the table and while waiting. It wasn't a long wait before each person gave his name, phone number, e-mail address if he or she had one, and preferred days to work. Most were putting down 'whatever needed', Ben noted. Each applicant also received a booklet of maps of the reservation outlining the proximity of clusters of houses, schools, clinics and various landmarks like upper and lower pastures and wooded areas. There was also a page of phone numbers and emergency contacts, including Chief Billie and several doctors at the camp.

The chief was busy talking with those in line, answering questions, and announcing that there would be a short meeting as soon as everyone had signed up. Dr. Black was directing several maintenance men who were setting up electrical equipment on a cobbled-together platform at the south end of the parking lot. It appeared there would be a couple mics on the ground in front of the pretend-stage for audience use. Ben checked his watch. He'd probably have to miss most of today's meeting but not the next one.

With the electric working and mics in place, Dr. Black climbed on stage. He said he hoped to answer most of their questions from the stage, but that there would be a Q and A period when he finished. First, he mentioned that the next meeting would be at the camp in five days. Then, teams would be assigned. Each team would consist of three people. Everyone would be tested daily and expected to wear masks—everywhere and at all times—and if contagion was suspected, then full protective gear. All PPE would be provided by Indian Health Service. There were known hot spots of virus break-outs around the reservation. Teams going to those designations would have a medical person with them—a nurse, emergency responder, or at the very least, a lab tech to administer testing.

Checks would be issued at the end of every five days' work. Gas vouchers would be handed out to all those bringing their own vehicles. Trucks and SUVs were recommended. Meals would be at the Two Sisters café and box lunches would be prepared if requested twenty-four hours in advance. Overnight facilities in the FEMA trailers would be scarce and on a first come, first served basis. Sleeping bags, pup tents, or mattresses that would fit in the bed of a pickup were encouraged. The theme of social distancing was repeated and underscored. Safety first. Personal phones were required, or if not available for everyone, at least one phone per search vehicle.

Dr. Black announced that flu shots would be administered at the field hospital and at all clinics on New Mexico and Arizona reservations beginning September first. He highly recommended getting one. Likewise, testing for the virus would be available daily in the triage area at the camp. Each volunteer would be given a set appointment time to receive the test—and all volunteers would be monitored judiciously. All results would be shared with participants within twenty-four hours. Anyone testing positive would be quarantined at the camp for fourteen days so as not to spread the virus outside the boundaries of the reservation. Likewise, anyone exposed to someone who tested positive, would also be quarantined. Socializing would be encouraged to include only the three-man search team each person had been assigned to and not others in the camp.

Everything seemed to be going well, so Ben helped hospital personnel empty trash receptacles from the parking lot into bins in the alley before taking off. He'd left his jacket and tie in the truck and was pleased that he didn't see any spatters of salsa on his dress shirt. It wasn't every day that you had an audience with the governor.

A lot was riding on his plan. He needed to articulate a good, workable approach to providing tangible help by way of supplies delivered in a timely manner and matching what was ordered. He wasn't being melodramatic and hoped he wouldn't be perceived that way. He hoped the governor was aware of the consequences if his plan wasn't put into action. It would be a major step in saving money and lives. A deep breath. He could do that—convince the powers that be to invest by providing the New Mexico National Guard as helpers. If the governor agreed, it was back to Albuquerque to meet with several dealerships.

* * *

Success! He had the promise that New Mexico's National Guard would be activated to protect the large shipment of gear that the reservation was desperate for. No one thought he was embellishing the facts. Yet, the governor simply had no idea that shipments of PPE meant for the reservation were either stolen or misdirected and replaced with inferior goods, or that drivers of delivery vehicles had been killed or maimed. Was it more important that a safe delivery was made? That the reservation would receive the supplies they so desperately needed or was it of paramount significance to find the killers? Thieves who let nothing stand in their way? Ben knew he had to trust law enforcement. But he was apprehensive and found himself looking over his shoulder. He'd be glad when this convoy was successful and safe on the reservation.

But how many knew of the threats, veiled, but nonetheless real? It always astounded Ben with the amount of inflammatory and shock-factor news that daily made headlines, the desperate plight of indigenous people literally living in the same state as those who could help never got the attention it needed. Could people be so callous as to ignore what would be an obvious strain on any health system that had to meet the needs of hundreds of thousands of individuals spread across miles of bad roads and inferior infrastructure?

He was feeling like a broken record, just repeating and repeating the needs of thousands of people. How many times had he presented the problems of a lack of sanitation, a decent water supply, or just simply funding by the federal government that in no way even began to alleviate the struggles on most reservations to have an audience refuse to believe in the severity of the problem. People would say things like, 'that just couldn't happen in the United States', and he was blamed for simply blowing a situation out of proportion to receive sympathy or as some saw it, more funding. He got tired of being branded a liar. Yet, here the Governor never questioned him but instantly saw what needed to be done. In addition to safeguarding the PPE, she was releasing state emergency funds to be used as he saw fit.

After finalizing the particulars and giving an estimated date of enacting the plan as ten days out, Ben borrowed an office and touched base with the car dealerships in Albuquerque to outline a time and meeting place. If Dr. Black was true to his word, and he was able to procure government issued PPE, it would be flown to Albuquerque and held in a guarded hangar at the airport before being loaded into vans and trucks to begin the trek west. The Governor promised ten, steel-reinforced, armored personnel carriers—one for every two transport vehicles. And guards would be armed. At last the plan was set in motion.

No one seemed to question the need for armored cars and armed escorts, and Ben wasn't going to share. Was it right to keep the ugly, dangerous side of the mission a secret? The possibility that there could be a threat to lives? He had more than a twinge of conscience and had to tell himself that this was a need that simply had to be met.

Chapter 34

"Doc, you gotta minute?"

"Sure, Oscar, come in." Ben got up to clear a stack of folders from a chair in front of his desk. "What can I help you with?"

"I'd like to volunteer—be a part of the chief's search and rescue teams. Not a lot of people know the reservation as well as I do. Seems like that know-how could be useful."

"I agree. Would you be able to find someone to take over the grocery and errand runs?"

"That would be easy. I got a cousin just waiting on me to give up that job. So, no problem. He's ready to go tomorrow. Think you could put in a good word for me with the chief?"

"Not a problem; I'd be glad to. How's the hangar coming?"

"Last delivery of steel trusses is due in today. The joists got here day before yesterday—all that's left is putting it together. But it's a big one, all right. Too bad there wasn't time to pour a cement floor."

"I agree but need outweighed 'nice to have.' There'll be time later to add a floor and maybe some partitioning inside. For the time being a two thousand square foot structure for storage is going to be a great help."

"I'm hearing that there'll be a warehouse foreman's job open when the building's done. Somebody said it was going to pay twenty an hour for the night shift."

Ben laughed. "You hear more than I do, but that sounds about right. I know the chief talked about three shifts. How are your computer skills?"

"Miss Otter offered to tutor me. Help me with bookkeeping and spread sheets and things like that—tips on how to keep up with inventory and submit reports."

"Chief's going to be tied up appointing teams today. I'll be meeting with him this afternoon; I'll tell him you're interested in a warehouse position. Better yet, walk over to the parking lot with me. You can volunteer as a team leader for the search and rescue operation. I think the chief will be glad to have you."

* * *

The parking lot was filling up. Several port-a-potties lined the south edge. Tables containing bottled water were arranged along the northern parameter. In one month's time the place had gone from being a wide spot in the road to a bustling mini-city. Four more contained septic tanks were going in behind the last row of ten trailers, which had been delivered Saturday. Hospital tents now numbered fourteen and the triage tent had been expanded to hold twenty separate examination cubicles. The newest well was providing good drinking water and another well was planned. It had been two days since Ben had lost Wi-Fi service and then only for an hour. Twenty-five miles down the road, another tower was going in. And the Two Sisters had just hired a dishwasher, a sous chef, and five wait-people. Menu items numbered over thirty dishes divided between breakfast, lunch and dinner. Outside seating now circled the main tent and was covered. Julie's 'couple hours in the afternoon' to relieve Trini in the office had turned into an eight-hour-plus daily stint. But her help was invaluable.

Today Trini and Julie each were manning a table offering gas and food vouchers, maps, and schedules for the week. Parking for search and rescue volunteers was in a field behind the last row of trailers. Ben counted thirty-one trucks and SUVs. The chief had gotten the number of volunteers that he'd hoped for. And with that number, the chief estimated connections with even the most outlying clusters of residents could be completed in two to three weeks. One round was planned, with two more possible follow-ups.

"Looks like everything is ready to go. Nice crowd." Ben had walked up to stand by the chief. "Oscar would like to help—maybe head up a team? Or just be on stand-by to step in wherever he can?"

"What do you say, Chief? Got room for me?"

"You bet. Right now, I need someone to help those needing to put up tents. Most folks are sleeping in their trucks or cars, but about fifteen individuals brought tents,

I'd like to put them on the other side of the port-a-potties. Think you could organize that group? Keep them all to the south of the toilets and make sure they're ten feet apart—more distance if there's room."

"You got it, Chief." Oscar took off at a trot.

"I've assigned five deputies to work the group, so to speak. We'll organize this afternoon in order to head out in the morning. I've asked the Two Sisters to put out a spread about five o'clock this evening and then we're going to show a movie starting at seven. The idea is to keep everyone fed and entertained."

"That's always a good plan." And it was. Ben wasn't just brown-nosing the boss. He watched as people interacted. Those who had already been tested were lining up at the café, grabbing a soft drink or bottle of water, then a sandwich before sitting outside with friends. Lunch, pitching a tent, setting up their bed, getting tested, and going over their orders made up a busy afternoon. Ben walked around Julie's table and whispered in her ear.

"Mutton stew? I'm in heaven. I think I'll be finished here by five." The line to Julie's table was finally getting shorter. The stack of paper masks had been reduced to just one box, and the movie tickets that were good for one bag of popcorn had disappeared.

"Looks like they've planned a double-feature." Ben had pulled a chair up to the table after sharing the highlight of the dinner menu. "I don't know any titles, but one starts at seven and the other at nine-thirty."

"I'm not particular. I'll probably fall asleep in the middle anyway."

"That's what happens when you start work at six." Ben was impressed with Julie's ability and willingness to throw herself into work, but there was a part of him that thought she might need to ease up. Or maybe he was just being selfish. Three days in a row she hadn't left work before nine in the evening. Watching a movie together in a parking lot on a reservation was the most exciting thing they'd done together in a week. Well, almost.

The movies were just all right. Not anything he'd want to pay money for, but both were rated as family-approved. One was an animated, action movie and the other a sports movie with a young protagonist overcoming a handicap to go on and eventually earn a spot on a professional football team. The audience was vocal—cheering the good guys, booing the bad. Ben idly wondered if they'd gone through a bushel of popping corn. The treat had disappeared early. And he'd noticed two empty, one-gallon containers of butter-flavored cooking oil in the trash bin.

"Showing movies was a great idea." Julie slipped an arm through his on the walk back to their trailer. "Perfect for the families that had to bring kids."

"Most, if not all, of the activities have been planned by the chief. I don't think this is his first time organizing large groups around a community task."

"Oh, damn." Julie had been looking for a flashlight in the tote bag slung over her shoulder but instead pulled out several pieces of paper. "I forgot to take these sign-in sheets to the office earlier. I know Trini plans to start on a master list early—earlier than I plan on getting in. I'll just be a minute or two. Go on ahead; I'll meet you at the trailer."

Julie rounded the office trailer and even with a flashlight almost stumbled over the edge of the slab that had been poured to extend the porch and connect it with the parking lot. The office was shrouded in utter darkness. No one had thought to leave on the perimeter lights—even the motion sensors were turned off. And another oddity—the front door was unlocked and open about six inches.

She and Trini had been manning the sign-up desks all afternoon. Could Trini have forgotten to lock up? Or worse yet, left the door ajar? Maybe she had given the keys to someone, like the chief? Or a deputy who got called away before making certain the building was secure. Well, she wouldn't forget. Once she'd left the sheets on Trini's desk, she was out of there—after she locked up.

But two steps into the waiting area she knew she wouldn't be getting home anytime soon. By the somewhat restricted beam of the flashlight, she saw the safe that was usually under Trini's desk had been dragged out of her office and was now open and laying on its side. Banded stacks of bills were scattered in a half circle, with a trail of packets leading to the back door.

Had she walked in on a burglary? Was there someone still inside the office? Julie fumbled for the wall switch and flipped on both banks of fluorescent ceiling lights—just as she heard the back door bang shut. She stood rooted next to the safe and called Ben.

for that week. This was our first delivery. It wouldn't take an Einstein to figure out we were working on a cash-only basis."

"Sorry for the delay. I took the time to get my camera out of the Bronco." Chief Billie paused on the porch steps with Ben standing right behind him. "I've sent a deputy around back to secure the back door. Other than Mrs. Pecos, has anyone been inside the building?"

"No one," Julie said.

"I think we were damned lucky that you forgot to leave the sign-in sheets on Trini's desk earlier. And you're probably luckier that the perps weren't still inside," Ben said. He put an arm around Julie's shoulders and gave her a hug.

The chief radioed for two of his deputies to come to the office. "We're going to try to lift some prints and get a copy of yours, Trini, for comparison. I guess I'd be surprised if we found anything we could use."

"So, you think it's probably a professional job?"

"Not sure I'd use the word 'professional' but look at the facts. Someone knew our schedule—I picked up funds in Shiprock yesterday. We announced that we would be paying for a partial week's work this Friday—three days from now. Someone knew there would be two pretty big payouts in the next three days because we also owed the construction workers. We brought in the money early rather than wait until the last minute. Someone also knew Trini would be in charge of the money and was familiar with Trini's office—knew she had a safe. A good guess that the money would be here—that she wouldn't be carrying it around. But more importantly, someone had the combination." The chief was standing over the safe. "This has not been forced open."

"You're kidding." Trini stepped forward to look at the safe's door. "Oh my God, someone just opened it."

"Looks like the first plan was to take the whole thing. Don't think they knew that these office models weigh about a hundred and fifty pounds. Only the outside is metal. The interior walls are cast cement—can't just tuck one of these under your arm and walk off with it. They dragged it this far before going to plan B. And the fact that it's out here in the entry makes me think there were at least two people moving it."

"I guess the question is who had the combination?" Julie asked.

"Exactly. Do you know if it was purchased new for the camp? Or preowned?" The chief turned to Trini.

"Used." Trini spoke up. "But it was in good working condition. It had been in storage in Albuquerque, at the Indian Hospital. There was a lab set up behind the hospital, but it shut down years ago. Dr. Black might know who used to have this item. He was the one who gave it to me."

The chief was busy taking photos, pausing to get down on his knees and take several shots of the door, the key pad, and the inside of the safe. "Interesting. The safe is still pretty full of money. Ms. Pecos, you're the hero. Your timing was perfect. A whole bunch of taxpayers owe you."

The chief moved out of the way for his deputy to dust for fingerprints, then pulled on a pair of latex gloves and proceeded to empty the safe and pick up the bundles lying on the carpet, motioning Trini to help him. He held out gloves. "Better take some precautions here before anything else disappears. I'm interested in knowing how much might be missing."

Trini stepped forward, pulled on the pair of gloves and carried several packets to a nearby table, sat down and quickly started counting. Finally, the table top was covered in stacks of fairly crisp, one-hundred-dollar bills.

"Would you believe I'm within one thousand dollars of the original amount. They didn't get away with much. Thank God--and Julie."

"Looks like we're done here for the day. We can't do anything until morning. We need to change the combination and bolt the unit to the floor. This time Trini will be the only one who has the combination. We'll decide on a backup person tomorrow. Let's put the safe and money back in Trini's office. I'll leave a deputy on guard for the night. I suggest we all get some rest. You know, six a.m. is going to get here rather quickly."

Chapter 36

The Two Sisters had a full crew on deck at six. Two stacks of paper cups beside three urns of coffee were at one end of a table holding several platters piled with pastries, mostly four-inch squares of fry bread sprinkled with cinnamon and sugar. All vehicles were lined up behind camp ready to roll once the chief gave the word and breakfast was over. The day promised to be perfect. No rain was forecast, there was going to be a break in the late August heat with highs only getting to the low to mid-eighties. Balmy for that time of year. Everyone seemed eager with maps in hand and supplies already in their vehicles. They would reconvene at six that evening for a debriefing to be held in the camp's parking lot. All had two-way radios or cell phones or even one of each if cell reception couldn't be counted on in the part of the reservation where they were headed. Ben had to hand it to the chief—the organization, outfitting, and feeding of around a hundred people was running like clock-work. That took expertise. Ben looked up and saw him headed his way.

"We've got a problem." The chief sat down next to Ben outside the café tent. "Ms. Otter tested positive. I don't have anyone to set up and supervise the testing that will be done at the schoolhouse, let alone, we need to disinfect. We've advertised that we'll be open for business tomorrow. That leaves a lot to be done without supervision in a short period of time."

"Why do I have a feeling that you're wondering about Julie and me? Maybe we'd like to volunteer to help you out?"

"Read my mind."

"I'd be speaking for Julie, who just stepped inside. She'll be out in a minute. But I think I know what her answer will be. Let me know what you need us to do."

"Get the place ready for patients—I'd like to offer drive-up as well as a more private, clinic atmosphere inside. I think we'll be able to handle the most people that way. And put people at ease. This is not something they will want to do. We're going to run into suspicion and opposition. I don't have to tell you that."

"I've wondered how people were going to accept all this—it's a major change to their routines, as well as a silent threat to their lives. Have you thought of having President Nez put out a statement? Something encouraging but stating the necessity of testing or going to the clinic? You could hand out flyers and post some. Of course, I'm assuming residents are familiar with written English or Navajo."

"Great idea. Most are fluent in English. And Nez is a well-supported leader. I think it would make a difference. Any chance Julie could contact the Navajo Nation offices and get someone started on putting a flyer together? I'll give her the contact information."

"I'm sure she'll be glad to do it."

"Otherwise, I think I'm ready when it comes to manpower and equipment. I have five techs standing by with swabs and testing equipment. We can replenish as needed on a daily basis for the time being, but I'll breathe easier when we get six-months-worth of supplies stored at camp. Any word from Dr. Black on how the shipment is coming?"

"I expect to hear later today."

"Let me know when you do. We're going to go through supplies pretty quickly. I want results turned around and back within an hour. That's going to keep everybody busy."

"I know we'll have to reconfigure the large classroom but any other changes to accommodate testing?"

"We'll have to have seating—we can move some of those benches we use as bleachers for games out of storage and put them up in the shade alongside the building. I'll have plenty of cold drinks, packaged snacks, and other amenities like separate tables set up on the basketball court for those filling out paperwork. I've had four outside port-a-potties installed. But the rest of it has to be set up and the disinfecting of everything has to be completed this evening. By the way, the two of you, as well as the techs, will wear complete protective gear when working with the general population. I'm not asking you to take any chances."

"I wouldn't think that you would. Let me know what you need to put in our truck. I'll load up and fill Julie in. We'll be at the schoolhouse in about an hour—meet you there."

"Dr. Pecos? I know I don't have to tell you this, but be careful. I think you'll be safe in a group, but just be aware of your surroundings. I think Skinwalkers were behind your wife's accident and that was caused by being too close to sacred ground. But I don't want something like that to happen again. And I believe J.C.'s death was the result of a fight over drugs—still, we don't know for certain. We can't relax our vigilance."

* * *

"I'd love to help. I'm glad Chief Billie thought to ask us." Julie was filling their ice chest with ice and cold drinks. "Should I go ahead and order a couple subs? From what you've said, I don't think we'll be getting away for lunch or dinner."

"Good idea. I don't think the compressor to run the pressurized hose for the disinfectant spray will be delivered until late afternoon. I think we might as well figure on some after-dark hours."

"Disinfecting a schoolhouse and several port-a-potties on a remote part of a Southwest Indian reservation—you really know how to wow a girl. That is date-bait if I ever heard it."

"Give me a break here." But Ben was laughing.

* * *

The school house smelled musty. The first thing that Julie did was secure anything in the main room that might fall over in a stiff breeze, and then she opened all the windows. The breeze felt great and cleared the air. The building hadn't been opened for a week or so probably. Two of Chief Billie's deputies were in the barn helping Ben untangle ten, twelve-foot benches that had been stacked together since spring. Julie carried in the bags of snacks, six-packs of water and soft drinks and put everything within easy reach in the kitchen area. She plugged in the fridge, a bank of lights over the counter and prayed the electricity was ready to go. Prior to this, a generator provided power, but with the cable having just been completed, the fridge came on with a hum. Once she checked all the bulbs, she turned the ceiling and counter lights off again. No use wasting energy.

The day went smoothly. She and Ben ate their dinner-subs for lunch, vowing to chow down on peanut butter crackers and bags of pretzels for later. Julie had just about run out of Pledge and Clorox toilet disinfectant by late in the afternoon. The framework to hang the dividing curtains on in order for them to form cubicles was up—twelve box-stalls now filled a part of the classroom. They wouldn't hang the white canvas curtains until after they had been disinfected and the spray had thoroughly dried. Which probably meant putting that chore off until morning. By nine that evening they were ready to call it a day.

"Looks great, inviting even. And it smells even better." Julie was standing in the middle of the large classroom, admiring its transformation from school to clinic. "I think the way it looks should instill confidence. And the flyers are a perfect touch. I'm so glad they could deliver them this afternoon. I've put up several outside."

"How about toilet paper in—"

"Done."

"I guess we should leave the fridge on. I'm sure cold water will be appreciated tomorrow. It'll get pretty warm waiting to get tested. I expect there to be lines. And that's it. We're out of here. I'll get the guys to help me move the sprayer to the barn and lock up."

* * *

They were beat. Ben had to remind himself that he was still in his thirties. But then, Julie had fallen asleep in the truck on the way back to camp; so, he wasn't the only exhausted thirty-something. Twelve hours of work with only a break for lunch took its toll. But it was worth it. The two of them and the techs would be able to walk in, hang the curtains and start to work in the morning—no waiting. And everything sparkled—the air safe to breathe and equipment, desks and chairs safe to touch. He was glad that part was done. With some of the close-in clusters of families needing testing, they expected to find people on the doorstep.

Still, morning came way too early. Julie had set two packages of thumbtacks, a roll of packing tape, and a whisk broom by the door. The first two items compliments of Trini, but all were things she could have used the day before. Lunch would be catered by Two Sisters so they didn't have to worry about hauling food around. With the kitchen at the schoolhouse, they had a fridge to keep food cold or a stove to warm things up if needed.

The schoolhouse sat below the road in a hollow which

gave it wind protection, so when Ben crested a small hill before going down the road that would take him to the school's front door, seeing the four port-a-potties on their sides didn't make sense. He was pretty certain that there hadn't been a wind storm and it would have to be a heck of a gale to topple those metal closets.

"Ben, look. What happened? Was this a prank? Some kind of early Halloween trick?"

"I have no idea." He pulled around to the back door and instantly knew they were in for a shock. Shattered vials littered the back steps next to a still smoldering fire that had fed on the canvas curtains and the wooden frame they were meant to hang on. Two wooden benches had been dismantled and split for additional kindling but just stacked to the side apparently not needed to keep the fire going.

"I'm afraid to go inside." Julie stood at the bottom of the steps.

"Me, too. C'mon, it's not going to get any better standing here."

The kitchen and storage area had been ransacked. If it could be tipped over or dragged out of a cupboard, it was. And that included the fridge. Julie walked into the classroom and stopped. Everywhere she looked there was a fine sifting of silt—on the floors, the tables, chairs—not a surface had been missed. And in the dust were prints. A cougar, a bear, what was maybe a fox, a deer, wolverine, the front and hind legs of a rabbit—a zoo of animals recognizable only by their feet.

"Who would do this?"

"Skinwalkers." Ben didn't hesitate. Ghost dust and their calling cards were the animal paw and hoof prints that were scattered around the room.

"But this is more like juvenile destruction, not evil, not something that would kill anyone."

"It's evil. Think about it. Seeing the mark of the Skinwalkers would scare away anyone coming here for a test or medical advice. The schoolhouse is tainted. If we can't get this turned around, people refusing help even by getting tested could die and spread the virus to others before doing so. This act of evil has the potential of doing harm to the greatest number of people. It's sly, diabolical even, and took some careful planning."

"What are we going to do?"

"Not let them win, for starters." Ben took out his phone and walked back outside to call Chief Billie.

<h1 align="center">Chapter 37</h1>

Ben never knew how they did it, but at ten o'clock, a mere four hours after finding the devastation that was the schoolhouse, a tent had been delivered and erected on the basketball court, all outside seating areas washed clean, tables sported white paper covering, broken glass vials were picked up, port-a-potties set upright and moved to be closer to where people would congregate ... and they were ready for patients.

In addition, the schoolhouse was locked. The front and back porch and inside floors were swept clear of any tracks. Extra ice chests were outside in the shade along with individual bags of chips and nuts close to the seating areas. A case of brand-new vials for collecting samples along with gloves, gowns and masks were safely inside the voluminous white hospital tent that came with cubicles already marked off. Each was separated from the next by curtains on rigid aluminum rods attached to a track that made a loop just below the peak or highest point of the tent's ceiling.

Chief Billie had provided six strong men, three of which now either directed traffic, checked paperwork, or were simply on call to step in and do whatever was needed. Success. No one would even guess that they had been the victim of Skinwalkers.

They agreed to shut down testing at four and spend the late afternoon and early evening putting the schoolhouse back in order. Cleaning equipment including the compressor for the disinfectant sprayer would be brought back and Chief Billie promised extra volunteers. By the morning the building and surrounding area would be in pristine, safe shape again. It would be great to let people wait either on the porch or in a partitioned room adjoining the main classroom. A portable air-conditioner made inside the schoolhouse a much more pleasant place to wait. And with an afternoon rain predicted, a much drier place to be.

Ben was in his truck just pulling out to return to camp for more test vials when he got the call from Dr. Black.

"It's a go. Everything we've ordered will be delivered to Albuquerque this weekend. Easier to get military transport on a Saturday, I'm told. I want the two of us to be there— we need to take inventory and see that everything is stored properly. I don't want any of the electrical equipment getting wet or dropped or in any way compromised. I'll talk with Chief Billie about guards. Looks like if everything arrives on time, we'll be ready to roll on Monday morning. I think it's safe to go ahead and contact your convoy participants and give them a heads-up as to time and location for pick up. I guess that includes letting the Governor's office know about where and when to have the Guards meet. I'm leaving it up to you to get Chief Billie to set up security for the warehouse at camp. I think we have all our bases covered. I'm excited. I think we have a plan of action that will work."

Ben promised to be at the Albuquerque airport by ten on Saturday morning and thanked Dr. Randy Black once again for all his help. Winning was everything—especially when it meant saving lives. Skinwalkers 0/Chief Billie and Ben Pecos 1. And they were about to add to that score. It felt good.

* * *

Two hundred and ten people had been tested that first day the schoolhouse was operational. Most tested negative. Others weren't so lucky. Depending on the severity of symptoms, individuals testing positive were either sent home to quarantine or taken to be admitted to the hospital nearest where they lived. Most hospitals were rapidly filling to capacity—both on the reservation and in nearby communities. The camp had gone from six hospital tents, to ten, then twelve, and finally fifteen. There was hope that with search and rescue teams identifying those that tested positive and then encouraging the healthy to distance themselves from them, the virus could eventually be controlled. Ben had heard that there would be a complete lockdown over the weekend—everyone quarantining in place for fifty-seven hours starting Friday afternoon. That would certainly reduce traffic when the convoy travelled across the reservation.

Having a trailer in the front row close to the office now seemed a luxury. Five new doctors had been added to the staff along with fifteen nurses and techs. The camp had become a tent city. There were also a half dozen strategically placed kiosks dotting the parking lot and living areas providing coffee, and several food choices from desserts to sandwiches. And its hospital tent complex was the center for a network of outlying medical service areas. There was steady traffic to and from the hospital tents. Dr. Black had his hands full.

At the end of the day, Ben and Julie checked in with Trini picking up any instructions for the following day and handing in their reports. Today, they waited while she paid the foreman of the temporary warehouse that was finally finished and waiting for Ben's convoy of supplies.

"It's great to see that done. It's hard to believe it will be full in another two days." Ben was breathing a sigh of relief.

"Did you ever find out who might have known the combination to the safe? I'm assuming you were able to get it changed?" Julie asked.

"A brand new set of numbers the very next morning. And it's bolted to the floor. But no one remembers who might have known the combination. Dr. Henry said it was just too long ago. He hadn't used the safe personally. His lab assistant at that time was a Shirley Running Elk. She had the combination and shared the safe, but she left Indian Health more than four years ago. He thought a couple techs also had access. He offered to give me their names and look up addresses but they have also moved on and now live out of state. I didn't see any point in following up.

So, a dead-end, I guess."

"Seems odd though. The person or persons not only had the combination, but also knew your schedule—when you would have money here. Have you ever made a list of people who use this office or have spent time here?" Julie asked.

"Never thought it was necessary. I just know I'm being extra careful now. I won't open the safe without the door to my office being closed."

"A good idea. I'm going into Albuquerque Friday night so I'll be able to help unload the supplies Saturday morning and do an inventory. I'll come back with the convoy on Monday. Do you need anything? Anything from the Indian Hospital?"

"Could you ask Gloria if she has another external drive for my computer? I'm scared to death I'll lose some information that we need. I know this one is close to capacity."

"No problem."

"If Ben is going to be gone over the weekend, how 'bout dinner at the Two Sisters Saturday? A girl's night out."

"Sounds perfect." And Julie meant it. She was already trying to come up with things to do when Ben was gone—other than work.

* * *

Saturday morning and Ben was loading up his pickup for the trip to Albuquerque. Chief Billie had gotten word that the transport wouldn't be landing before one o'clock that afternoon so it gave Ben another evening at home. Julie walked Ben to his truck. She always hated their separations. But at least they had carved out time for a Friday date night, if walking across the parking lot to a restaurant in a tent and then a movie on the thirteen-inch screen of Ben's laptop counted.

"Be safe." She handed him an unopened box of six masks. "Share these so I won't worry about you." A hug and a long kiss and he started the pickup. "Let me know how things go."

And then she was standing alone, waving as the truck disappeared. Maybe she should have gone with him, but she had too much to do at camp to take a weekend off. She owed the *Herald* an update on the news story that she'd sent them last month. She'd spotlighted the New Mexico/Arizona field hospital and the medical outreach program that supported it. It was time to readdress. The news department had contacted her twice about what changes might have taken place. National news was finally including stories of reservations struggling with the virus across the US.

The Navajo Nation was not atypical, just bigger. The Florida Seminole tribes were also struggling. This time she thought she'd build a story around the schoolhouse and its transformation into a clinical testing center. Of special interest might be the so-called identify and rescue mission. It wouldn't dawn on readers that all aspects of meeting the crisis would have to be brought to the reservation—a captive audience totally dependent on care from the outside. Only those in urban settings would have access to community amenities and not have to wait for services to arrive.

This was a unique problem she hoped would have an automatic human-interest element. The story she was planning would rattle a readers' 'poor me' attitude and reiterate the extreme challenges of the pandemic. It was important to point out inequities.

The clinic was open until noon both Saturday and Sunday. Already after being open for only two days, supplies needed to be replenished. She'd take gowns and gloves with her and disinfectant wipes and spray. Trini was going to try and get away to go with her, but her elderly mother had just been admitted to the hospital and Trini felt she needed to stay close. In fact, this new development had caused Trini to cancel their girl's night out. So, Julie was on her own for the weekend.

Trini, knowing she would be at the hospital all afternoon, loaned Julie her car—a Jeep Wrangler from another era. Actually, that wasn't nice, Julie upbraided herself. It was a sweet and helpful gesture. It wasn't like she was taking off cross-country. And Trini said that all the dents and scrapes gave it character. In fact, Trini talked as if the Wrangler was family—she'd even named it, 'Butch'. Naming a car wasn't something that Julie had ever done. She'd felt real love for a little BMW convertible once, but she hadn't named it. Julie knew that all that open-air character didn't mask the fact that Butch also needed a new muffler. Not that she was planning on sneaking up on anyone, but the noise drowned out the radio. Still, wheels were wheels. She gassed it up at the tanker-station, and checked the tires hoping they stayed inflated.

So, here she was pulling into the parking lot in front of the schoolhouse. At least this time she had her best camera with her—two cameras, in fact, a choice of lens, and her laptop. The yard and porch in front of the building looked great. Not even a hint of the ghost dust and animal prints that had been there so recently. She wished she'd gotten photographs of those. Two techs were just finishing up, putting vials in cold storage and syringes in a disposable metal refuse container marked hazardous. Dressed in full hazmat gear, they consented to several photos involving their work. Then they changed clothes, and in blue jeans and t-shirts, they were out of there for the weekend.

Julie walked out on the porch, then to the end of the road taking photos of the sign announcing the clinic, the sign directing cars to approach single file if requesting to be tested without coming inside, and the sign directing anyone interested toward refreshments and outside tables—a place to wait their turn if the clinic's foyer was full. Back inside, she grabbed a clipboard with a supply checklist and headed toward the barn or outside storage area. A pictorial inventory was just for her records, not something to be published. She'd attach the photos to the report she was working on for Trini. An hour passed before she knew it.

Back inside, she downloaded the photos to her laptop and started a cursory division of them into categories. She was thinking of the newspaper article as more of a feature in the Leisure Living, Sunday edition. She was in the kitchen getting a bottle of water out of the fridge when she first heard it—a scratching sound—not pleasant, more like fingernails on a chalk board. But probably an animal with claws hoping to open the back door. The smell of food was no doubt enticing. She'd check the dumpster on her way out later. She doubted it had been emptied.

And just to make sure the building was secure, she'd check the back door. She thought she'd locked it and engaged the deadbolt, but best to make sure. She pushed back from her computer and walked back into the kitchen. She didn't remember what happened next. The sound of her screaming as the huge hairy paw burst through the glass in the top half of the back door, exploding in a burst of slivers that sprayed over her and littered the floor; or the head, enormous, tiny eyes fixed and staring, three-inch fangs yellowed and menacing as the bear tossed its head and growled, leaning inward.

She didn't even realize she was still holding the bottle of water until she threw it. Dead aim, straight throw hitting right between its beady eyes—and the bear backed away, disappearing down the steps, and the growling gave way to silence. She reached out to steady herself grasping the edge of the kitchen counter and stood there until her breathing slowed and she stopped shaking. She had a half dozen scratches from the flying glass on her right arm but that was all. The bear was gone. She stood quietly and listened, but there was no sound.

And when she could think clearly, the question that was forming popped to the surface—what was a Grizzly bear doing in New Mexico? It could have simply been a brown bear but its size was too big, but not big enough. A Grizzly easily attained eight feet in height when standing on its hind legs. This animal barely reached six foot. Still, the huge head, tiny ears and pin-point eyes of this bear that threatened her would have been more at home in Alaska.

She'd lost all interest in staying at the schoolhouse any longer. But she needed to close up the broken window and clean up the broken glass. A deep breath and she reached for the broom leaning against the wall. This was a place to start.

With the broken glass in a pile, she found a dustpan under the sink, swept the shards up and emptied them into a wastebasket. Now, she needed to find something that would block the gaping hole where the door's window had been. Ever so gingerly she unlocked the door, pulled it open and stepped out onto the porch. She looked in all directions. Nothing. Not a hint that there had been a very angry animal in that very spot some fifteen minutes before.

A part of her wished she could just whistle for Butch and he'd gallop around the corner and they would be off for home. But there were a few things the Wrangler couldn't do. With a last look around, she walked down the steps and into the barn. She'd noticed plywood in a corner earlier and hoped there would also be a hammer and nails somewhere.

After admitting that carpentry just wasn't her thing, she stood back and admired the somewhat crooked piece of plywood that now covered most of the back door. Not pretty, but it would work—discourage any hungry, meandering four-legged creatures. She walked back inside and pulled the door shut putting the deadbolt in place. Picking up her laptop and cameras, she walked out the front door, secured it, climbed into the Wrangler, and took her first deep, steady breath in over a half hour.

Chapter 38

Julie could never have imagined anything feeling as good to her as the trailer at the camp.

Home, if you could call it that. At least it equated to safety. No bears in a camp now serving some one-hundred-fifty people—and growing. Crowded, a little noisy, but filled with helpful friends. She'd made up her mind not to tell Ben about her encounter with wildlife; so, when he called, she left out the bear part of her afternoon. He was maybe half way finished with an inventory of the million plus dollars-worth of supplies. Work was going quickly. But he was more excited about Zac's soccer game. They were now first in their league. And Nathan had made the basketball team; first team, not second, and the prize position of center at that. He'd tested into the eighth grade and Raven had celebrated by treating the boys to their choice of dinner and a movie. Congratulatory gifts included a down jacket and snow boots. Ben was thrilled that Nathan was fitting in so well. And, of course, there were several pictures of Romo. Ben missed Julie, wished she was with him in Albuquerque, but thought they were on schedule to load the convoy and take off Monday morning. He'd be home by early afternoon.

She would have asked Trini if bears were ever sighted in this part of the desert but didn't see her around the office. She couldn't shake the image of that huge head at the school's back door. And the breaking glass, was it going to kill her? And why her? What part did pure coincidence play in the fact that it knew where to find her? Or would any human have been acceptable? But the worst question of all? Was it a real bear? And if this was the second time her life had been threatened, would there be a third?

After leaving the Wrangler parked outside the office, what was left of the afternoon Julie devoted to laundry, washing windows across the front of the trailer—those that seemed to collect dirt from the road—and scrubbing and disinfecting both the kitchen and the bathroom. Action seemed to clear her head and force her to not focus on what had happened. By six she was done and headed to the Two Sisters for some carry-out. The special was a 3-cheese pizza with sausage, mushrooms, and black olives. Not the healthy meal she'd promised herself with emphasis on broccoli, but a favorite she couldn't pass up.

She checked the Netflix App on her computer but nothing caught her eye. Her iPad was loaded with books and that sounded more exciting, as well as relaxing. She was finding it difficult to push the image of the bear from her consciousness again. She'd close her eyes only to 'see' the large brown, hairy paw breaking through the glass in the schoolhouse door—shouldn't that have been reported? Chief Billie was with Ben but maybe she should have said something—had them contact someone here at the camp. She'd make that decision tomorrow. If she felt the same in the morning, that someone needed to know, she'd call Ben. But tonight she just wanted to put some distance between what had happened and have a quiet, undisturbed evening at home.

She changed into t-shirt and yoga pants, ate two slices of pizza, finished a bottle of cherry-flavored water, took the garbage to the outside bin and finally at seven-thirty settled back to enjoy her book. By nine she couldn't keep her eyes open and had reread the preceding chapter twice, and still couldn't keep the main characters' names straight. She needed to go to bed. The camp was quiet this early on a Saturday night. A lot of people were spending some time inside their trailers.

She'd awakened twice—once to go to the bathroom and return to bed—but the second time close to midnight, it was a bad dream that startled her awake. Bears with big bulbous heads were stalking her. She felt clammy and shaky and sat on the edge of the bed until her heart rate returned to normal. This time she took a trip to the kitchen for a glass of water. She got a glass from the cupboard, turned the tap on, then leaning against the sink, she took a couple sips before the noise fully registered. Growling. She whirled around and the glass of water flew from her grasp drenching her bare feet. She was staring at the bear as it moved silently toward her shuffling out of the front bedroom, into the living room, waving its paws, clawing at the air in front of it. She opened her mouth, but the scream was more of a whimper.

"Hey, move it. Get away from there."

Someone outside the front window was yelling. Confronting someone standing by the trailer? Suddenly, the bear in front of her simply disappeared, dissolved into air. It had been less than ten feet away, and now it was gone. The knock on the front door startled Julie into action. Willing her knees not to buckle, she lunged for the front door.

"Who is it?" She quickly turned on the porch light.

"Deputy Ashkii. Mrs. Pecos, are you all right?"

Julie opened the door. "Yes, I … uh … heard someone out front."

"Someone who left this behind." The deputy was holding a hologram projector. "My kids want one of these for Halloween. This model will project full 3D images on a wall or transmit them free standing. Pretty spooky, or at least the kids think so. I'd promised to get one if there was a party at the schoolhouse, but it doesn't look like there'll be a celebration this year. Any idea what he was doing out front here with this machine?"

Julie was leaning against the door jamb. Holograms— the bear was a hologram. She was so relieved she couldn't think of anything to say. She just nodded before adding, "he was trying to scare me with a really realistic bear."

"Damn. I'm sorry. I should have gotten here sooner. I do a couple or three turns around the compound every night. The place is usually quiet. You know, I'm thinking I'll just borrow this machine. Actually, confiscate. The guy leaning in your front window was up to no good—I'm sorry he put you through this. I'm sure it was quite a scare."

"No harm done. Thank you for keeping an eye on things. I feel safer." And she did. She had no idea that there was an evening patrol, but it was obviously a good idea.

The deputy said good night and left with the hologram projector under his arm. Julie walked into the front bedroom. Had she left a window unlatched when she'd washed them this afternoon? The scrapes along the metal below the lock indicated the window had been forced and with the window open and the projector resting on the sill, a very menacing 'air' bear could walk into her living room. And scare the shit out of her—the deputy was right about that.

There was no going back to bed now. She put a coffee pod into the machine and got the milk out of the fridge. Did she feel better? Yes, and no. Yes, because she hadn't been injured, but, no, because she felt targeted. She knew the bear at the schoolhouse hadn't been a hologram, but now she was convinced that it wasn't real either. A Skinwalker? Probably. That was her guess, but the real question was why? Who stood to gain anything by scaring her to death? It wasn't like she could be driven out of camp. She could understand wanting to close the schoolhouse clinic down; it would allow the Skinwalkers to wreak havoc on a vulnerable population and perpetuate their hold on evil.

Was she being punished because of Nathan? He had thought enough of her to save her life by pushing her out of the path of the boulder—and put his own life in danger. And then Ben had offered Nathan a chance to leave, go to school, become successful. Wanting to get even made sense. And, if that was true, it wouldn't be their last attempt.

Chapter 39

Ben and the convoy rolled in at exactly noon. They had gotten an earlier start than originally anticipated and with an escort of National Guard vehicles, the trip went smoothly.

Not that he hadn't been absolutely jittery checking in with other drivers every half hour, and almost losing it when the highway patrol pulled them over to check paperwork. Luckily, written permits from the governor's office got them back on the road quickly. But there was a huge sigh of relief by everyone when the convoy pulled up next to the newly constructed warehouse on the reservation and they were met by hospital personnel eager to help them unload.

Julie was there to help with check-in. Each pallet of

supplies had to be accounted for and signed off. Nothing was missing. Mission accomplished. The building filled quickly and after all the trucks and SUVs were empty, about forty volunteers were ready for lunch. Ben and Julie and the chief found a table outside. Julie needed to alert the chief about the broken window in the back door of the schoolhouse and that meant telling him everything—even about how Nathan had saved her life.

"I didn't know who pushed me out of the way of the boulder. Not until Nathan came to the house that night asking for our help. It was the bracelet—sinew and sea shells—I remembered it clearly. In fact, I think the bracelet came from Zac. Anyway, I was able to thank Nathan. When I saw the bracelet, he knew that I knew who had helped me. Because he had on the mask-head of a fox including the skins and paws, I believe that he was on some sort of training mission that afternoon—the incident with me was a setup to prove his loyalty to the Skinwalker's society."

"I don't want you out there by yourself … ever again. Not the schoolhouse, not the ruins or anywhere on the reservation that you won't have people around." Ben was adamant. "I don't understand why you've been singled out. But it's dangerous, life threatening."

"I think Julie's idea that these latest bear incidents might be retribution for some real, or perceived, part in helping Nathan have a new life, of taking him away from here when his uncle died might be a stretch. I do think you're right that setting you up to get clobbered by a boulder was a test for Nathan—a test of his ability to inflict evil. And it was obvious that he thought more of you than of being an accepted part of the Witchery Way," Chief Billie said. "I guess I just want to add that this attempt at harming you might not be the last. But I need to look into the bear incidents. I'm not saying it couldn't be a Skinwalker's ploy; I just find it suspect."

"Isn't there some way to stop it?" Julie asked.

"If you mean arrest a Skinwalker, no. There's a certain anonymity that goes with being a member of the Witchery Way. Basically, they hide in plain sight. Often, they're a family's best kept secret. Nathan's uncle was a renowned Shaman in his younger days. Many Skinwalkers start out saving lives only to become entangled with evil later."

"You're saying the position can be inherited? Passed down to future generations?" Julie was intrigued.

"Exactly. In this case the honor fell to Nathan, his nephew. And I don't use *honor* lightly. The family with such a tradition is revered."

"Do you think J.C. was in training?" Ben asked.

"I thought so but I saw him as an embarrassment to the old man. J.C. was brash, self-indulgent—what is it they say today? Not the brightest crayon in the box? As a teenager he was out of control and there didn't seem to be anything his grandfather could do about it or wanted to do. Something interesting though—because J.C.'s body was in a car parked along an interstate highway, there was an autopsy performed. It wasn't drugs that killed him; he was, in all likelihood, murdered—probably a drug deal gone wrong. That's the only explanation that makes sense."

Ben looked at his companions and made a decision. He would be breaking his word, but the chief needed to know what he knew. He needed to know the truth.

"I need to share something and I'm breaking a trust to do so. I have to ask that the information stays here— among the three of us."

The chief and Julie both nodded, and Ben began with the story Zac had told him about that afternoon when the two boys surprised the Skinwalkers, or maybe it had been planned-- they had been followed, lured into danger. It didn't change that whatever brought them together in the caves, the ending was death—one boy killing to protect the other. And each child now safe and far from the reaches of the witches. Ben finished his story and sat back.

The chief slowly nodded. "I believe Zac's story. Nathan saved his life. The hyoid bone, upper part of the throat, was literally nicked, a chunk taken out of it. A spear thrust upward into the neck with force could do that, as well as, lay open every artery in its way."

"So, with J.C. gone, a twelve-year-old boy was the last in line to follow his uncle."

"Exactly. Thanks to you and your son, Nathan got a glimpse of a family he never had—and a future that had surely seemed beyond him until you offered to make it happen. I think more than Zac's life was saved."

"Would Skinwalkers try to get even? Lash out at those they saw as standing in their way?" Julie asked.

"It's not beyond them with the old man gone and Nathan out of the way, they may have changed their focus to a broader application," the chief added.

"But why would Skinwalkers place a bear at the schoolhouse? Or use a hologram machine to scare me here? Frankly, I don't see a hologram projector as part of a Skinwalker's arsenal," Julie said.

"Nor do I. That's why I said earlier that I need to do some research. Not saying that Skinwalkers couldn't embrace twenty-first century technology, but it's pretty unlikely. Let me see if I can catch up with the deputy who chased the guy away from your window. He doesn't get off until seven a.m.; so, I'll give him another couple hours of sleep. Ben? You up to tagging along? And Ben? Thanks for sharing Zac's story. It's safe with me."

* * *

Deputy Ashkii was a new recruit. Not a lot of locals wanted the night shift patrolling a medical field camp's parking lot and trailers, especially when the money was just mediocre. But he thought that Deputy Ashkii aspired to bigger things, since he had added a hope to move into a more permanent position with law enforcement on his application. Chief Billie had made a note of that and shared his excitement about this recruit with Ben. This was the kind of kid that you could throw something a little more challenging his way and see how he handled it. Law enforcement was tough on a reservation. Drugs, domestic violence, alcoholism—he needed all the good people he could get.

"I forget how difficult recruitment might be out here."

"Yeah, some just want the money—there's no real feel for helping others, making it safe for families."

"Isn't that our man?" Ben pointed.

The deputy was standing beside his truck in the parking lot brushing his teeth.

"All the comforts of home, right?" The chief smiled.

Deputy Ashkii laughed. "It's not so bad. I was thinking I might borrow my brother's travel trailer. He's got one of those little egg-shaped things. Sleeps one but has a fridge and a toaster oven.

"I'll find a spot for it if you decide to bring it to camp."

"Thanks. Electricity would be the main thing I'd need. I'll let you know."

"I'd like you to meet Dr. Pecos. It was his wife that got spooked by the air-bear last night. As you can imagine he's hoping you can identify the guy who was running the projector."

This time an elbow bump between Ben and the deputy seemed appropriate.

"Yeah, I caught up with the guy. Seems like it was just a prank he was playing on your son and the other kid who lives with you."

"Used to live there—both kids are away at school now. They've been gone two, maybe three weeks. Did you get a name for this prankster?" Ben couldn't believe the farfetched story about scaring Zac and Nathan. Who thought that up? And why?

"Yeah, the guy's name is Oscar Begay."

"You sure? The guy who runs errands? Brings in groceries?" Ben couldn't believe it. Oscar was a great help to the community.

"I guess so. He said he works in the camp, mostly hangs out over at the main office. Seemed nice enough. Maybe a little simple but eager to help me out. I got the feeling he was really embarrassed that he'd gotten caught. Even offered to fix the window lock on your trailer."

The chief and Ben both thanked him and complimented him on handling the situation. It put a wrinkle in things for sure, Ben thought. They said their good-byes and headed back to the office.

"I can't believe that." Trini was only voicing the chief's exact same opinion. The idea of Oscar as a Peeping Tom directing holograms through a window in order to scare anyone was just crazy.

"He's off on a grocery-run this morning but should be back before five. No offense, but your new deputy just has to have it all wrong. Couldn't someone have used his name? Just said they were Oscar thinking the deputy might not check?"

But when the chief showed back up at the office at five and waited until six-thirty with still no Oscar, he was getting a jab of cop-intuition. Something was wrong. Trini was fielding calls from people in camp looking for their groceries and prescriptions.

"He's never been even the least little bit late before. I know Oscar. He would have called if something came up."

"Do you know where he was going?"

"After picking up the grocery orders at Safeway, he was stopping at CVS for some basics—aspirin, ibuprofen as well as several prescriptions. I think he had a request for shampoo, maybe some other toiletries, too."

"Call the pharmacy. See if he showed."

Trini dialed and finally got through to a clerk. The chief couldn't hear the other person, but Trini shook her head and mouthed "no show". Oscar made a run to that particular store once a week so there was no mistaking whether or not he'd been there. They knew him and there was a box filled with orders under the desk waiting on him.

"What do you think has happened?" Trini was visibly shaken. "This is just so unlike him. I hope he's okay."

"I'm putting out an APB. I'll let you know what I find out." The chief walked out to the parking lot and got into the Bronco and then just sat there. Something was wrong. He picked up his two-way and texted messages to five of his deputies who would be closest to the camp. He hated inaction but couldn't think of one thing to do that would produce positive results. He really was going to have to sit and wait.

The wait was short. Within forty-five minutes he heard from an officer outside Shiprock. Oscar Begay's truck had been located, and Oscar Begay was deceased. Details to follow.

Chapter 40

The body was brought back to camp because of the pandemic. But there shouldn't have been any fear of the virus; this was a murder—one shot to the back of the head while Oscar was stopped at a stoplight at the edge of town. Shiprock. Not a place known for gang-type murders. Witnesses said the shooter was in the passenger-side seat of a pickup—something old, used to be white—and the driver wore a cowboy hat. No one seemed to have gotten a clear view of the shooter because the bed of the pickup was full of garbage cans, fifty-gallon rubber containers. The truck had been reported stolen from the city's maintenance yard just thirty minutes before it became a get-away vehicle after a murder. And it was discovered across town abandoned another thirty minutes after that—wiped clean, not a set of prints to be had. Were the driver and shooter both Navajo? Maybe just one was a Native? No one knew. Drivers and passengers in the two cars closest to the pickup had been too busy diving for cover or pulling away.

'Oscar's murder is tied into what happened last night.' It repeated itself in his head like a mantra, but the chief knew it was the truth. But proof? That was another thing. Had someone threatened Oscar's life if he didn't shine a hologram through the window? Offered him a fortune to do it? Threatened to 'off' his mother if he refused? What in God's name could have prompted Oscar to do something so truly out of character?

The text from Deputy Ashkii caught his attention— could they meet at his pickup? He had something that the chief would be interested in.

"This will give things a name and a timeframe." The deputy handed Chief Billie a receipt from BestBuy, Albuquerque, NM. "It was folded up and slipped inside the case of the projector. Looks like the thing was purchased via credit card the first of August. I sort of inflated my title and got a store manager to give me the name on the card. Does Curtis Henry mean anything to you?"

"Dr. Henry. Yes, if it's the same individual, we have a doctor by that name here." Another surprise ... no, maybe shock. And this made absolutely no sense. Again, the chief thanked Deputy Ashkii. Impressive. He needed to hire him full time. But now he needed to visit Dr. Curtis Henry.

* * *

"I purchased that for what was going to be a terrific Halloween party at the school. I go into Albuquerque every once in a while and Miss Otter requested that I pick it up for her. She wanted me to make sure the projector came with a USB connector to send images from her iPhone or laptop. Seems she'd been working on some pretty scary stuff. Oscar took it out to the school and I haven't seen it since. Of course, the pandemic put a stop to any party planning. I have no idea what happened to the projector. In fact, I don't remember Miss Otter even letting me know she'd gotten it."

Dr. Henry was more than courteous and offered his condolences to Oscar Begay's family. An unfortunate turn of events. An understatement, Chief Billie thought. But he really couldn't think of any pertinent further questioning. The doctor's explanation made sense. What was he missing? Every avenue of questioning seemed to be either a dead end or had perfectly good logic behind it. He thanked the doctor and left but knew he couldn't let it go. He needed a sounding board—someone involved but outside looking in. He called Ben and asked him to bring Julie and meet him at the Two Sisters for dinner.

Over a beer and some far better than average guacamole, the chief shared what he knew with Ben and Julie.

"Doc Henry made sense. I can't think of any reason he would have to lie. And now we won't be able to question Oscar. But something just isn't adding up. What am I missing? I thought maybe you guys could help fill in some spaces."

"It's plausible that the projector was meant for Halloween. It would have been a big hit with the kids. Did you run it by Miss Otter?" Julie asked.

"Tried to, but she's in the ICU at the Shiprock hospital. And it doesn't look good."

"I'm having trouble trying to tie Dr. Henry into any of this," Ben said.

"Oh no, I think I can help there, and I may have really goofed up." Julie put down her fork. "Things have been so crazy that I forgot to tell you I finally heard back from AMSA."

"AMSA?" The chief looked puzzled. "Should I know what that is?"

"I'd forgotten that I'd asked Julie to chase down the particulars to the corporation that calls itself the American Medical Suppliers Association. They act as a warehouse storage and clearing house for foreign medical supplies—anything entering this country—and then they disperse across the US. The government has procured them for the gargantuan effort of dispersing PPE statewide. As you can imagine they are doing a bang-up business thanks to the pandemic. When we were having trouble getting the correct shipments in a timely fashion—they were being stolen or we were getting the wrong articles—it seemed the most problematic deliveries were directly linked to AMSA. So, what did you find out?" Ben asked.

"In brief, the founder and most recent CEO—and I might add, biggest investor—is our very own Dr. Curtis Henry."

"Money. Why do I feel that things might be falling into place?" Chief Billie paused. "Of course, proving wrongdoing and making it stick to the doctor will be difficult. But who would stand to gain more? We know we've had leaked inside knowledge as to schedules, even monies on hand—don't forget Trini's safe was originally in his lab. He knew where she kept it in all likelihood."

"You know, before the three of us prosecute the guy, I'd

like to run what we have by Dr. Black. He was Dr. Henry's boss during the Hantavirus epidemic. I know we have circumstantial suspicions—I can't really call it evidence—and that adds up to almost nothing at all. Anybody have any problem bringing Dr. Black in?" Ben asked.

"Not if you think he can help." The chief paused. "Are we looking for a character reference for Dr. Henry? I'm not sure I see how that can make a difference."

"I guess I want to know if he's capable of something nefarious. Are we trying to implicate a squeaky-clean person in everything from robbery to murder? Maybe someone or some group is impersonating him—just using his name and position. We're dependent on federal money during this pandemic, character assassination of someone the Feds have placed with us in a strategic position wouldn't go over well. We might very easily lose a key player in our recovery from the virus," Ben said.

"That's a good point. Just because he's the major stock holder in a company the government is doing business with, doesn't mean he's corrupt," Julie added. "But why try to scare, or even harm *me*?"

"I think Ben was the intended victim here. You were set up. I think the belief was that if you wanted out of here, Ben wouldn't let you go alone and both of you would leave. Ben has been too good in safe-guarding shipments of PPE. He certainly made it more difficult, if not impossible, to sidetrack this last multi-million-dollar delivery. And that must have cost someone a bundle." The chief turned to Julie, "You'll excuse me but if that 'bear' had wanted to kill you, you'd be dead, Mrs. Pecos."

Julie didn't want to admit it, but she knew the chief was speaking the truth. It had nothing to do with her having taken deadly aim with a ten-ounce water bottle. The incident was only meant to frighten her.

"There's Dr. Black now. Should we invite him to join us?" Ben asked. At the two nods, he waved his old boss over.

"Dinner? I can recommend the company," Ben offered.

"Believe it or not, I'm on a coffee break. This has turned into a late night. Let me grab a latte. I'll be right back." In five minutes he was pulling up a chair. "This is a serious looking group. Problems?"

The chief went first, listing their concerns, as well as the facts as they knew them. Ben concluded by leaving their questioning open-ended. Did Dr. Black know anything that would lend credence to what he'd just heard?

"Give me a minute." Dr. Black took a sip of his latte before pushing his chair back. "I need to know that what I say will stay in this group. Do I have your promises on that?" He looked from one to the other. Everyone nodded.

"Okay, then, I'll fill you in on Curtis Henry. Ten years ago he was at the top of his game—a leading epidemiologist, published, awarded in his field, department head at a major university and then he got caught misappropriating funds. Oh, not putting money in his own pocket—at least not directly—but the monies were redirected to his projects, feathering his own nest, as it were, but in more general terms. In two instances funding dried up at the peril of closing down a very viable, much touted pet project of a Congressman. And there was no fighting city hall. Dr. Henry was worse than fired; he was demoted, stripped of any access to positions of leadership. A sort of excommunication at the university level. No one would touch him. He had taken advantage of colleagues, ruining a person's life's work by doing so. Unforgivable. There were no job offers coming in until this one. The government often can't be choosy. They needed Dr. Henry to fill a slot setting up a field hospital on an Indian reservation. Not a cushy position at a John Hopkins R&D establishment, but here—out in nowhere. I think to say the man is angry would be an understatement. Even if it was of his own making, getting caught and then chastised has been difficult for him to accept."

"So, you're saying we're not off base by what we suspect?" The chief leaned forward.

"I'm sorry to say this, but, no, not at all. Especially since Dr. Henry turned in his resignation this afternoon and took off."

Chapter 41

A call to the Albuquerque International Sunport and Dr. Curtis Henry was detained by local law enforcement— literally taken off of a plane and held until Federal Marshals could get there. A trip to Tunisia had been thwarted. In the days that followed, several off-shore accounts were uncovered, each containing millions. The confiscation and sale of PPE had been exceptionally lucrative.

Thanks to fingerprints on the gas cap in the stolen pickup and checked against the usual maintenance crew, the driver of the truck was apprehended and he gave up his partner, who he claimed was the shooter. Both of the men involved in the killing of Oscar Begay were behind bars. Both had a history of incarceration and both were linked to Dr. Henry via cell phone records.

But the links to local mayhem didn't stop there. Raids of the apartment shared by Oscar's killers revealed schedules and names of an organized group of marauders, who thanks to exact information of shipments, could run trucks off the road, beat up or kill the drivers, and steal the contents.

The chief had stopped by the office to share the good news.

"One part of the mystery solved," Ben added.

The three of them were standing in the waiting room when Deputy Ashkii burst in.

"Sorry, but I just had to stop by. I knew you'd want to hear this. After Dr. Henry was stopped at the airport, I was assigned to go through his trailer here on site. Guess what? I found one very realistic bear costume in the closet. I guess we know who was the bear at the schoolhouse and who ordered the hologram. But that's not all. Lists of possible resale opportunities were in a safe in his office. Corporations in the US and abroad—all putting in orders for PPE. There were even receipts. This was one big, lucrative operation. One that unfortunately cost lives."

There were sighs of relief all around. The stealing of goods was a thing of the past; Dr. Henry was locked up. Julie was safe and together with Ben; and Zac and Nathan had won another soccer game—safely living some fifteen hundred miles away.

* * *

Dr. Black, feeling somewhat guilty for not cautioning his friend, Ben, about Dr. Henry's reputation, took over the field operation until someone could be found to head it up.

And Ben and Julie promised their time until the holidays. Then, after a Christmas trip to Washington to spend time with Zac and Nathan, home would become Florida.

+ + +

Thank you for taking the time to read *Ghost Dust*. If you enjoyed it, please consider telling your friends or posting a short review. Word of mouth is an author's best friend and is much appreciated.
Thank you,

Susan Slater

What's next for Ben and Julie?

Ben Pecos is heading for South Dakota, where it seems a Lakota religious ritual—the SunDance—is somehow tied in to the killing of several people. Can Ben get to the bottom of the mystery? You won't want to miss *Paper Arrows*, coming next from award-winning author Susan Slater.

Books by Susan Slater

The Ben Pecos Mystery Series
The Pumpkin Seed Massacre
Yellow Lies
Thunderbird
Fire Dancer
Under A Mulberry Moon
The Thaw
Ghost Dust
A Way to the Manger (a Christmas novella)

The Dan Mahoney Mystery Series
Flash Flood
Rollover
Hair of the Dog
Epiphany

Standalone Novels
0-60
Five O'Clock Shadow

+ + +

Visit Susan's website at susansslater.com where you
can sign up for her free mystery newsletter and a chance
to win some very cool stuff.

Contact Susan: susan@susansslater.com
Follow Susan on Facebook

Kansas native Susan Slater lived in New Mexico for thirty-nine years. Her Southwest mystery novels reflect her extensive knowledge of the tribes and pueblo culture in the area. As an educator she directed the Six Sandoval Teacher Education Program for the All Indian Pueblo Council through the University of New Mexico. She taught creative writing for UNM and the University of Phoenix. She retired to Florida to write full time, continuing her Ben Pecos and Dan Mahoney mysteries, along with the occasional stand alone novel. Visit her website at susansslater.com

www.ingramcontent.com/pod-product-compliance
Lightning Source LLC
Chambersburg PA
CBHW061556100726
47898CB00002B/394